My JoeSmith: Anonymity, Book One

By Pebbles Lacasse

My JoeSmith: Anonymity, Book One

This book is to be sold to ADULT AUDIENCES ONLY. It contains adult situations, explicit sexual scenes and graphic language which may be offensive to some readers.

This is a work of fiction. Names, places, characters, and events are the product of the author's imagination. Any resemblance to any persons, living or dead, is entirely coincidental. All sexually active characters in this work are 18 years of age or older.

ISBN 978-1-989979-17-4

Cover photos and design by Pebbles Lacasse
Photographs by Pebbles Lacasse
Cover Model J.M.
Edited by Jody Freeman, Off The Shelf Editing
Published by Pebbles Lacasse
www.pebbleslacasse.com

Chapter 1

My Secret Life

Master JoeSmith has me belly up over an oversized barrel, literally.

The oak wood is cool against my arched spine. Rope binds my spread ankles to one side, and my wrists, also bound, are secured to the other. I'm bent backward, unable to move. Being vulnerable is exactly how he prefers me.

A wooden clothespin pinches each stiff nipple. From time to time, he flicks one to add discomfort to my sensitive little buds. It hurts and yet a ping of desire shoots directly to my clit. He enjoys it when I flinch. My pain arouses him.

My thighs and belly are hot and flushed bright pink after the flogging with a long-stranded leather flogger. I remained silent through the whipping because it pleased Master. If I don't call out, he'll reward me. If I do, the punishment is harsher. I've learned to absorb the pain and release it with my orgasm, which he'll provide when he deems me deserving of such pleasure.

If he asks a direct question, I must answer. If I don't, he might duct tape my mouth closed. He's done that *once*. I quickly learned my lesson.

I'm blindfolded, as usual, when he plays with me. He forbade me from seeing his face and insists on his anonymity above all else. I enjoy my time with him and wouldn't want to jeopardize it by peeking, but I wish I could put a face to my delicious torturer.

Still, it adds an element of excitement of not knowing who's watching, or when or where Master will touch next. It can unhinge me if I allow myself to fall victim to anticipation.

I listen carefully to every sound he makes. His feet shuffle toward me and stop directly in front of my upside-down face. He's so near I can feel the heat from his body on my nose, which is at crotch height. Adrenaline courses through my veins as I await his next move.

Something tenderly brushes along my top lip and I instinctually open my jaw. His thumb gently pulls on my chin, urging me to open wider.

"I'm going to fuck your mouth."

Master only speaks in hushed whispers, adding to the alluring mystery of his anonymity.

He guides the puffy head of his warm penis between my lips. Gentle fingertips trace my jaw. Slowly, but with purpose, he works his cock in until it's in my throat and his balls rest against my nose. He brushes his fingers along my exposed throat and it tickles. Each time he pulls back, he allows me a breath. I'm amazed at how this position, nearly upside down, allows me to effortlessly take all of him.

His shoes scuff as he rounds the barrel and snaps at each clothespin, and he snickers when I twitch. He stands between my legs and drags his hot palms from my breasts, down my tummy, over my thighs and to my ankles where they remain.

Hot breath brushes my clitoris, and I bite my lips to restrain a moan. He gingerly spreads my labia and my clit twitches as the cool air stings it. His fingers glide between my folds before dipping into me.

I want more. I want him inside me.

JoeSmith's whisper cuts through the silence that stilled my thoughts. "You're wet. This pleases me." He pauses to spin his fingers back and forth as they slowly glide in and out. "When I fuck you, you won't cum until I permit it. If you do, I'll punish you. Do you understand?"

His words don't frighten me. In fact, I'm happy to receive either a punishment or a fucking.

"I understand, Sir."

I feel the firm mushroom head press against my opening. One thrust and he's buried deep inside me. My chest heaves but I don't dare cry out. My ankles pull hard against the restraints with each of his powerful thrusts. He's relentless.

Suddenly, everything stops. He holds still. I stay as mannequin-like as possible, but my heaved breaths allow an errant whimper to escape from between my clenched teeth.

"You'll remain quiet," he whispers. His fingertips glide from my lips, down my throat, and stop at my clavicle. "You're a good pet and deserving of release. Soon, but not yet."

Master grips my shoulder and continues pounding into me. He yanks the clothespins from my nipples and my breath catches. As blood rushes through them, it's nearly impossible for me to restrain my orgasm. I know he savours the control I allow him to have over me.

He presses a small vibrator against my clitoris and my body bucks and pulls at the bindings. I cry out even though it's not permitted, but I can't stop myself. I want to let myself go, to fall into my pleasure, but I need his permission first.

Finally, his hoarse whisper sings sweet words. "You may cum now."

My muscles burn. Strangely, the world darkens beneath my blindfold. There's so much tension deep within my core that I erupt.

The world seems to spin at warp speed. A scream escapes me and snaps me back to reality. He pants above me, readying to release his seed. His hips heave against me one last time before he collapses heavily onto me.

Tender kisses peck between my breasts. He's in no hurry to lift off of me, but when he does, he releases my left ankle first and rubs it lovingly. The warmth of his lips calms the hot indents that linger in the rope's absence. He repeats his tenderness with each binding.

In his gentlemanly way, he helps me rise. I clutch his arm when dizziness has me unsteady. I was upside down for some time, and I'm still blindfolded. With an arm around my waist and the other gripping my hand, I'm guided ten steps away. I hear him sit on a creaky wooden chair as he continues to steady me. He guides me between his legs and has me sit on his lap.

"You've pleased me once again. Did you enjoy yourself?" JoeSmith whispers as he brushes a tuft of my hair off my shoulder and glides his warm hand down my back, where it comes to rest on my opposite hip.

"Everything was wonderful. Thank you, Sir."

My hands are no longer bound. I could reach up to remove my mask and finally see his face, but I won't out of respect for Master's rules.

He kisses my shoulder. "I need you."

JoeSmith tries to keep our relationship professional with little emotional connection. He's usually stern and domineering. I know he appreciates me, otherwise, he wouldn't ask me to return week after week. Perhaps his way of showing affection is by always ensuring I'm completely satisfied.

Our arrangement is strictly meant for pleasure, but my feelings sometimes blur. There are moments when he's gentle and his touch has me wondering if he feels a loving connection with me.

I jolt back to reality when a paper ball soars from the cubicle next to me. I was daydreaming and replaying what happened last weekend, only this scenario was about to become more heartfelt than the reality was.

I nod in the direction the paper missile launched from to thank my best friend and coworker, Sam, for waking me from my midday zone-out.

My thirty-something, unbelievably sexy boss stands with one hand in the front pocket of his well-tailored dress pants. He's looking at me from behind the plate-glass windows lining his second-floor office, which overlooks twenty-two cubicles. He wears no expression on his handsome face as our eyes meet.

Is he upset that he caught me daydreaming, or is he curious about what stole my thoughts from my job?

He sips from his mug, and his eyes drift to the right. His black suit does nothing to hide his exceptional body. I have so many naughty fantasies involving him, but I'm way too shy to admit to him that I find him attractive. He's my boss, and office romances seldom work. Besides, a boyfriend would never allow another man—a dominant master—to mark his woman's body, let alone fuck her or share her with other people.

And that's why I stay single. Well, that and most men bore me.

Despite the office closing an hour early on Fridays, I'd swear time always moves slower. My patience was put to the test today, but the workday is finally over.

As I pack my belongings and prepare to leave the office for the weekend, I wonder what JoeSmith has planned for me for tomorrow evening. When I get home, I'll read his email, which should contain a vague description of the weekend's BDSM adventure.

I dare not open my email at work. The boss could be monitoring our computers; some companies do that. I don't think my super sexy boss Ben Manning is snoopy, but I won't bet my career on it. If he discovered my dirty little secret, the embarrassment would surely kill me. I doubt he'd blab, but if he did, it would spread like a wildfire and I couldn't bear all the judgemental stares and whispers.

I rush out the door toward the parking lot, and I've almost made it to my car when a familiar voice pulls me from my thoughts.

"Terri!"

Dammit!

My pace slows, and I groan as I stop and turn. Sam is hurrying toward me with a wide smile and her dark brown hair flowing in the breeze.

"Wow! What's your hurry?" Her shoulders droop as one arm hangs and the other clutches her chest, exaggerating her heavy breathing even though she's only slightly winded. "As usual, a bunch of us are going for drinks tomorrow evening to blow off some steam. Don't rush to say no. Give me a minute to try to guilt you into coming."

Her fists perch on her narrow hips, and she glares.

Strands of wavy hair cling to the film of sweat on her face brought on by the sun's baking rays and high humidity. If she weren't only 5'2", her intimidating stare might convince me.

"Look, you haven't partied with me in a long time, and I'm feeling a little unloved." Her voice lowers as she leans her weight on her left leg and rolls her eyes. "Bob made me promise to tell you he'll be there."

She knows I'm not interested in Bob, but a promise is a promise.

Nobody knows about my sexual exploits with JoeSmith, not even my best friend. It breaks my heart that I've been lying to her for a year. It's difficult to think up new excuses as to why I'm always too busy to party with her on Saturday nights. I'm surprised she hasn't demanded a solid explanation or spied on me to find out.

What would happen if I told her my secret?

It could go either way: she might disown me or possibly want to join in. I don't doubt she'd be entertaining for JoeSmith and he'd enjoy her tight little figure and small, perky breasts. I wouldn't mind watching her lose herself to his skills and knowledge of the female body.

We've been best friends for seven years, ever since we met in college. Lucky for us, we were both hired to work here fresh out of school and her cubicle is right beside mine. I can always count on her to tell me the nitty-gritty gossip from the secret-spilling-water cooler-judgment-crew.

Aside from Sam, I'm a bit of a loner, which has helped keep me off their radar. I banish thoughts of being the subject of workplace gossip. For that reason, I keep my personal life separate from my work life.

Sam bounces like a toddler setting up to have a tantrum. "Please, please, *please*!"

All the begging in the world couldn't convince me to forego a Saturday playdate. It's rare, but occasionally JoeSmith doesn't invite me to play. He never offers a reason why and I don't ask. It's not my place, and I know that. I'm a plaything; a toy he can set aside and take out when it suits him, and I like it that way.

"I can't make any promises because I already made plans. If they fall through, I'll come." I squint and cross my arms over my chest. "And will you please stop giving Bob hope? I could always talk to the creepy guy who stares at people and doesn't look away when their eyes meet and tell him that you like him."

I snicker when her face contorts. She gasps and places her hand over her heart.

"You wouldn't dare!"

My shoulders lift and my eyes widen. "I recommend you don't fall asleep after you two have hot, sweaty, sloppy sex. You might wake to find him dancing after he's cut off your skin and made a tight Sam-suit." We both shiver and I grimace. "That was too far, wasn't it?"

Her face scrunches for a second time. "First off, I'm not giving Bob hope." She laughs, lowers her voice, and points at me with both of her index fingers. "Bob Hope! See what I did there? Huh? Huh?"

I roll my eyes and smile. "Uh-huh."

"And that creepy guy—"

She studies my face to question my bluff, so I raise an eyebrow in defiance. She pouts and skips toward her Jeep, which suits her energetic, happy-go-lucky personality. She'll be a great catch for some lucky guy if he can pin her down long enough to call her his.

"Hear this, missy!" Her finger points at me as she opens her door. "One day, I'll insist you introduce me to this mysterious friend that robs me of your Saturday nights."

She waves goodbye and sags into the driver's seat and shuts her door.

I'm free!

Chapter 2

Satisfaction Guaranteed

The drive home seems painstakingly long, and each red light is torture. Every green light is a reason to celebrate. My muscles are tense with anticipation. I want to ram cars driven by people out to enjoy the scenery instead of driving the speed limit.

I jam the key in the lock on my front door and push it open. The knob smacks against the wall with a loud bang, and the door rushes back at me and the handle snags my purse strap.

"Motherfucker!"

I wrestle to free it and then slam the door behind me and flip the lock. I sprint to my laptop, flip it open, and push the start button.

Normally, I would have plopped myself in the chair and tapped my fingers on the desk while I waited impatiently for the computer to load. Today, however, I really need to pee.

I kick off my high heels as I dash to the bathroom. My arches ache as they flatten to the floor. My nylon-clad feet slide on the hardwood as I whirl myself around the corner, hearing that familiar computer jingle and force my urine out as fast as possible.

The computer will be ready for my password any second. Yanking up my panties will waste time so I fling them in the hamper. I'm so glad I wore stockings and not full pantyhose.

No surprise that my computer's password is *JoeSmith*. I plant my butt in the chair and take a deep breath. There it is; my email icon staring at me, taunting me. I don't dare click it for fear it will slow the loading process or cause the computer to freeze. That would be unbearable.

It's ready! *Tap, tap.*

My body heats with excitement. I can hear my heart try to beat its way out of my chest. I hold back the urge to click on his name simply to torture myself. I'm a masochist, after all.

With a tap of my finger, the email opens.

Hello, Pet.

I request your presence at the castle. If you accept this invitation, you'll reply with the words, "I accept."

You must follow the same rules as always:

-You'll attend your pre-scheduled wax appointment.

-You'll be picked up at five o'clock tomorrow evening.

-You'll remain quiet upon arrival.

Lady Catherine will prepare you for my arrival. Expect to be very uncomfortable tomorrow. I will grant you much pleasure if you behave. I might choose to put you on display for others to enjoy. Your flesh will sting and your muscles will ache. I'll use you until you have nothing left.

Do you accept?

Always,
JoeSmith

I consider declining, but my curiosity holds me prisoner. Besides, I trust him: he'll take me to my limit but never push past it. I type "I accept" and send the reply to my punisher.

There's pain in our sessions, but nothing I can't handle. A hard spanking until my butt goes fire engine red. A typically violent and exciting fuck. Anal sex here and there. But what does he mean by *uncomfortable*?

Being displayed is nothing new to his games. I've had audiences watch my humiliation unfold more than once, and it's exciting. Will the audience take part this time?

Why will Lady Catherine tend to me? She never has before. She's the extremely intimidating woman who runs the castle. My mind spins with an infinite number of scenarios. I hate yet love the unknown.

My pussy clenches. I need an orgasm.

I rush to the bedroom and around the bed to the bottom drawer of my nightstand in search of my favourite sex toy.

There it is right on top; my trusty vibrator that always satisfies me. I drop my skirt to the floor, plug in my friend, and then flop on the bed. A pillow flops onto my face and I leave it there as a makeshift blindfold.

I click the vibrator to the lowest setting. There's that sweet hum that promises me pleasure. I touch it to my pierced clitoris. The bouncing stainless-steel ring intensifies the vibration and I let my thoughts drift and picture myself bound to something. My ass cheeks burn from a spanking and something big is stuffed in my vagina. I imagine myself pleading with my unknown captor to let me cum.

An intoxicating tickle begins in my lower belly and slowly rises through my core. I click the vibrator to a faster speed. It's louder, more violent, and much more exhilarating. A click higher, and I'm so close.

I whisper to myself. "Not yet."

There's no better feeling than those few seconds before an orgasm overwhelms.

I flip it on high.

My toy attacks my clitoris like a devil with a mission. A split second later, the heat roars inside me and takes over my entirety. Every muscle from my toes to my eyelids flexes from the intensity.

The world disappears around me, and the fire in my belly reaches volcanic heat. I scream and shake but keep the vibrator pressed to my clit until I beg myself for mercy.

After a quick shower and an even faster bite to eat, I slide on a denim skirt and a violet shirt that reads, *I'm Trouble.* I can't be late getting to the salon because I'll have to wait even though JoeSmith pays them well to take me next, no matter what time I arrive. Still, the later in the day it is, the longer I have to wait.

Chapter 3

JS

My Confession

I had a restless night of sleep because I anticipated his touch. JoeSmith never ceases to satisfy me. He doesn't leave me until I'm utterly spent. But I wonder what fantasy roleplay game he's chosen for us tonight. What will he have me wear?

After a large cup of coffee and a yogurt, I stick my earbuds in and find my favourite workout music. I begin with a medium-paced walk on my treadmill and gradually increase to a steady run.

I've lost time reminiscing about the different scenarios Sir has acted out with me. I've been running hard for nearly an hour, and my legs ache. The steamy shower feels wonderful as water washes the sweat from my skin. I let it pound on my back before I bring the showerhead to my pussy. I select a steady stream, put my left foot on the edge of the tub, and point the stream at my clit. It isn't long before I cum.

I call Sam while I slip on a well-worn pair of jeans and an oversized pastel blue t-shirt with the words *Don't Judge Me* on the front.

"Hey, Terri!"

Sam's peppy, as usual.

"Hi, Sam. What are you up to?" I ask while I slip my foot into an ankle sock.

Sam always talks fast. "Not much. I'm just leaving my mother's, and my afternoon is free until I go to the bar tonight. What did you have in mind? Do you want to do something?" She gasps and adds, "Oh, hey! Are you coming tonight? Please tell me you are."

"Sorry, no. Do you want to meet for lunch? You'll need a hearty meal before you go out drinking tonight. If you eat now and not just before you go out, you won't have a food baby when you slip on that hot little dress you were telling me about." Sam never turns down a free meal. "I'll buy if you meet me in about half-hour at Andy's Pub."

She ponders momentarily. "Half-hour is tight for me. Forty-five minutes would be better."

"I'll see you in forty-five at Andy's."

My tummy rumbles when I think about their chicken club sandwich meal.

I gather my hair and affix it with a clip, brush my teeth, and rush out the door. I've known Sam long enough that I'm sure she'll get to the pub with plenty of time to spare. Can I beat her this time?

Rushing was a waste of my efforts because she's already here, sitting at a patio table for two overlooking the street and the steady stream of people scurrying about. We both love people watching and being watched. It's fun to see how many men—and women from time to time—will stop and offer to buy us a drink. We usually turn them down, but it's great for our self-esteem.

Sam's drink arrives at the table as I walk up. She's dramatic when she looks at her watch and stands.

"You may be early, but I was earlier."

I roll my eyes and hug her. "You said you couldn't make it in half-hour."

She shrugs and sits. "It appears I could."

*****

Our bellies are full and I'm more relaxed after drinking a margarita. Sam had two. She bites her lip and shuffles in her chair.

Louder than I should, I ask, "Butt rash bothering you?"

Without missing a beat, she replies, "It's about cleared up. How's the herpes?"

She snickers. I shake my head when the two people at the adjacent table stare open-mouthed. Sam exhales heavily.

"If I ask you something, will you answer honestly? Like, will you swear on our friendship to tell the absolute truth no matter how uncomfortable it makes you?"

What if she asks me where I'm going tonight? Should I confess my secret lifestyle? What if she wants to experience it for herself? I think our relationship could withstand it, but what if it couldn't?

I hesitate and she crinkles her eyebrows together as if questioning our friendship. Reluctantly, I nod my head. What else can I do? I don't want my secret putting a strain on our friendship any longer.

"I've gone to your house on several Saturday nights when you said you were staying home. Your car was there, but you weren't. Where do you go?"

She holds my gaze without blinking and my heart pounds in my chest as a hundred thoughts rush through my conscience. I'm a terrible liar. She claims I have a tell but won't say what it is.

"Just tell me. Do you have a boyfriend, or *girlfriend*—no judgment!"

"I don't think you really want to know. If I tell you, it'll change how you think of me." I pause and hope she'll tell me to forget she ever asked, but she stares unblinking. "You're better off to stay oblivious."

Sam doesn't back down and raises her eyebrows to insist I confess.

"I don't know where to start."

"Tell me what he or *she* looks like—again, no judgment."

Here goes nothing!

"Okay, he's about 6'2" and has dark hair. He's physically fit but not ripped like a bodybuilder. He's Caucasian and his voice is deep, I think. He only whispers to me and never speaks in his normal voice." My eyebrows furrow, and I shake my head when her eyes widen. "I can't honestly tell you what his face looks like because I've never seen it."

Her hand rises to stop me. "Okay…" Sam's eyes search the sky momentarily and then she crinkles her face. "Wait, what?"

My lips twitch when I try to smile. "He insists on his anonymity. I'm forbidden to look at him, even if he wears a mask. His masks have eye holes but mine never do."

"Um, okay." She bites her cheek and leans toward me with her elbows on the table. "Your boyfriend sounds hot, I think."

I shake my head and pull on my earring. "Definitely not my boyfriend."

"Okay, I understand. I think. Wait… no, I don't." She takes two big gulps of her drink. "So how did this all start?"

"It all started about a year ago when I opened an email at work." I tuck a tuft of hair that escaped the clip behind my ear. "My life felt stale and I craved excitement. So, after some communication and research, I agreed to a meet-up with—"

"Are you crazy?" she barks, alerting the same two people. "You met someone from the Internet without at least telling me you were going or taking me with you for safety purposes?"

"It was stupid and dangerous. I know."

I fiddle with my straw. She drags her finger around the salted rim of her glass and pops it in her mouth, and then she waves her hand, urging me to continue.

"His name is JoeSmith; one word, and he emails me on Fridays. I'm to follow his instructions, otherwise, he'll punish me." I pause when she opens her mouth to speak but doesn't. Instead, she urges me to continue. "We always meet at a mansion just outside of the city somewhere. It's more like a castle. Before you ask, I'm not sure where it's located. I'm picked up and driven there in a limo with a hood over my head."

With the straw bound tightly between her pursed lips, Sam looks concerned and yet intrigued, so I continue.

"When I arrive, I sign some waivers. It's just a formality. After that, I'm led to the shower. While still naked, I'm brought to where people dress me, apply my make-up, and do my hair to his exact specifications."

A slurp startles Sam from her trance. Immediately, she waves her hand to our server and points to her glass.

"I'll need another drink to get through this."

She nods, and I continue.

"When I'm ready, a leader brings me to whatever kinky room suits his fantasy. There are rooms for bondage, wet rooms, dungeons, et cetera; just about any kinky fantasy you can think up."

I wave my eyebrows while sporting a crooked grin. She looks past my head as if searching the sky for a memory or fantasy she's hidden away.

"I'm chained, tied, or positioned how he requested. Only then does JoeSmith come into the room." My hands wrap around my glass and I snicker. "You can guess what happens from there."

We sit silently for a full minute before Sam speaks. I can tell she has questions and she's trying to decide what to ask first.

"Who is he and what's his name?"

I shrug, rather aloof. "JoeSmith. Like I said, I've never seen his face and I don't know his real name. If I'm not blindfolded, he'll wear a full mask with eyeholes. Sometimes I can see the back of his head and his jawline when he tells me to watch him, like when we're in the mirror room."

Her eyes widen and her head tilts to the left. I bite my lip as the memory of his sweaty body pounding against mine as I was faced away from him and bent at the hips floods back.

"That's one of his favourite rooms."

It's a lot for her to process, so I patiently wait while she watches a crowd of chattering people walk past. She's halfway through her third drink and her eyes are glassy.

Sam's louder than what's appropriate for our conversation as she finally says, "Why didn't you tell me about this? I could have lived vicariously through you this whole time! Oh, my god!" She flings her arms wildly. "You've been letting me go on and on about how great my sexual rendezvous are, meanwhile, you've been having the mother-load of kinky sexual experiences this whole time!"

She leans back and crosses her arms over her chest, but quickly resumes leaning her elbows on the table. Her voice lowers, much to my relief.

"All this time, you could have been spilling to me and getting me all hot and bothered. You *know* you have to fill me in, detail by detail about absolutely everything!"

Sam seems to be more than okay with my confession, and I regret not telling her sooner. I could have saved myself a lot of aggravation. She's right, though; her typical sexual flings are dull in comparison to mine.

"So, tell me..." Sam's glossy eyes are wide with excitement. "What are you going to be doing tonight? You're meeting him, right? I mean, that's why you aren't coming out with me. But, shit! I wouldn't go out with me either!"

I tell her everything that was in the email and she's as excited as I am. She shifts in her chair and bites her bottom lip. It's obvious she's aroused. Sam slumps back on her chair as if lounging in a recliner and stirs the remainder of her third drink with her straw. Her eyes narrow and her expression has *horny* written all over it.

"Do you think I could ever do what you're doing?"

I nearly spit my sip of water at her.

She whispers, "Would I be able to come along sometime? I wouldn't want to impose if your mystery man is special to you; like a boyfriend or something." Her shoulders bounce. "But I'm curious."

Her eyes don't leave mine, but her eyebrows slowly rise with desperation when I don't immediately respond.

I nod and reply, "I can ask."

Chapter 4

The Preparation Ritual

I have plenty of time to grab a coffee in the bistro on the corner before the limo arrives. I try to be at the pickup point ten minutes earlier than expected because tardiness is unacceptable to JoeSmith. When I break his rules, harsher punishments ensue.

At exactly five o'clock, the familiar white limo stops alongside the curb. Jim, the driver, jaunts around the car to open the door for me. JoeSmith considers it ungentlemanly if a woman's male escort allows her to open her door. I'm quite capable, but rules are to be followed.

I'm sure Jim is not his actual name. This whole experience is about fantasy role play, and he's just one pawn on the board. If I know Sir at all, he loves to control every aspect; no detail is too small, and no act is unaccounted for.

Throughout the journey, I wear a blackout hood, and no matter how careful I am, my coffee always spills on my shirt. I don't think I'll ever perfect the task.

The drive to the castle takes approximately an hour. Do other submissives receive the same limo ride, or are they allowed to drive themselves?

My eyelids weigh heavily. A memory floods my thoughts about the night JoeSmith had me straddle a vibrating saddle. It looked like it could have come off a horse except that saddle had two dildos protruding from the seat.

Master inserted the biggest one in my pussy and the smaller one in my ass. My hands were tied behind my back with my elbows together so my tits jutted forward. Clamps donned my nipples and heavy weights dangled from them. They were painful but also stimulating.

I allow him to own my body because I trust him to keep me safe. He vibrated the seat on a slow setting while he pinked my skin with a leather strap, gradually turning up the vibration. I sucked his cock down my throat with his fingers weaved in my hair for guidance. I was forbidden to orgasm, and I fought hard to obey. He didn't cum despite how much he enjoyed the way his prick blocked my airway, throwing off my concentration. It's always a game to him.

He stood aside and tugged on the weights he'd clamped on my nipples and I couldn't help but cry out. Master turned the vibrating seat on full. I could hold off no more and came hard.

He kept up the speed, which forced me into three more orgasms, and caught me as I slid off the saddle; I was passing out.

I remember he told me to breathe, but the extraordinarily wonderful pain he caused when he removed the nipple clamps overwhelmed my senses. He then untied my bindings, pulled me onto his lap, and rocked me until I was calm, and carried me over to a mattress on the floor. He kissed and fucked me, but was so aroused that he was quick to let himself go. I love his games!

I jolt from my daydream when Jim says, "We've arrived at the castle, and it's safe to remove the hood."

As I step out, I run my fingers through my hair and squint to ease the burn from the sunlight reflecting off the white cement.

The stone-shelled building looks like an antiquated romantic castle. The windows are newer but designed to look centuries old. The driveway, large pathway, and wide steps that lead to the building are newly poured cement and cleaner than any I've ever seen.

Songbirds and the scent of roses on the breeze defy the wildness of pain and pleasure occurring just behind these stone walls. If I didn't know better, I'd picture people sipping tea from hand-painted china in the study or quietly reading in a magnificent, elegant dining room.

My leader's bright red lips lift at their corners to greet me as I approach. She has her role to play, just like the rest of us.

The thin Asian woman wears a sexy, white latex nurse's uniform with the word *Slave* written on her I.D. badge. Her make-up is applied too heavily, which seems to be the theme. Her hair is short, straight, and chocolate-brown, and her gorgeous pale-blue eyes are lined in black. She's beautiful and sensuous as she moves.

A leader can be anyone; male or female. This castle is enormous and difficult to navigate, and submissives are forbidden to roam about unaccompanied. Sometimes, I'm told to walk down a dark, vacant hallway until I see an open door. Usually, JoeSmith is waiting inside, hooded, dressed in sexy leathers, and ready to punish me for roaming the halls alone.

The "nurse" takes me to the front counter, where I sign the usual paperwork and hand it back to the blonde wearing a sexy schoolgirl outfit. I'm then led to the locker room so I can put all of my belongings in a locker, including my jewelry. She smiles as I pass her to enter the cleansing room. I now have fifteen minutes.

The cleansing room beams with soft light. The floors, walls, and sink are marble. It's cold and seems sterile, like an operating room.

On the counter by the sink is my cleansing packet. It contains a mild vaginal douche, enema, toothbrush, toothpaste, a tiny bar of soap, and mini shampoo and conditioner bottles. When finished, I'll smell like fresh-cut flowers.

On a shelf beside the sink is a face towel, washcloth, and a large towel—they're always white. There is no actual shower stall. A spout juts from the wall beside the toilet. A small red button is how I turn the water on and off, and it's never quite warm enough.

I run through my routine and then dry my skin and prepare for the next stage. I have almost a minute to spare. That's a personal victory. Towels are to be put in the hamper and never to be used to cover my indignity as we go to the next station. My wet hair drips cold water down my bare back and I shiver.

Most of the time, the same leader stays with me from the limo to the playroom but not today. The new woman wears a red leather hat with a long black ponytail flowing from its top. Around her neck is a leather choker with small chains that loop down her chest, and her nipples bear red pasties with tiny chains that sway as she moves. Her tight, red leather belt has several metal loops on the front and back.

She isn't wearing panties and a horsetail butt plug hangs from her backside. It sways as she walks. Her shiny red boots rise to her knees; too high for me to walk in.

I'm led down a corridor and past several rooms with familiar sounds of wild sex, moans and screams from both men and women. I hear the snap of a whip and my body tingles with excitement.

As we descend, my bare feet slap the polished wood lining the winding staircase. I follow her down another smaller corridor to a set of large, hand-carved double doors, which also look aged. She pushes them open and stands to one side to allow me access. Then she closes the doors, and I'm alone.

I've been in this dressing room a few times. Here, my preparers will do my hair, apply my make-up, and dress me exactly as JoeSmith requested.

Both of my preparers wear off-the-shoulder designer evening gowns; one's blue and the other yellow. Both gowns are perfectly fitted on each woman. Their hair is shiny and thick, swooping across their foreheads. They look as if they could walk the red carpet in their elegant spiked heels.

I'm familiar with the routine. I sit in the preparation chair with my arms resting on the armrests. The two women will tend to me without a single word spoken.

My hair is piled atop my head in a loose bun with random curls left to dangle. A light powder, mascara, soft charcoal eyeliner, pink blush, and bright red lipstick are applied to make my lips look thinner.

The blonde takes my hand and escorts me to the high table. She chooses a lotion from the vast assortment. I spread my feet and grip the edge of a table. She stands behind me and squirts a glob of lotion onto my back, and then rubs it in from my neck to my toes.

Next, the brunette slips on latex gloves, lubricates the fingers, and pushes two into my vagina. She explores my hole, then examines her fingers. I'm not sure why this is done because JoeSmith doesn't care if I'm menstruating. She glides one finger into my behind and pauses until I can relax enough to accept two fingers. She's very clinical, but it's still exciting.

The brunette laces my corset tighter than I'd like. I laugh as I step into white bloomers. I find the word *bloomers* comical, and my outburst is quickly halted when the blonde woman clears her throat.

They drape a heavy dress over me and lace it from the back. The powder-blue silk gown trimmed with white lace is elegant and fits as if it were made just for me. I step into three-inch high tan ankle boots.

My heart thumps loudly in my ears and I fist my hands, hoping to ease the tremor.

I fucking love this!

Chapter 5

The Elegant Lady Catherine

I'm led down a brightly lit corridor and instructed to wait. I crack each finger as I watch my leader strut away. Stand in silence, I wait for something to happen, expecting the elegant Lady Catherine to glide around the corner. JoeSmith's instructions said she'd be the one to prepare me, but I have yet to see her.

The two doors suddenly swing open and Lady Catherine glides through them with a leash in her hand. Following behind her is a muscular man crawling on his hands and knees. He's dressed in tight black leather shorts and wears a dog collar around his neck, attached to her leash.

She jerks the lead and tells him to sit. He immediately drops his face parallel to the floor and sits back on his heels, resting his giant hands on his thighs. She's so tiny, and he's massive. He could easily overpower her, but he chooses to submit.

She's a goddess, and I wonder if she wakes looking just as beautiful as she stands before me now. Her long, silky hair is held in a tight ponytail that drapes down her back like a black waterfall.

Lady Catherine's eyes lift at the outer corners and black liner emphasizes their dark brown hue. Her cheekbones are high and prominent, covered with smooth, milky skin teased with a hint of rose blush. She's painted her plump lips blood red. The movie industry would adore this woman.

Her dresses are always long, flow softly, and are designed for seduction. Today, she wears a tightly fitted red gown with a flared bottom trimmed in fine black feathers. The side slit starts just below her waist, leaving her entire right hip exposed. The front is so low cut it shows off her ruby belly-button jewelry. Most women would stagger from the height of her red leather shoes, but Lady Catherine is perfectly balanced. I envy her elegance.

"Are you ready to be JoeSmith's toy?"

I smile and nod. She motions for me to spin. I slowly turn so she can examine me.

"Very good. Your master will be pleased. Follow me."

She pivots and gives the leash a quick jerk. Her dog-man is quick to trail behind her on his hands and knees. I walk behind him, careful not to get too close and risk stepping on his toes.

Lady Catherine glances over her shoulder. "Do you have any questions?"

"Yes, a question for Master."

"I'll mention it." She stops and tells her dog to heel, jerking her head toward the black-tiled bathroom without a door. "Keep in mind he doesn't like a lot of chatter."

She stands at the archway and watches as I wrestle with my dress. I can't get the bloomers down. I'm sure peeing on them will earn me a nasty punishment.

Success, finally! That coffee I had on the way here has run right through me.

While she looks down the hall, I assess her dog. The massive man's hair is very long, blond, and tied back in a loose braid. From what I've seen of his face, he's supermodel handsome. I wish I could see his eyes but he's obedient and doesn't look up from the floor.

When we arrive, Lady Catherine sits her dog-man outside the door before we enter the playroom. I finally see his sparkling blue eyes when he tilts his face up, allowing her to place the handle of the leash in his mouth and tells him not to drool on it.

A floor-to-ceiling metal pole is in the center of this room. Ropes I believe to be made from jute drape down. A leather-covered spanking bench sits to the left of the pole. It also has ropes fastened to it. Candle sconces line the walls, casting a dim hue about the room.

I'm sad there isn't a bed in this room. From past experience, no bed means he won't be at all tender and loving.

As usual, I'm nervous but know I can back out at any time. This imagined sense of no control over what's about to happen to me… Well, I love it. I crave it.

What will he do to me tonight and for how long? Who will be here? Will other people touch me or just him? Will Lady Catherine join our party?

She's never joined in before. I wonder what it would be like to be dominated by her. Wonderfully challenging, I assume.

There are five tall-back wooden chairs lined in the shadows along the far wall. Are they here so people can sit and watch my fate? My tummy flutters and I inhale sharply. As long as I remember to breathe, the rest is easy.

Soon I will give myself up to JoeSmith. Everything done from that moment on will be his decision. I'll be his to use however he wishes. I am in complete control, always. I can simply walk out if I'm not tied to something.

If I speak my safeword, it'll immediately end all play. I permit him to do things to me, and he is grateful for my submission. If I say no, he must obey me.

That's how this works. It's all based on trust: me trusting he'll stop and him trusting I'll speak up if I need it to end. I trust him completely.

Lady Catherine instructs me to stand facing the pole and ties my wrists with the rope that dangles from the top. She pulls it taught, which stretches my arms over my head, and secures a feathered blackout mask over my eyes.

"Have fun, and be a good little submissive," she whispers as her hand glides down my spine.

I hear her heels click as she struts away, followed by a thud when the door closes.

The room falls silent. I listen for him but the drum of my heartbeat pounds too loudly in my ears.

Finally, I hear muffled voices coming from behind a different door but can't understand what they're saying. The door opens with a sharp creak and the voices fade to silence. Shoes shuffle on the hardwood floor as people make their way to the chairs. They sit, and all goes quiet except for the hard-soled men's shoes that make their way toward me.

That strut is familiar. It belongs to JoeSmith. My body shakes with anticipation. I close my eyes and breathe deeply.

It's time to let go and give myself to him.

Chapter 6

A Teacher's Prop

I sense him behind me.

The tiny hairs on my back stand on end from the electricity building between us. I yearn for his touch. From now until completion, he will tell me how and when to do everything. Whatever happens, will be at his bidding. He makes all the decisions. I can let go of everything.

He lifts my dress until the back of my bloomers is revealed to the onlookers and then fastens it in place. The back of his fingernails graze the bare skin of my arms and neck, and I shiver.

He cups my ass through the bloomers and I stifle a moan to adhere to his wishes. His finger glides up and tucks the cotton material between my cheeks.

JoeSmith presses his body against mine and I can feel his arousal on my ass. The stark contrast between the cold pole and his superheated body has me shivering. He raises his arms, drags his fingertips from my wrists down my armpits, and abruptly grabs my breasts through the tight clothing. The pole remains buried between them. His breath is hot behind my ear.

He whispers, "My pet, your safeword today is the same as always; *zebra*." His soft lips brush my neck. "You will obey me. Repeat the safeword, Pet."

JoeSmith calls me *Pet*. It's extremely rare for him to address me by my real name.

"The safe word is zebra, Sir, and I'm yours," I reply with a tremble in my voice.

He kisses the back of my neck between words. "Repeat. The. Safe. Word. Again. My. Delicious. Pet."

I whimper. "Zebra, Sir. The safe word is zebra."

His shoes shuffle as he steps away and returns almost immediately. A loud clap accompanies my stinging derriere. My pussy tightens. He swats the same cheek again with the paddle, and it stings gloriously hot.

Oh, fuck! Yes!

Over and over the paddle alternates between my cheeks until both sides are tender and flaming hot. I don't dare scream. That would displease JoeSmith.

I hate the silence that fills the room. Anxious anticipation can build too monumental proportions if I were to give in to it, and he knows this is more torturous to me than the actual physical punishment. Master's accomplished in many forms of torment, but he never pushes me further than I can handle.

I'm about to come unravelled when his palm tenderly caresses my stinging ass. This brings me the sense of security I need to bring me back from the edge of panic.

My bloomers are swiftly torn at the seam to expose my crimson ass to all who look on. The white cotton material hangs in tatters from the tied waistband.

He loosens the rope just enough so he can reposition me. I'm bent at a ninety-degree angle with my hands bound at the wrist, clutching the pole. He stands behind me and swiftly pushes my feet apart until they are wider than shoulder-width. The shoes prove this position difficult to maintain.

I think I hear the snap of a latex glove. Suddenly, I'm sure of it when the gloved hand whacks my already burning ass cheek. My yelp is louder than he approves of but the latex adds another level of pain to the slap, and I couldn't hold back.

"Bad girl."

He swats my ass ten more times as punishment. I bite my lips together but my yelps are still audible.

The sting is nearly too much and I fear my knees will give out. He reaches ten and brushes his fingers in tiny circles over my clit, completely distracting me from the burn. I'm dripping wet.

JoeSmith steps away and whispers to the people as if teaching a lesson in a classroom. "Arousing her is the goal. If she isn't wet, you may have spanked too much or too little, or your technique needs work."

He glides his palm along my lower back as he continues in a hushed tone. "Each submissive is different so you'll need to pay close attention to find the perfect balance. My pet is soaked, as you can see, but we've been together for quite some time, and I know her body well."

A finger pushes into my pussy and wiggles as it reaches my depths. His knuckles press against my opening. I relax to allow three of his fingers to delve into my needy pussy. I crave him, any part of him deep inside me. A moan lodges in my throat. This feels so good.

He begins fucking me in a slow rhythm and waves his fingers, tapping my g-spot with each flutter. His pace quickens until my legs shake. I moan despite my instruction not to.

An orgasm builds even though he hasn't permitted me. I can't hold it back even if he demands it. My mind darkens as an orgasm rushes through every fibre of my being.

He abruptly withdraws his fingers before my orgasm concludes and cracks his palm on my welted ass, ruining my orgasm. I've disappointed him. I hadn't earned the right to cum, nor had I asked permission.

JoeSmith drops my gown to cover my ass. The silky material feels scratchy against my tenderized skin. With his hands placed on my shoulders, he urges me to straighten and then turns me so my back is against the pole before he pulls the rope to secure my arms over my head.

He wraps a belt around my waist and pulls it snug to hold my core to the pole. My left leg is tied to the pole at my knee and ankle. Then he wraps a rope three times around my right knee, knots it, and lifts as he ties the rope up by my hands, lifting my bent leg to my chest. With a light tug, he's sure I can't wiggle free.

The front of my gown's lifted and clipped to expose my torn bloomers, which likely don't cover my vagina anymore.

I hear the distinctive lovely and intimidating sound of leather fingers cutting through the air as the tassels slap against themselves and finally me. The tips of the flogger's tassels bite at the inside of my left thigh. I'm struck repeatedly with the many tresses of soft leather.

Floggers are my favourite of JoeSmith's tools. My pussy twitches each time the leather strikes my silky flesh. The slaps begin on my right thigh to make it just as red and hot as the other.

Deafening silence.

My pants fill the room as anticipation of another brush from the flogger is almost more than I can bear. The silence is broken when my master scuffs his shoes as he strolls away.

My bottom leg shakes under my weight while I continue balancing on the high heel. He returns and stops with his face a mere inch from mine. I can feel the heat of his breath on my cheek. If I pucker my lips I could kiss him, but he would punish me for that.

It's so quiet. If I listen hard enough, I might hear his eyelashes cut through the air as he blinks.

Will he kiss me?

My lips await his, but he disappoints when his hand wraps around my throat. He could kill me and I would have no way to stop him. I am completely at his mercy. This is where trust comes in. His grip eases and his hand slips down to my cleavage.

With a violent yank, he tears the dress to expose my breasts. The shock forces a sharp yelp from me. I should have expected the unexpected. I press my lips tightly together to stop my jaw from quivering.

He slaps my left breast with his latex-covered hand and it shocks me. I gasp and squeeze my eyes closed behind the mask but JoeSmith presses his body against mine. His breath is hot as he whispers in my ear.

"You seem to have forgotten that you're to remain quiet?" He takes in a long breath and slowly releases it as he caresses my raised thigh. "Don't make another sound."

He kisses the inside of my knee and pinches my left nipple firmly, pulling it to test my silence. I don't make a sound but the sensation shoots straight to my clit, and I like it.

"You will not forget to abide by my rules." His palm cups my cheek and I lean into it. "You are my one and only, Pet, and I treasure you."

Master slaps my pussy gently, then slithers his middle finger between my folds, leaving the two opposing fingers to ride outside the outer labia. His digit slides into my pussy, gaining lubrication before he rolls gentle circles over my clitoris.

If he keeps this up, I will lose my fucking mind!

He whispers slightly louder when he speaks to his audience. "You should always reward your submissive for abiding by your rules. Pets love to be rewarded."

My pussy flinches as my clit swells under his touch. I breathe as calmly as I can, but it's difficult to maintain control.

His freshly shaven cheek presses to mine and he whispers so sweetly, "Do you want to cum?"

Yes, dammit!

I nod.

When I'm close, he slows long enough to pull me back from the edge. I want to scream and beg him to let me cum, but I don't dare speak. As if reading my thoughts, he knows when to stop and start. He'll control when I orgasm. He's pulled me back several times, frustrating me to no end. He knows how much I want this—need this.

I won't beg. I can't!

"Do you want to give in? I can make you hold it if you'd prefer." His exhale does little to hide his amusement. "Speak, my pet. Tell me what you want."

He's entrancingly seductive. At this moment, he owns my mind, body, and soul. I belong to him. I'm safe under his watchful eye. Safe in his arms. Safe from insecurity, self-doubt and indecision.

"Please, Master JoeSmith," I beg. "May I cum?"

"Yes, and you may scream if it's what you desire." He nips my earlobe with his teeth.

He removes his finger from my firm clitoris and I scream, "No, please!"

His hot mouth engulfs my pussy. The tip of his tongue traces under the hood that shelters the most sensitive part of my body. He gently sucks while caressing my clit, urging me closer to the edge where my mind will fall numb to the world I exist in.

How exciting is it for the audience to watch JoeSmith give his slave such a lavish reward? I picture it and it's enough to push me into the weightlessness of orgasm.

Every muscle tightens beyond my control as my limbs pull viciously at the ropes to keep from floating away. My lungs burn, desperate for a breath. As my head pushes back against the pole, my mouth gapes and a scream echoes about the room.

The delirium eases and leaves me exhausted and gasping for breaths. My muscles continue to twitch.

He lowers my leg and asks, "Did you enjoy that, Pet?"

I nod, unable to form words. His fingertips brush from my cheek to my clavicle.

"Now that she's climaxed, she'll do just about any twisted act my dirty mind can think up."

He isn't lying. I'll do almost anything to please him with the hope he'll reward me with another orgasm.

He saunters away and a different set of footsteps approaches. *Click, clack. Click, clack.* I hope she's Lady Catherine. The woman stands close to me and an overwhelming scent of her cherry blossom perfume fills my nostrils. She's not who I was hoping she'd be.

Small hands touch my skin as she frees me from the rope bindings. I wobble and her gentle, cold hands grab my waist to steady me.

"Are you okay?" she asks in a voice as soft and sweet as her perfume.

I nod.

She reaches around me to undo my dress and relieve me of it. She also removes the corset, tattered remainders of my bloomers, and my shoes. Other than my mask, I'm stark-naked and completely exposed to gawking eyes.

Chapter 7

JS

A Couple's Fantasy

While I'm still blindfolded, the woman guides me away from the pole. I feel for the bench and lie face down on the cushioned leather pad. She binds each ankle in soft cuffs and spreads my feet before fastening them to the base of the bench. My hips rest on the edge while my legs dangle.

I startle when JoeSmith clears his throat behind me. I didn't know it was him and not her who'd positioned me. He wraps leather cuffs on my wrists and fastens them to the sides of the bench so they hang straight downward. He lays a thick strap over my back, which hugs my waist to the bench. I rest my cheek on the cool leather.

I love to be vulnerable, to be at his mercy and not know what he'll do. Being bound quiets my mind like nothing else can.

He speaks. "I want to show you just how *accommodating* the vagina can be."

I tense, knowing he's going to stretch my pussy. I love it and hate it. The fullness of a fist inside of me can't be compared.

He pats my welted ass. "Relax."

The cap to the bottle of lubrication pops and the fluid gurgles when squeezed. His warm hand smears the cold liquid, coating my labia. Three fingers push in and my walls clamp around them. He clears his throat, a signal for me to relax, and he pulls and stretches my pussy as he fucks.

Four fingers slip in and I silently remind myself not to tense. There's a lot of pressure but it's not painful. He spins his fingers and spreads them inside me. The pressure veers more toward pleasure as he expertly expands my vaginal walls.

With slow, gentle pressure, he pushes. Just as I doubt it'll happen today, his palm slips into me. Only his thumb prevents him from pushing wrist-deep.

Pain, pressure, and yet so fucking mind-blowingly awesome! I force my body to sag limply on the bench. His hand continues to spin, push, and stretch my opening

His hand pushes past the tight opening and is instantly swallowed to his wrist. I yelp but JoeSmith doesn't punish me for my outburst. He holds motionless to give my body time to adjust to the incredible invasion.

The onlookers' whispers are hushed. I'm jealous of them because I'd love to see his hand entombed in my body.

Gently, he spins his relaxed fist. The pleasure and pain ride a fine line and teeter between both.

My wail echoes about the room when he cautiously slides his hand completely out, then back in. Nothing I've experienced has made me feel so completely lost in my own body. How can something so painful feel this marvellous?

Sir's whisper snaps me back to reality. "Pet, you don't have to remain quiet. Enjoy yourself."

That's all I need to hear.

As if I've held my breath for an hour, a blast of carnal moans claws through the silence. I'm out of my mind. The longer he fucks me with his hand, the more animalistic I sound. I have lost the ability for rational thought as an orgasm slowly builds.

I snap back to reality when Master removes his hand. People mumble but in my cloud of ecstasy, words have no meaning.

The snap of a latex glove grabs my attention, as foggy as that might be. I hear the familiar *squwoosh* of the lubricant bottle and then high-heels click on the floor as they near. Is this the same candy-scented woman who undressed me?

A cold hand glides up and down my backside. I gasp when the woman's icy hand glides into my stretched pussy. It feels like she's poured ice water on a burning fire. I've never had a woman invade me with her entire hand. My female preparers penetrate me, but it's not to pleasure me and never done with a fist.

The petite size of her hand allows for a more pleasurable experience, yet I'm still full. Pleasure builds as she spins, pulls almost completely out, and pushes back in. Her gentle, rhythmic motion builds an urgency in my belly.

My moans beg her not to stop; not to speed up and not to slow. I moan with each penetration. She has me so turned on. I know Master watches over me and I feel safe.

I become weightless as I float higher and higher out of myself until I fall over the edge into the blackness of euphoria. I scream and fight to buck free of my restraints. My walls grip her hand, hoping to pull it deeper. She pushes and fucks fast, hard, and with a slight spin. I cum again, and conscious thought ceases to exist.

Oh, yes!

I've forgotten how to swallow and a bead of saliva leaks onto the leather pad. My vagina pulses and throbs around her hand, squeezing it relentlessly. I hear a sexy giggle. She's excited at how easy it was to bring me to two powerful climaxes.

Her hand holds still inside me and I hear inaudible whispers not far to my right. My thoughts are mushy, like I'm trying to think through jelly. I call it ecstasy fog, and it's fabulous.

A finger slips into my asshole and it yanks me from the fog. The finger slides in and out and is soon joined by a second. The digits pull at the rim to stretch it. It's uncomfortable, and yet so extraordinarily naughty and taboo that it's fucking exciting.

With her wrist deep in my pussy and three fingers in my ass, I don't think I can take much more. Her hand slowly fucks.

I feel exposed and violated like a cheap whore. I love it!

"Pet, what's the safeword?" Master whispers beside my ear.

My thoughts are scrambled. I struggle to remember. "Zebra! The safeword is zebra."

His fingertips gently stroke my cheek. He kisses my cheekbone and then his shoes drag as he makes his way behind me.

The fingers leave my ass but are replaced by something else, something thick and warm. It glides into my backside and a hard groan barks out of my throat. The insertion slows to a snail's pace but is still being slid into me. Hands grip either side of my waist on the bench just as someone's hips press firmly against my ass cheeks.

I have a cock in my ass, but who's? I don't care as long as he fucks me. That's all I want. I know JoeSmith will keep me safe.

The unnamed cock fucks deep with his hips slapping hard against my ass cheeks. I have no control over what's being done to me. This is so exciting! The hand begins to roll inside my pussy while the cock slams in and out of my ass. I'm filled to max capacity.

Just when I think it can't possibly get any more intense, a vibrator is pressed against my clit. It sends me over the edge. I've lost control and moan and scream. It doesn't sound like it's me who makes these noises. It sounds like someone's in sheer agony or utter ecstasy; perhaps it's a wounded animal.

I'm lost in the nothingness of euphoria. I quiver violently as my muscles flex, hoping to defeat the restraints. He moans and fucks me harder. The pressure is incredible.

I am nothing. I am but a vessel for his pleasure. Do to me what you desire and I will cum at your beckoning. I am yours.

He grabs a wad of my hair and pulls my head back. "I'm fucking your asshole, bitch, and there's nothing you can do about it! Tell me you love my cock in your ass!"

I don't recognize his voice and he isn't whispering. He's not my master. Who is this wild man?

This feels so good, so dirty.

"I love your cock in my ass!" I repeat.

My mind is lost and my body writhes below him, hindered by my shackles.

Orgasm overtakes me again. My muscles tense and my pussy walls force against the fist. She yanks it out and a flood of my hot cum follows. It trails down my shaking legs.

With an obnoxiously loud grunt, the man slams his pelvis violently against my ass for the last time. His cock swells and twitches inside the condom. He groans with a heavy exhale as his prick slithers listlessly from my asshole.

My body is my own again: stretched, tired and used, but satiated. I hear whispers followed by the crowd exiting through the door.

Silence. I hate the silence. Did everyone leave, including my master? I didn't get to pleasure him.

Is he disappointed in me?

Chapter 8

JS

A Question for Joe Smith

I startle when a voice whispers, breaking through the silence, "You've been a very good girl. This was a fantasy come true for that couple. You should feel very proud of yourself."

He unties my hands, waist, and finally my feet. I stand on rubbery legs and remain blindfolded. I hear him remove his pants.

He sits on a squeaky chair. "Take your mask off, so I can see your painted eyes."

I remove my feathered mask and set it on the bench. My make-up is surely smeared terribly at this point. The light is blinding, even though candlelight illuminates the room.

Master sits in a chair in front of me. He wears a full-face black mask bearing tiny eye holes and a slightly larger hole at his mouth. I want to rip it off his face to reveal the identity of my fascinating master, but I don't dare.

His shirt resembles one for a wealthy nineteenth-century man. He leans back on the chair with his hips resting at the edge. His legs fall open, and his erection is fat and stands at attention.

"Come to me," he whispers. My legs are unstable. "Take your time, Pet. You've been through quite an ordeal."

He leans forward and outstretches his hand. I take it and stagger toward him. He hands me a condom and leans back on the chair.

"Suck my cock. Then put this on me, and ride me."

JoeSmith's whisper is deep, sexy and assertive. How could I possibly resist?

I sink to my knees and gently grasp his solid cock. I admire the soft, warm skin that covers such a fiercely hard organ. I tilt my head and glide my tongue along the underside, then swallow his cock deep into my throat until I can take no more and then fuck his cock with my mouth. I cup his testicles in my hand and roll them gently.

He gathers my hair and pulls my mouth off his shaft. As he sits forward, he tips my head back and kisses me hard.

"You're very good at that. Maybe a little too good. Put the condom on me. I can't leave here without having been inside you."

Sometimes, when he speaks, I think he cares more for me than just as a sexual plaything.

I roll the condom on him, rise, and straddle his strong thighs. He cups my ass cheeks and holds them firmly. I am so tired. I hope I'm able to please Sir.

I guide his cock into my pussy that's shrunk back enough where he's snug inside me and hook my feet on the rungs of the chair. Gripping the backrest, I slowly move my hips back and forth, never lifting my body.

"Look at me. I want to watch your expressions. You have control over me."

Even behind a whisper, his words cut to my soul. He appreciates me and is giving me free rein to take from him what I desire.

I stare at the hood while my tummy flips feverishly. This is the first time he's allowed me to look at his eyeholes. I can't see his eyes because they're shadowed in darkness, but I sense him looking at me and it's tantalizing.

I'm unable to hold his gaze because he intimidates me, but that's his role as my master.

He strokes my cheek with the softest caress. "Look over to the chair on your left. Do you see her?"

A lone woman sits in the far corner in the shadows. I thought everyone had left.

"I don't want you to take your eyes off her until I tell you to. Will that be easier for you than looking at me?"

Because he did not ask me to speak, a nod will do. I admire her pink feathered mask. How erotic is this? I have a newfound energy that urges me to fuck him with vigour.

He holds my ass tighter and forces me to fuck him faster and harder. I throw my head back in an uncontrollable contortion. He braces my lower back to prevent me from toppling to the floor.

I'm coming!

He sucks my nipple hard and then the other one. My hips slam him to the chair. I fear it might crumble beneath us.

The woman's legs are crossed and her hand is between her thighs. She's masturbating. She's a voyeur.

My pussy walls strangle his cock as another orgasm takes me. My body twitches and jerks spastically. He's watching my face while I fuck him and take my pleasure.

Who is that woman to him? Maybe she's another pet or his girlfriend; wife, perhaps. Is she the woman whose hand was inside me?

"Get on your knees and suck my cock. I want to cum on your tits."

I roll off the condom and keep it in my hand. He stands and pets my head. I part my lips and slide the head deep into my throat and try not to take my eyes off her, as instructed by my master.

My mouth slides along his shaft until my nose thrusts against his firm abs. I stick my tongue out and try to lick his balls. I repeat three more times.

"You're a good woman and my favourite little plaything."

He grabs my hair and forces my head back until my chest juts out toward him. He strokes his shaft with one hand and holds my hair with the other. I can almost see the shape of his lips through the hole in the mask.

Heavy groans erupt from deep in his chest. His belly jerks and hot seed splatters my chest. He pants and sits.

The strange woman stands and quickly exits. JoeSmith and I are alone. He takes my hand in his and I sit on his lap. He wraps his arms around my waist and kisses my shoulder.

"You've earned a special treat, which you'll get the next time we meet. Did you enjoy yourself tonight? You may speak freely."

I nod and smile. "Yes, Sir. Very much so. Thank you, Master."

"I enjoy your smile." His finger glides along my bottom lip. "Lady Catherine told me you want to ask me something, so ask."

"I have a friend, and she wants to," I pause to clear my throat, "take part."

His voice is harsh. “How did she come to learn about this?”

I swallow away the sudden dryness in my throat. “It’s been very difficult keeping this from her. With her persistence, I finally broke down and told her.” I look at him but quickly cast my gaze to the floor. “She’s intrigued.”

JoeSmith brushes loose strands of hair from my cheek and tucks them behind my ear. “Are you willing to share me and my attention with your friend?”

“If it pleases you, Sir.” I look at his eye holes and see him blink. “She’s my closest friend, and I trust her completely.”

We stand and he faces me away, then hands me his hood. My heart pounds.

Will I be allowed to see him? He kisses the back of my neck.

“I’ll consider your request.”

It’s quiet, and then his shoes scuff the floor by the exit door before it closes with a click.

I’m alone but content… even with the silence.

Chapter 9

JS

Sam Needs to Know

This week at work has been nothing short of boring, as usual. I wish I was given tougher assignments that didn't numb my brain with tedium. The only exciting moments are when I talk to Sam about my adventures. She insisted I tell her everything that happened in my last encounter with JoeSmith and in great detail, while she sniffed the white rose JoeSmith put in my locker. I'm always gifted a rose after a playdate, which I place in a crystal vase on my desk. It's a happy reminder, until it wilts.

I stand at the window in the lunchroom while I wait for the kettle to boil. It's raining and isn't expected to let up until later this afternoon.

I've caught Sam staring into space a lot this week. She loses herself in her imagination, perhaps putting herself in my tales of pleasure and pain. Every time I catch her, I throw a wadded piece of paper at her head just like she does to me.

Will I be jealous if she joins us? Talking about it is one thing, but to watch him touch her is another. Would I lose both of them if he prefers her over me?

I can't bear the thought of losing him, even though I know he's not mine to keep. He's my master and despite my efforts to keep my emotions in check, I've developed strong feelings for him.

I'm so thankful it's Friday morning. Today I got the email from him with clues for Saturday's adventure. I wonder if he'll accept Sam. I sit at my desk, lift my mug to take my first sip of tea, and who sneaks up behind me?

"So?" she blurts out.

I nearly jolt out of my skin and spill some tea on my skirt that immediately sinks onto my thigh. She looks at me as if I can read her mind while I stare at her with angry eyes and pursed lips.

"What?" I hiss.

I know what she wants but I act oblivious so I can prolong her agony. I love watching her twist in the wind, so to speak.

"You're killing me, woman!" she says and my expression doesn't change.

Sam's arms flop to her sides and she pouts. She slides her butt onto my desk and I bite my lips to hide my amusement at how excited and anxious she is.

Her voice lowers. "So, can I come with you? Did he write yet? Oh, Terri, please say I can join you. Tell him I promise not to be a pain in the ass. I'll do everything I'm told, I'll never complain, and I won't cry."

She looks at her knees and chews her fingernail. Sam always chews her nails when nervous or telling a lie.

I look around to make sure there are no prying ears. "You can't promise not to be a pain in my ass." My eyebrows rise. "What if he directs you to finger fuck my asshole? You'd be a pain in my ass, literally."

I joke, but her wide eyes and gaping mouth are priceless.

"Do you think he'll make me do that?" Her fingers lace together and she holds them against her lips. "He'll break me in slowly, right?"

I shrug. "Maybe. I never know what he'll do. He likes to keep me guessing. Would you be all right with penetrating me?"

I watch her face to see if she cringes; instead, she looks curious.

"Yeah, I'm okay with that. I've never touched a girl sexually, but I'm willing to try anything." She rests her hands on the desk beside her knees. "Lesbianism must have something going for it or there wouldn't be any lesbians, right?"

She looks sexy with hooded eyes. The corner of her lip twists into a crooked smile.

I'd have sex with Sam. If I know JoeSmith at all, he'll have us licking and fucking each other in no time. The thought intrigues me.

"So, did he write to you?" Her arms lift to her waist, palms up.

I roll my eyes in frustration. "I checked my email before I came to work and nothing. He'll skip a weekend now and then. I might not hear from him for two weeks. It's happened."

"Check it again," she demands and waves her finger at my computer screen.

"I won't check my email at work. It's too risky. What if Bossman has someone monitoring the computers?" I lean toward her and scan for listeners. "We'd be humiliated by the water cooler gossip crew and/or fired! I need this job, Sam. I'll check it when I get home."

"I can't wait that long! This is torture! Just check it, please! I don't think the boss cares what we do as long as we get our jobs done and we do that, so no worries." She slides her ass off the desk. "Besides, I read through my emails all the time and he's never confronted me about it."

She's acting like an unruly child and I won't give back her balloon. I know how much she wants this, but she doesn't realize the anticipation is torture for me, too.

"Sam, no! Think about this: if I get found out, it's just a matter of time before they realize that you're involved. We'll be fired or forced to quit due to humiliation."

She scrunches the left side of her face, doubting anyone would know she's involved.

"Think about it. You're my only best friend. He'll say whether I can bring a friend along—*a friend*—meaning you. Bossman will put two-and-two together because he has a brain." I shake my head and wave my hand to dismiss her. "I don't want him to look at me like I'm some weird freak. He's hot, single, and you never know. Maybe one day he'll see me as more than just his employee. A girl can hope."

She bites her lip and waves her brows. "That's true, but he might like a wild, crazy girl who'll try anything. It is a selling feature." She winks.

"Yeah, but…" I shake my head. "He doesn't seem the type, Sam."

She won't give up easily. As a last-ditch effort, she stands behind my chair and wraps her arms around my shoulders.

"Neither do you, sweet and innocent, Terri." Sam disappears into her cubicle and returns, rolling her chair next to me and sits. "You can use my phone. Bossman can't check that way unless he has magical powers or a computer hacker hidden in the back room."

"If I get caught using a cell phone, I'll get written up. You know that's a huge no-no."

Like usual, she begs relentlessly and bounces in her chair. "Please, please, please, please!"

I hate childish behaviour, but she breaks me.

"Fine! I'll check it when everyone leaves for lunch. Okay? Are you happy?"

She smiles exaggeratedly and shows off all of her teeth. "Hell, yes, I am!"

I chuckle. "I'll stay after everyone leaves. Just leave me your phone. I don't have any data left on mine."

"Yes!"

Sam leaps up and dances around like a teenager who just got asked to the prom. She's so damn cute. I really can't wait to watch her writhe at his touch. I bet she's a screamer, but JoeSmith will break her of that.

Chapter 10

Does He Know?

It's 12:15, and almost lunchtime. I look to see if Sam's nervously chewing her fingernail while staring at the clock, wishing the seconds would tick faster, but she's not there. Just then, she hops her ass onto my desk, startling me, and I yip.

"Dammit!"

She grins wide. "So, are you excited? I'm excited. I asked Nancy to save us seats in case we're late for lunch."

I glance at her and then back to my computer so I can save my spreadsheet before logging out. "You can't stay back with me. Everyone'll notice your absence; mine, not so much. You should go with the crowd. I'll stay behind and meet you there after."

She smiles excitedly. "Okay, so what do you want me to order you for lunch? I think I'm going to get the soup of the day and Caesar salad with chicken."

Sam can hardly contain herself. She's pure high energy, like a kid on a sugar high. I swear she vibrates perpetually.

She speaks fast and in a higher octave than usual. "This'll be so fun. I didn't get much work done today.

Hopefully, they won't check because I'd get in shit for not pulling my weight." She frowns and jerks her eyes up at the ceiling. "Maybe, I felt a little sick or had cramps. Men don't like to hear about lady issues."

"No, they don't." I look over at the clock; 12:27. "Order me what you're having and hot lemon water."

She looks at her watch, then slides off my desk and strides to her desk to retrieve her purse. With a wink and a little wave, she high-tails it out the door among the crowd of hungry souls.

I act like I'm looking for something so nobody questions my loitering. My heart's pounding. It's not only Sam who's anxious to know if she's invited.

Fuck! Sam didn't leave her phone! Should I use the computer? I look up at the wall of windows that line Ben Manning's office and overlook our cubicles. He remains at his desk. If I stay and he sees me, will he be curious why I've stayed behind?

"Aren't you coming to lunch, Terri?"

I jolt and squeal. Rick's right beside me and looking at my computer screen. Thankfully, I wasn't reading the email. He might have read it over my shoulder.

"Ah, I'll be there in five minutes, tops. Sam will order for me."

I'm a terrible liar so I didn't even attempt to. I smile as he walks away. He's the last to leave the room, so now's my chance.

I quickly load my email. My heart pounds loudly in my ears. What if someone forgot something and comes back? They'll see I'm on my private email. My head swivels as I scan the room and then up to the boss's office. He's on the phone and not looking my way.

I hurriedly find the website and sign in. I scan down the list of emails and find the message from JoeSmith. Usually, I wait to prolong my agony but not now. There's no time for that. I click to open it, then scan the door one more time before I read it.

Dear Pet,

You must be at the pickup point by 5:30, Saturday evening. You will not be late as a punishment will be enforced if you are. You must go to the salon today and get waxed. As usual, if you skip my instruction and shave, I'll enforce a strong punishment.

You'll be expected to adhere to all rituals and procedures, and you'll be prepared and posed in time for my arrival.

You'll show yourself, you'll entertain, and your beauty will be admired, but you'll be mine.

Do you accept?

Yours,
Master JoeSmith

Without hesitation, I hit the reply icon. My hands hover over the keyboard as I consider how to word my question. Short and to the point will be best.

Dear Sir,

I accept, but wonder if you've decided if you'd like my friend to attend.

Always,
Your Pet

I need to get to the restaurant but wait anxiously for a reply while I search the room for any stragglers. When I look up at the boss's office, he's looking at me as he slips his arm in his suit jacket.

Does he know? Did he secretly watch what I did on my computer? He waves to me as a kind gesture. I force a smile and wave back. I quickly shut down my computer, grab my purse, and flee out the door.

I rush down the block toward the restaurant and tell myself that he doesn't know anything. He seemed relaxed, which is the opposite of what he'd be if he found out I used the company computer for personal use. Besides, I think he would've been more upset about the email content than anything, and he waved; therefore, he must not suspect any foul play.

I reach for the restaurant's door handle but an arm reaches from behind me. I turn to see who it is and thank them. It's my delicious boss, who may or may not have watched me open an erotic email. I freeze, but only for a second, and wonder if he noticed.

A shy smile lifts my lips as I thank him before rushing inside. I can sense him following me toward the table filled with our colleagues. We arrive just as our food does. Someone must have ordered for him just as Sam did for me.

Nobody questions my tardiness, which is odd since I've never stayed late. If I haven't finished by the time I leave, it waits until my return. Sam must have calmed any concerns.

Everyone chats amongst themselves but Sam stares at me with huge eyes. I reach for the edge of the seat to pull in my chair but it slides under me before I can. When I look back to see who is so gentlemanly, Mr. Manning holds the backrest. My face flushes crimson when his sexy eyes meet mine.

He's always made me nervous. He's one of the smartest, sexiest men I've ever known, and he's way out of my league.

"Thank you, again," I say with a chuckle.

Sam anxiously waits for me to start talking. It's fun to make her wait. After I set my purse under the table, I glance at Sam and then Mr. Manning as he takes his seat while he taps on his phone, deep in thought.

That man is all business. I'd bet he works until he closes his eyes at night.

I'd love to lie next to him in his bed as he drifts off to dreamland. To watch his bare chest, rise and fall, lit only by the moonlight seeping through the window. That'd be intoxicating.

"Terri!" Sam elbows my ribs.

"Ouch!" I realize I've been staring at Ben.

She elbows me again. "Did you do it?"

"You forgot to leave me your phone."

"Oh, shit!" Her hand slaps to cover her mouth before she digs in her purse and hands it to me. "Check it now."

"It's okay, it's done."

"What do you mean, it's *don*e? What's *done*? How would you do it if I had the phone?"

We both veer our eyes to nonchalantly glance at Mr. Manning, who stares past the phone in his hand at his water glass. What's he thinking that has him so lost in thought? I'd give anything to be inside his head, especially if he's thinking about sex!

She leans closer to me. "Did you use your computer?"

I shrug and rush to say, "You didn't leave me any other choice." I nod and look at her lip held tightly by her teeth. "Yes, I checked it."

"I'm sorry," Sam whispers but gradually grows louder as her words spew quicker. "So, he must have written to you, right? What did he write? Did you write him back? What did you tell him? Can I come, too?"

So many questions!

I scan the table to see if her outburst got anyone's attention. Sure enough, almost everyone is looking at her. Even Bossman looks up from his phone. He nearly always comes to lunch with us on Fridays. It's his way to keep the friendships with his employees strong, I guess.

Sherry sits beside him and, as always, chatters feverishly at him even though he isn't paying her much attention. I don't think she cares if anyone listens. Our peers say she talks just to hear her voice. They might be right.

I meet eyes with him and he immediately drops his head to look down at his phone. The edges of his lips turn upward in an awkward grin. Slowly, his eyes meet my gaze from under his brow.

How much of our conversation did he hear? I try to remember what she said and if any of it was taboo. What did she say?

My cheeks flush hot. What would he think if he read that email? Would he fire me? He's too respectful to embarrass or blackmail me into some torrid affair—which wouldn't require blackmail. A mere suggestion would have me naked in seconds. But to ask would require a real in-depth conversation. He hasn't done that since last year's Christmas party.

I don't know why we don't talk anymore. Maybe I've been too preoccupied with JoeSmith that I haven't been sending out any vibes. We used to talk in the lunchroom at work when we'd run into one another. We were friends, or so I thought. Perhaps back then he wanted to get to know me to see if he felt a spark. I'm probably just overthinking it like I always do.

I couldn't ask for a better boss. He gives excellent bonuses when we've earned them, and he treats everyone equally and fairly. Quite often I look up to see him staring down at us and lost in thought. Maybe that's why he doesn't get upset when he catches one of us daydreaming.

I've compared many men I know to my master, including my boss. Ben's physical attributes are similar, but sadly, the differences cancel him out as my mystery man.

Although Ben stands just over six feet tall, JoeSmith is taller and my master has more muscle. JoeSmith's hair is always messy and his eyes might be dark but I'm not sure. Ben's short, and his dark hair's never out of place and he has the greenest eyes I've ever seen. Both men are always freshly shaven but Ben always smells like a delicious, musky woodsman and JoeSmith smells of soap. Ben's probably thirty years old and I believe JoeSmith to be older.

Ben's a well-dressed man in designer suits tailored perfectly to accentuate his strong, lean, manly build. He's definitely a good-looking man and he'd be a hell of a catch for some lucky woman. So far, nobody's been good enough to land him.

I have fantasies about him bending me over the back of his sofa or lying me on his desk so he can fill me with his steely-hard cock while everyone works below unaware of the orgasms being had by me. Each powerful thrust would have the feet of his desk squealing as it slides along the floor.

My pussy clenches, alerting me that I'm staring at him for the second time. I have to look away but his shirt does nothing to hide his strong chest and tiny nipples; it's hypnotic.

What's wrong with me? Why can't I blink? Do I want to look up to see if he's watching me undress him with my eyes?

No!

"Terri, woohoo!" Sam waves her hand in front of my face to wake me. "So? Are you going to tell me what he wrote, or are you going to keep me guessing?"

I reply in the lowest whisper I can manage. "I asked him if my friend can come along because he didn't say either way."

The waitress sets a glass of water in front of our boss and he thanks her. His eyes meet mine and he smiles. I return the gesture and then jolt when an arm glides past my head holding a white mug. He snickers and I blush.

Sam asks, "And?"

"And what? He didn't write back right away. I doubt he sits in front of his computer staring at the screen, desperate to hear from me." I pause to sip from my mug. "Now we wait until I get home to check it again. Hopefully, he'll have responded by then. Please don't get upset if he doesn't invite you to join. He didn't seem open to the idea."

"He won't refuse!" she declares with eyebrows raised. "What man in his right mind would say no to having two women at his mercy?"

Sam turns back to her plate and starts to eat her lunch without so much as another word about it. I join in on another conversation and leave her to her thoughts.

She's unusually quiet and people have noticed. Sam's always been a social butterfly. She's the bouncy, chatty person who loves to be the center of attention. People seem to like her for it. If a crowd needs livening up, she's the woman to do it.

Today, however, she's lost in the fantasies in her mind.

Chapter 11

Career Advancement

Sam's still unusually quiet when we arrive back at the office. She sits at her desk and gets right to work. I can tell the tales of my experiences are playing in her imagination.

I remember when I waited for my first instructional email. It was torture. The only difference is she's waiting to see if he'll accept or deny her, which would be worse. She'll be so disappointed if he refuses. We only have to be here for an hour and a half longer, but that seems like a lifetime to wait for something of this magnitude.

Time ticks by slowly. It's one of those afternoons when the minutes seem like hours. My work phone rings, waking me from my gloomy thoughts.

Sam's probably calling so nobody'll bother to listen to her conversation because they'll just think it's a work call. Normally, when she comes to my desk, people watch us and try to listen in. It's not that they're necessarily nosy, but that work is boring and human movement breaks the monotony.

"Terri, can you come to my office, please?"

The blood leaves my face and my hands shake. It's Mr. Manning. Did he read my email? Oh my God! I take a deep, cleansing breath to ward off the nauseating panic threatening to hurl my lunch from my body.

He's never called me to his office without at least one other person. Every time I've been up there has been to discuss a case along with another co-worker, except for the day I came in for an interview. He hired me in less than ten minutes.

Am I about to get fired?

"On my way." My heart pounds feverishly.

I will my shaking legs to lift me from my chair and hope they won't quit on me. Sam notices the colour drained from my face. Her eyes widen with concern as I walk past her desk and toward the stairs that lead to his office.

I hear her mumble, "Oh, shit."

I walk up the stairs on trembling legs and stand outside his closed door. I squeeze my shaking hands into tight fists before I lightly knock on his door and slowly push it open.

"You wanted to see me?"

My voice doesn't sound like mine; it's a few octaves higher.

Without lifting his face from the contents of a manila folder, he offers me a seat. I'm grateful that I don't have to continue trusting my weakened legs won't give out.

"Hi, Terri." He looks at me with a lopsided smile. "How are you?"

Small talk—the introduction to the slaughter will come soon enough.

"I'm fine, Mr. Manning. How are you?" My voice seems to have returned to normal.

"I'm doing well." His voice is deep and strong. "I do, however, have something I'd like to propose to you."

"Propose?" I ask and wonder if he meant to say, *I propose you should get a new career.*

"You're doing a great job here. You could easily advance in this company."

Wait, what?

My thoughts shift into sex mode and all I can do is picture him throwing me on his desk to make my fantasy come true.

Rid the thought! Pay attention!

"Are you busy tomorrow in the late afternoon, around four o'clock? I know it's Saturday but," he leans back in his chair and holds the ends of a pen with both hands, "I have a heavy load, and I think you're the best candidate to assist."

Mr. Manning waits for me to respond, but my mouth can't catch up to my racing thoughts. He wants me to help him with a *heavy load*. Is that a sexual innuendo?

"We have a new client, and there's a lot of information; too much for one person to get through in the allotted time frame. He wants it handled as quickly as possible." He leans forward and taps his pen three times on the desk before gripping it in his fist. "I would only keep you for a few hours, maybe until seven o'clock. You don't have to say yes."

I could drown in his dreamy emerald eyes.

He must have overheard Sam and me discussing plans tomorrow night or he read the email and thinks I'm an easy lay. Am I a wild woman he can have if he gets me alone? Yes, probably, but I doubt he heard any of our conversation from across the table. I try to remember if she said what our plans were for Saturday, but it's all a blur.

I try not to squirm, instead weaving my fingers together and dropping them on my tightly squeezed thighs.

It's rare, but occasionally we come in on weekends. He usually plucks people from the work pool that are reliable employees and hands them client cases that would better suit their proficiency than someone else's. A new client's case is rarely handled by anyone but him, so he must think I'll be an asset to the client or he wouldn't have asked.

"Um, I'm sorry, but I have a commitment for tomorrow evening. I'll come in early any other day or stay late. I can probably stay an extra hour today to get started," I pause, hoping to slow my ramble, "if that would be something you'd consider."

He blinks several times before looking at this hand resting atop a brown box file.

"But tomorrow… I'm sorry, I just can't."

Mr. Manning leans back in his chair and taps the pen on his chin while one side of his mouth lifts.

What is he thinking? Should I get ahead of this and confess and apologize for the email before he questions me about it? Perhaps I should try to explain it away as something innocent. How would I even do that? There can be no other explanation than I'm going to have a very intense sexual romp tomorrow night, and I've asked to bring my friend along so I can drag her into my corrupt world.

"It was just a thought. I'd ask you to come in earlier—around three o'clock—but I can't make that work." He takes a breath while he looks at me with a tilted head and an innocent smile. "I see everyone as employees and sometimes forget they have lives outside of work."

I nod and try to look professional but when my pussy clenches, I bite the left side of my lower lip.

"We can tackle it Monday morning." His eyes drop to my chest but quickly jerk back to meet mine. "Enjoy your date."

I make a weird sound, like a snort crossed with a laugh, followed by fast-talking, word-vomit. "Oh, don't be fooled. I really don't have a life outside of this office. I mean, I'm not a crazy cat lady or anything. I'm not saying that's a bad thing. I just don't go out much. I don't really go on dates. I mean, I'm not a shut-in. I have gone on dates. I'm not a virgin or a prude, if you know what I mean." I wink.

What the actual fuck!

I press my lips together to stop myself from rambling further. I cannot believe I just said all that. I'm so embarrassed. No matter how much back peddling I try to do, I can't erase that blunder.

"That's good to know," he says, fully amused. "I'll let you get back to work. Thanks for your time. Perhaps you can start on it Monday morning."

"Sure, definitely. I'm sorry I'm not available tomorrow. And, I'm sorry… for the… um, *that*," I say while swirling my finger around my mouth.

I should leave immediately. Hopefully, I won't further my indignation with a stumble and faceplant on his carpet. I still don't know if he snooped and read my email, but he might fire me simply because I'm a buffoon.

Chapter 12

Can She Come?

As I descend the stairs, I grip the railing tightly so I don't fall all the way down. I come into Sam's line of sight, and she scans my face for either a smile or evidence of shed tears.

Sam is out of her chair and holding papers in her hand as if to show me something. It's a little trick we often use to make it look like we're working when we're just gabbing. Her hands shake so much I wouldn't be able to read the paper if I tried.

"What did he say? Did he read the email? Are you fired? Tell me! Tell me, now!"

While still a little flushed from my uncharacteristic rambling, I tell her what he said but omit my insane blunder. She stares at me for several seconds before she speaks.

"Do you think he read the email?" Her finger slips in her mouth and she begins to chew on the tough skin beside her nail.

"I don't know. He didn't mention it, so maybe not." Mr. Manning is at his desk watching us. "We should get back to work. We'll chat later. He's watching."

I walk back to my desk and pretend I'm hard at work. It takes all my willpower not to look up to see if he's looking down. Fortunately, the remaining hour speeds by rather quickly and I don't get much work done. I had to reread everything several times before I could comprehend it.

Sam and I walk to our cars in silence. We parked side by side. Nobody's within earshot so we can finally talk freely.

Staying quiet over the past hour must have been torture for her. It's not in her character description. I don't think she knows that JoeSmith insists his subs remain perfectly quiet, no matter what he does to them until he tells them to be verbal. She'll have a hard time with that, but she'll learn quick enough; otherwise, she'll be punished until she does.

She hands me her phone and sways side to side. "Check your email, right now. I can't wait much longer. I need to know."

"If he tells me it's a go for tomorrow, you have to come with me to get waxed tonight. He hates stubble. You don't make the appointment or pay; he handles everything." I pause and rest my hands on her shoulders to stop her from swaying. "You're making me dizzy. All we have to do is show up. Are you good with that? It's non-negotiable."

I take her phone and log into my email while she talks.

"Yeah, I'll do anything. Is he hairless, too? Please tell me he doesn't have a huge bush." She shivers. "If he does, the deal's off."

I chuckle. "No, he's not Sasquatch. I'm sure he waxes because I've never felt any stubble. His balls are always smooth as a fine Italian leather purse."

"You have such a way with words." She giggles and wrinkles her nose. "Do you think he waxes his junk? Wouldn't that be more painful for a man?"

I shrug while I wait for her slow-ass phone to load. "I don't know. Maybe. He's too soft and smooth to be a shaver."

Finally, the screen loads. She leans in.

"Well?"

"Yes, he's replied. Keep watch for any stragglers who might sneak up on us." As I tap on his email, I look at her and scrunch one side of my face. "Here we go. It says: *Bring your friend with you to get a wax treatment. I'll arrange everything. She must be with you when the limo arrives. If she's late, the invitation will be retracted. She's your pet, therefore, it's your responsibility to teach her the rules. What shall I call her?*"

I lower the phone while she stares at me with parted lips and wide eyes. Maybe she didn't expect him to invite her, after all.

"That's it," I say and shrug. "So, what do you want your name to be? You can be anybody. I asked to be addressed by my name—it works best for me—but he prefers to call me Pet. It's rare, but he'll call me Terri as a reward."

She looks lost as her eyes shift as if searching her thoughts for a suitable title. "I… I don't know. Just use my real name, too." She waves her hand dismissively. "I'll come to your place at four-thirty tonight. Does that give us enough time to get this waxing business on a roll?"

I reply to his email with just one word, "*Sam.*"

After I log out, I hand her the phone and hug her. She's shaking.

"We're going to have so much fun!" I set her free and slide into my car.

"Absolutely!" She smiles and squares her shoulders to appear more confident.

On the drive home, I run through the whole conversation with Mr. Manning. My fingers go numb when I consider how badly it could have gone. He could have fired me. I analyze every word, smile, and facial tics. I will never open my personal emails at work again!

I park and sprint up the few steps to my front door. The key seems to have a mind of its own, flipping in my fingers but not turning the right way up. I finally get the key in but it won't turn.

"Oh, come on!" I should change this damn lock! Frustration overwhelms me and I growl. I stop, take a breath and try again. "Yay!"

I shut the door and lock it, then toss everything onto the chair while I kick off my shoes. Home at last! A comforting sense of safety and serenity warm me like a blanket.

As the computer revs up, I turn on the kettle and drop a Chamomile tea bag in the mug my Secret Santa gifted me last year that says *Fuck Off, I Need Coffee.*

I half expect a very anxious Sam to call and flash a hundred questions at me in a few seconds. But there's only silence, aside from the kettle. I squat my butt on the computer chair with the hot cup of tea and click to open my email. He sent a reply.

Dear Terri,

There are a few things I'd like to mention. There's a possibility Sam may be freshly shaved. If that's the case, she's not exempt from experiencing the waxing session; if not for hair removal, then for the excitement of the ritual, and you know I adhere to rituals.

I expect you to instruct her on my rules. Keep in mind I may ask you to perform sexual acts with each other.

Be sure she understands that before or during our session, if she, you, myself, or any witnesses feel uncomfortable for any reason, they are to speak up and the problem will be discussed immediately.

Terri, you'll always be my favourite pet. That will not change, even if your time with me is shared with her. At some point, I'll share her with others, just as I do you, but she is primarily yours and, therefore, your responsibility.

I will call her Slut or Samantha, as I assume that is her full given name. Tomorrow, I will do what I please to you... to both of you.

Is this acceptable?

Yours,
JoeSmith

I guide my arrow to the reply icon and click it, and then write, *I accept*. That doesn't look right. *I accept* is no longer suitable—*we accept* is the proper terminology. I make the alteration and send it.

I slurp my tea and re-read his message multiple times. The Chamomile tea won't calm my sexual craving.

After I make another tea with the hope this one might calm me a bit, I call Sam. There's barely a ring before her loud, giddy voice rapes my eardrum.

"You called!" she jokes. "I'm just getting out of the shower. I'll be leaving here in fifteen."

"He wrote me back."

"What?" she screeches, forcing me to yank the phone from my ear. "He said that you're my trainee and I have to teach you *all* the rules. You'd best learn them quickly, missy. I'm not taking a butt-bruising spanking because you can't remember the proper etiquette."

She laughs. "I'll do my best!"

I set my mug on the counter and run my fingers through my hair. "The salon gets busy around five o'clock and I hate waiting. So, we can meet there. Do not be late! I can't stress that enough. That's rule number one: never be tardy."

Sam squeals so loud my eyes vibrate. "I'm *never* late! Okay, where's the salon? And what are they going to do to me, like, what do I ask for? This is so exciting but fucking scary, too."

"Do you want a few quick tips?"

Another squeal. "Yes!"

"Here's what you do. When your anxiety piques, masturbate. If you're anything like me, you'll be jerking off five times before you see JoeSmith tomorrow night. Trust me, it helps."

"Yeah," she says with a heavy exhale. "I should do that."

"Perhaps slap one off before we go for our waxing. And tonight, wear a flowing skirt without panties. Your lips might be tender. Take a sleeping pill so you aren't up all night. You don't want to be lagging tomorrow."

"Okay, Terri. Can you bring one? I don't have any. Just so you know, I already came once in the shower and it didn't seem to calm me down *at all!* My adrenaline is zipping!" She giggles. "I'll meet you there, and you know I'm never late."

I tell her the address to the salon before we hang up. After a shower, I quickly rush out the door. Time's flying.

I pull up and see Sam waiting outside the door to the salon in a flowing, mid-thigh length, multi-coloured skirt. I think she's afraid to go in without me. She's flushed and twitchier than usual.

We check in, and I request to share the room. Sam might be more at ease if she can see what they do to me so she'll know what to expect. She attempts to tell the technician what to do when I stop her and tell her he's already informed them of his instructions and he does not allow us to alter anything.

Sam watches with wide eyes as I lie on the table. She asks questions when she has any, otherwise, it's mostly quiet and uneventful. When it's her turn, the woman looks at Sam's face after she glances at her giblets.

In a strong Italian accent, the middle-aged woman asks, "What am I supposed to do with you? You shaved. There's no hair for me to pull."

I answer. "It's not about the hair removal so much as her having the experience. Don't worry, you'll be paid just the same as if she had a woolly mammoth down there. Just wax her as is."

The woman looks at us as if we each have two heads. She shrugs, then spreads the first strip of wax on Sam.

Sam yelps when the technician rips the first wax strip. An even louder bellow follows when she pulls the wax from around her asshole where she had a bit of hair. I chuckle and watch her break into a sweat. Her horror is entertaining.

I remember my first time vividly. I reacted the same way, except I swore a few times. In my defence, I had hair. It's not my favourite activity, but it's not as dreadful as it once was. JoeSmith has put me through much worse. She'll adjust, as I did.

We walk over to the coffee shop across the street. Sam sits quietly and listens as I run through the rules. I try to remember all of them so we won't face any unforeseen surprises.

She's ready, at least she thinks she is. If not, he might punish me for her faux pas.

Before we separate, I tell her to call me if she has questions or doubts tonight.

A tiny sleeping pill washed down by half a glass of wine, and I'm lost in dreamland.

Chapter 13

JS

Prepare for JoeSmith

It feels like I've just shut my eyes when the morning sun wakes me. I follow my normal rituals of coffee with a piece of toast, a workout on the treadmill, shower, masturbate, and then sit down at my computer for a little relaxation. My emails have piled up and need some serious thinning. Too many people constantly send me crap that disinterests me. I should delete them from my contacts list.

Before I know it, it's almost time to go. Sam will be here soon and likely be a nervous wreck. This promises to be so much fun! I can't wait to see her expressions when JoeSmith makes her orgasm.

Sam walks in and looks dishevelled. Her eyes are huge, like saucers, weighed down by the dark circles hovering beneath, and she's ghostly pale, which accentuates the tired eyes. She's wearing an old pair of jeans and a vintage t-shirt with a superhero logo on the front. She looks like she stepped out of the 80s. She's super cute, but then again, she'd look good if she wore a potato sack.

I hand her a vitamin shake from the fridge. Her brows lift and she tilts her head as she points to the drink box usually served in nursing homes.

"It'll give you the energy you look like you need."

She holds it and scowls. "These are old people's drinks."

I open mine and take a swig. "Don't knock it until you try it."

She gulps it down, looks at it, then waves her brows appreciatively. We stop to buy a coffee and walk silently, side by side, to the end of the street to wait for the limo. As soon as Sam sees it come around the corner, she begins shaking. I hug her back to my chest to comfort her.

"You know you can say no. You don't have to get into the car. It's completely your choice, and if you choose not to go, I won't hold it against you. All I can say is that I hope you don't let fear hold you back." I take a breath and ask, "What do you want to do?"

I hope she doesn't change her mind. I don't want to call her a chicken tomorrow and for the rest of her life because even though I said I wouldn't, I'll still tease her. Isn't that what best friends do?

Sam pulls away from me and turns to look at me with her shoulders back, head held high. "No. I'm not giving in to my fear, not this time. I'm coming. I'm glad I'm with you. I can't even imagine doing this alone. You must have been terrified."

"I was scared, but in a good way. Believe me when I say I was torn. I had to decide whether to stay here and wait for that limo or run back to the familiar safety of my boring life. I almost didn't get in when the driver opened the door for me."

"You researched them first?" she asks.

"I made sure this business had a good reputation. My fear wasn't about what he would do to me; it was more whether I'd be strong enough to accept whatever he put me through. It was a challenge I put upon myself."

She turns on her heel to look at the limo as it waits at the red light.

"If it's any comfort, Sam, I still get butterflies before each meet, but they're excited butterflies rather than fearful ones."

Hopefully, this will be as satisfying for her as it is for me. She seems to take comfort in my confession of weakness.

The limo driver hops out and rushes around to our side of the car and opens the door. He addresses us with a smile.

"You must be Samantha. You may call me Jim. It's lovely to meet you."

"Nice to meet you, too," she says and sinks into the limo.

"Hi, Jim," I say with a smile, and pat the hand he holds the door with.

He smiles and nods. "Hello, Terri. I hope you're doing well."

"I am. Thank you for asking."

I slip in and pull on my seatbelt. Sam's wide-eyed as she looks in the flip-up console and then touches anything within reach.

"I've never even been in a limo before. This is awesome!" She sits back and looks out the window while she chews on her fingernail. "Why aren't we moving?"

I tap her arm to get her attention and hand her a hood. "Jim's waiting for us to put on the hoods. Remember when I said that they don't allow us to see where we're going? It's all part of the adventure. It's not so bad unless you get carsick. If you get too warm, ask Jim to turn up the air conditioning."

She takes the hood and slips it on her head. I pull mine on and sit back, close my eyes, and try to rest while I sip my coffee. Sam feels for my hand, intertwines our fingers, and gives it a little squeeze.

The ride doesn't seem to take as long this time, maybe because I have company other than Jim, who doesn't talk much. The car door opens and I pull off my hood and reach over to relieve Sam of hers. I put my finger to my lips to remind her that she isn't to talk. Sam nods, but her eyes are open wide and she looks like she's about to throw up.

I lean closer and whisper, "Breathe, Sam."

She takes a deep breath and forces a smile but the fear behind her eyes is real.

Our leader is nearly nude, wearing pasties over her nipples, a skirt that's way too short, and a pair of five-inch heels. Her eyes are painted with black eyeliner and her lips are dressed in bright red lipstick that shimmers in the sunlight.

Sam's told to read the contract thoroughly before she signs and dates it. As we make our way further into the castle, her lips remain parted as her wide eyes take in all the fancy woodwork lining the magnificent walls.

We're brought to the clinic room where Sam sees the doctor to get her exam and bloodwork done. This saves her from a trip to see her doctor to get her yearly physical, so she's happy about it.

I watch the leader's ass cheeks sway as she guides us to the change room. We each store our clothes, purses, phones, and jewelry in a locker. I try not to stare but Sam has an even better body than I thought. I wouldn't consider myself to be into girls, but she's sexy.

Our leader guides us to the cleansing room. She sets a timer for twenty minutes. It's five minutes more than usual so I can guide Sam through the process.

We have a different leader take us to the next stage. She's nearly nude and just as beautiful. We're taken down the corridor past many rooms, some of which have the sounds of hollering men and women seeping through.

Sam looks at me and bites her lips together, desperate to quiet her anxious giggle. She laughs when she's nervous, and it's never been an issue until now. On a good note, she finally has some colour on her face but I think she's just flushed from the embarrassing sexual noises.

Our leader guides us down a smaller corridor to a set of huge hand-carved doors. She pushes both open and steps to the side to allow us to pass. She closes the doors behind us and we're alone.

This preparation room is the same one I've been in many times. I get my hair done, make-up applied and dressed exactly how JoeSmith has requested. He typically allotted two preparers half an hour to make me beautiful and dress me in the proper attire, but today there are four.

The women wear snug-fitting, strapless designer evening gowns, each a different colour. They look as if they're ready to walk a runway in their elegant spiked heels. I watch Sam as she ogles each woman. I think she's in awe of their elegance.

They leave our hair to hang down but soften it with oils to make it silkier and then blow-dry it.

I'm eager to find out what the scenario will be tonight. He's never allowed me to have my hair down in a soft silky style before. I like it better this way. Our make-up is applied with a loose powder base, a little mascara, light eyeliner, pinkened cheeks but no lipstick; just a touch of gloss.

After our make-up and hair are finished, I take her hand and bring her to the next stage.

Sam watches as I lean over the desk, just like I have many times before. As usual, she squirts a blob of lotion on my back. While donning latex gloves, she spreads the lotion over my body from my neck to my toes.

Another woman brushes Sam's arm to get her attention. Sam stands as I am and watches me receive two fingers in my vagina. When she glides a finger in my asshole, Sam giggles. I scold her with my eyes and she mouths an apology.

The woman, who had her fingers in me, puts on a fresh glove. She places her fingers under Sam's chin and lifts her face to meet her eyes. Without uttering a word, she asks her for her trust. She bends her over and prepares Sam. She bites her bottom lip hard when the fingers enter her ass. I think she's aroused by all of this. Who can blame her?

Aside from the fluffy pink slippers, we're naked when she leads us to a place to await our master. I'm usually fitted in an outfit of JoeSmith's choosing and almost always teetering on a pair of high heels. Today, we don't role play; at least, I don't think we will.

She leads us to a bright corridor and simply walks away. We wait with our skin chilled from the cool air. Sam nervously bites her fingernail. I take her hand and shake my head.

"He'll break you of that habit."

She's just about to say something when a thin, handsome man in an expensive suit pushes open a set of doors and signals for us to enter. We hurriedly rushed over.

We enter a large bedroom with tall ceilings designed with calming comfort in mind. A queen-size, dark wood bed rests in the center of the room. The top of its canopy is draped with elegant off-white lace that doesn't hang down the thick wooden pillars. Instead, a dozen eye-bolts protrude, which contrasts with the theme of feminine comfort. The walls and quilt match; white with tiny blue flowers dancing about. Three white and blue throw-pillows have been tossed in the center of the bed. It's a place I would be happy to spend the night in.

"Remove your slippers," he says in a voice deeper than what suits his smaller-than-average stature.

He collects them and sets them out of the way. The fluffy white rug is soft under my feet. Sam isn't as close to the bed as me, so she takes a few steps so she too can stand on the rug and not the cool hardwood floor.

A woman with two long blonde ponytails comes from behind another door and casually saunters toward us. She's dressed in a tiny halter top, micro-mini schoolgirl skirt, above-the-knee socks, and shiny, black, flat-soled shoes.

"Hello, ladies! Are you both ready for JoeSmith?" She smiles wide to show off her big white teeth. "You two are naked as jaybirds." She stands in front of Sam and runs her hands down Sam's arms. "You're cold; you have skin prickles. Don't worry. He'll have you sweating in no time!"

Sam's chest expands and she swallows before exhaling. The woman turns away and Sam quickly turns her head and mouths something at me but I have no idea what it was.

"Would you two lovely ladies please follow me?"

She bounces on her toes, nearly skipping out the door she originated from. We follow and she points to a door. She smiles and spins a ponytail around her index finger.

"If you have to pee, go now."

Oddly, we're doing this now. I usually do this on the way to the playroom. Perhaps we didn't pass one on our way here.

We follow her back to the bedroom and the peppy woman has us stand at the end of the bed, each by our own pillar. She ties our wrists behind our backs to secure us around the poles.

Sam glances at me and flashes a nervous smile. She looks like she's either going to cry or vomit.

The woman must know Sam is new because she stands in front of her and asks her if she has any questions before we get started. Sam shakes her head, so the woman scampers out of the room and closes the door behind her.

Sam stares straight ahead and whispers, "Here goes nothing."

Her giggle lets me know she's okay, but I shush her anyway. The room goes silent and we strain to hear anything to signal that JoeSmith is on his way.

Sam breathes quickly.

"Deep breaths," I whisper.

Just then, the door opens.

Chapter 14

Be Careful What You Wish For

JoeSmith slowly walks toward us, donning a snug-fitting white mask that nearly covers his entire head. It has tiny holes for him to see from. They're smaller than usual. The bottom edge of his lower lip is visible, but only when he opens his mouth, which stretches open the slit in the mask.

He's wearing nothing beneath a lightweight white robe. His thick cock is moulded by the satin material as he nears us. He's barefoot, like us. I've never seen his feet.

He glides over to Sam, who's visibly shaking. I can see her in my peripheral vision. He stops mere inches from her. I'm sure she can feel his heat.

His face hovers above and looks down at hers. She's so tiny compared to him. He entwines her hair in his fingers and slowly tips her head back. Her mouth opens as she exhales with a whimper.

He slowly whispers in his sexy, deep voice. "I will call you Slut. I might also refer to you as my pet's pet. You will always be second to her." His free hand glides slowly down her arm and her breath quivers. "As we get to know each other, you'll matter more to me than that of a dog, but until then, you're here for her amusement and at her request, not mine. Do be on your best behaviour."

He clears his throat. In my peripheral vision, I see him turn to look at me.

"Pet hopes to watch me take you at my will, and she'll get her wish soon enough." He looks back at her and tilts his head so he can admire her body. "There may be days when you won't be invited to attend. Jealousy will not be tolerated. Do you understand? You may respond."

Sam's voice is faint. "I understand."

"I understand, *what*?"

"Ah," Sam pauses, then quickly replies, "I understand the rules."

He stares at her and clears his throat. She suddenly remembers what it is he's waiting for.

She adds, "Oh, um… Sir."

"Your safe word is zebra. If for any reason you wish to stop, you'll say zebra. Immediately following, I'll free you from any restraints and everything will cease." He glides his fingertips over her forehead to brush stray hairs off her face. "If you're too close to your limit, say yellow or mercy, and I'll ease off. Do you understand?"

She nods and his fingers graze her arm.

"I'll send a checklist to Pet's email for you to fill out before our next session. Today, I trust you'll use the word mercy or yellow if need be. Tell me your safewords and that you understand the consequences of using them. Speak now." Sam looks up at his masked face, and he says, "Don't look at me."

She drops her face and repeats the safewords and their purposes with a strong voice. Just when I think she's finished talking, she adds, "I can handle it. You won't hear a safeword from me."

She's determined to let him know she's not a delicate flower but he might take that as a challenge. I hope she knows what she's doing.

His tone is wicked. "We'll see about that. Is there anything you wish me to avoid, any triggers?"

She shakes her head. "Nothing I can think of, Sir."

He lifts a wad of her hair and breathes it in. "I hope you enjoy the activities."

JoeSmith stands in front of me and strokes my cheek with the back of his fingers. "My lovely pet, your safeword is also zebra. If you've changed your mind and you don't wish to share my time between you and your friend, you may recant your request now, before we get started. You may speak."

"I understand the safeword is zebra, Master. I definitely want Slut to enjoy your pleasure," I pause and lower my voice, "even though the thought of losing you to her scares me worse than any punishment you can test me with, Sir."

I sigh and shake my head. Why did I say that?

He stops breathing. His warm fingers lift my chin. With his other hand, he lifts his mask slightly and with incredible tenderness, presses his lips to mine. It's his first heartfelt gesture toward me and tears blur my vision. Why am I so emotional?

His forehead rests on mine. "I won't let you go that easily. Don't you know that by now?" He wipes the tears from my cheeks. "Shall we get started, or do you need a minute?"

I sniffle and nod. "I wish to continue, Master."

He takes a few steps back so we can watch him. "Let us begin."

He opens his robe to expose his semi-erect penis. His feet are shoulder-width apart, turned slightly outward. His stance emphasizes the thickness of his thighs, and his abs are tight and perfectly formed. Sam gasps. She approves.

As he watches Sam, he strokes his cock until it stands at full attention. Although I desperately want to, I don't dare turn my head to watch her reaction. He wants us to focus on him, to see *him*. If I know Sam, and I do, she loves his confidence. She's always wanted a dominant man in the bedroom.

Be careful what you wish for.

JoeSmith rushes her and she gasps. He presses his body against hers, forcing her back to the pole. Her breathing sharpens and I swear that even in my peripheral vision I can see her shaking.

He growls in her ear. "Don't look at my face!"

His hand quickly grabs her throat and she yelps. After he unfastens the rope that bound her hands, he forces her to walk backward with his hand on her throat and spins her so she and I stand belly to belly with my lips lined up with her eyes. Her skin feels cooler than mine, and her breasts are firm and rest slightly below my own.

With her hair gripped tightly in his hand, he tilts her head up toward his. He releases her throat and lifts his mask so he can press his mouth onto hers. I watch as his tongue gently slips into her mouth and he moans.

It isn't long before he's kissing her with a ravenous appetite. Her body stiffens against mine. He stops, drops his mask into place, and snickers softly as he caresses my cheek.

"Good girl."

He did that to gauge my reaction; as a test to see if I'd be jealous and beg him to stop.

Kissing isn't something we did at first. It wasn't until the second time we were together that his mouth touched mine and months before there was a shred of emotion behind it. I think he believes it a more emotional act as opposed to erotic.

He kissed her with force, so it was nowhere near an impassioned act. It turned me on to watch him force her mouth open for his tongue's invasion. Had he kissed her lovingly, I might have reacted differently.

"Kiss."

She lifts on her toes and kisses me with fire behind it. Her lips are hot and wet with his saliva. Sam's getting into this. I lose myself in how soft her lips are compared to a man's. She's more delicate with her tongue. Her breath sharpens and her stiff nipples press against my skin.

"Slut, I want you on your knees in front of my pet. Do not sit back on your heels."

Sam sinks to her knees. Her face is mere inches from my excited pussy. My thoughts swirl as I imagine her soft tongue fondling my clitoris. I'm surprised to realize just how enthusiastic I am for her to touch me and how much I desire to touch her.

JoeSmith chooses a leather-clad paddle and swings it through the air as he crosses the room back to us.

"Stick out your tongue, Slut," he orders.

Sam complies. He gently guides her face toward me until her tongue slips between my labia. I gasp when the tip of her tongue touches my clit.

"Do not pull away, and do not move your tongue."

With a swing of the paddle, a loud crack fills the room. Sam jolts and moves her tongue from where he placed it. She drops her head and winces.

"That won't do."

Master grabs her hair in his fist and moves her face back into place and continues holding her hair so she can't move her head. He swats her again, harder than the first time, and her wince is seen more than heard. He checks to see that she kept her tongue in place.

Sir releases her hair. "That wasn't so difficult, was it?"

He doesn't swat her hard but repeatedly until tears flood her eyes. She holds fast. Saliva drips from her open mouth. Sam remains in his desired position, unmoved while he returns the paddle to its place.

My pussy twitches with need and my excitement have my knees weak. If she sucks my clit between her lips, I'll probably cum in seconds. I knew seeing Sam at his mercy would be thrilling but I underestimated just how much.

She can't see what he's doing, so the fear of the unknown has her eyes wide. He picks up a medium-sized butt plug and a bottle of lubricant. He dollops the lube in his right hand and then slips the bottle into the pocket of his robe. When he stands her up, she wipes away the drool with the back of her hand and he immediately grabs her forearm, spins her around, and wrenches it up behind her back. Her face presses firmly against his chest.

"I did not tell you to wipe your face." He grabs her hot pink ass cheek and she winces. "You willingly gave yourself to me. You are mine. You do what I tell you, when I tell you."

He eases the pressure on her arm, walks her to the end of the bed, bends her over it so her face presses onto the quilt, and places her hands over her head. His left hand resting on the small of her back holds the butt plug. He caresses between her legs to coat her with lubrication.

"You're soaked, Slut. It would appear you enjoy the taste of my pet's lovely cunt." His voice raises just slightly. "Pet, I want you to watch me fuck her."

I turn my head to watch and my pussy clenches.

He watches my reaction as he buries his finger into her vagina. She remains unmoving. He explores her with two, then three of his digits.

"She's tight. I'm going to stretch this little cunt wide open."

He takes the butt plug and lathers it with lube, then aims it at her pussy. He pushes slowly so her vagina will stretch to accommodate the impressively sized object. She moans aloud and he swats her ass, hard.

"Quiet!" he hisses. "Just relax, little slut."

The plug slips in and she bunches the quilt in her fists and presses her mouth to the bed to hush any future errant moans.

He caresses her pinked buttocks with his fingertips to admire the radiating heat from her punishing spanking, then steps back and looks at her with his head tilted and his hard cock poking free from the gaped robe.

He slips his hand around her arm and helps her to her feet and stands her several feet in front of me. Pushing her shoulder, he has her sink to her knees facing him. While he watches my face, he opens his robe wide enough that the tails hold behind his calves. His fingers grip her hair and guide her face to his cock. She eagerly sucks while I watch her.

"Pet, look at me," he demands.

I look at his eyeholes. She sucks him in as far as she can and pulls back, leaving his rock-hard cock slick with her saliva. She greedily pumps him in and out of her mouth.

My pussy tingles and I bite my bottom lip to keep from moaning. I'm surprised at how exciting it is to watch *my* JoeSmith get sucked off by my best friend. I had worries that maybe I'd be jealous but I'm not at all. I'm aroused, incredibly aroused. He pulls himself from her mouth and orders her to crawl to me, but he doesn't follow.

"Pet, bend your knees and open your legs. Slut, lick and suck her clit until I tell you to stop."

I spread my legs and Sam's tongue immediately lashes at my stiff button with wanton lust. He watches with his arms crossed over his thick chest. His feet are still more than shoulder-width apart. The way he stands has his thick thighs flexed and it turns me on even more. The mask hugs his parted lips.

Sam sucks and flicks my clit. I look down and she's looking up. She waves her brows to signify that she's enjoying herself. I nod and flash a quick smile to show her my appreciation for her talented tongue.

She laps and sucks on my pussy and I can't hold back much longer. I look at JoeSmith, my eyes begging for his approval to orgasm. He chuckles under his mask and nods just once. That's all I need to send me over the edge.

My muscles flex as my mind fades from everything except Sam's mouth. My thighs vibrate under their strain until they give out and I slide down the pole. Sam tries to hold me up by my thighs without moving her mouth from my sweet spot, but I'm too heavy for her frail body.

I slip down the pole until I'm squatting and bent forward. My arms remain tied to the pole and lifted behind me. It's the only thing preventing my ass from touching the floor. My shoulders strain but I couldn't care less. We burst into breathless laughter.

"Contain yourselves, ladies," JoeSmith warns as he nears us. He helps Sam to her feet, then unties my hands and rights me. "Pet, I want you to sit on the bed with your back against the headboard. Face me with your legs stretched out toward us. Slut, I want you face-down on the bed, arms over your head, holding Pet's ankles."

We position ourselves as he requested while he puts on a condom. My legs are slightly parted and she lies between them with her head resting on my thigh. He grabs her ankles and with ease of effort drags her down the bed until her hips rest at the edge. He sets her feet on the floor and removes the butt plug from her pussy and hands it to me to hold.

"I'm going to fuck this slut, and you're going to watch," he tells me, and positions himself behind her.

She squeezes my ankles tighter.

He abruptly slams his rock-hard cock into Sam's eager pussy and she gasps louder than he'll allow.

"You'll remain quiet and you will not cum until I say so," he commands before he slaps her several times on her right ass cheek.

The cracks echo about the room. Sam doesn't make a sound. Having her face buried in the comforter helps muffle any protest that might mistakenly escape her.

With his left hand bracing his weight at Sam's waist, his right makes its way around her thigh to seek out her clit. She sucks in a full breath and releases it even faster. He pounds into her while he fondles her clit. He isn't gentle with his thrusts.

She holds my ankles with a death grip and I swear she's cutting off the blood supply, but I don't care, this is so fucking provocative! A few minutes in, he rests his left elbow on the bed and twines her hair in his fist. He turns her head to the side so he can look at her face.

In a weathered whisper, he says, “Cum… now.”

She writhes beneath him as he slams his hips down onto her. She screams out in pleasure and my eyes flit up to his mask, anticipating the spanking sure to come, but it doesn’t. He groans but doesn’t pause to swat her.

Her face tenses in a pained expression as her orgasm grows nearer. Her fingers dig into my ankles, but I don’t pull away. I press my hands onto the mattress to brace myself to prevent her from pulling me down the bed.

She shouts, “Yes! Yes! Oh, yes! I’m coming!”

My mind snaps from the hypnosis of it all, alerting me to the harsh reality that he didn’t give her permission to speak, and yet, she did. He’ll surely punish her now that she spoke. A moan is one thing but actual words…

I wait with eyes wide and watch his mask pull in between his parted lips as he pants heavy breaths, but he doesn’t slow his pounding thrusts, and he doesn’t punish her.

When she’s completely spent, he steps away from her. I wonder why he didn’t allow himself pleasure, too.

“Stand and put your hands together,” he whispers through quick breaths.

He binds them with one of the ropes we used earlier. He feeds the rope through a loop at the top of the right post at the end of the bed and pulls until she’s standing as tall as she can.

She glances my way and looks concerned as to why she’s being manhandled so aggressively. I’m forbidden to make a sound, let alone explain in great detail, so all I can do is watch.

I wait until I’m sure he isn’t watching me and then furrow my brow, open my mouth and curl my lips between my teeth and bite down. A dry swallow pulls at the tendons in her neck as a wave of understanding overrides her questioning eyes. She understands she's being punished.

He stands before her while he pinches her left nipple hard enough to make her wince, but her lips don't part.

"I told you to cum, not to speak. You took advantage of my kindness. If it happens again," he pauses to pinch the other nipple just as hard, "I won't permit you to climax at all. I'm going to punish you so you'll remember to abide by my rules."

He strides over to the table and chooses a heavy flogger. He returns to a wide-eyed Sam as he swings it through the air. With his finger under her chin, he lifts her face to look up at his mask.

"Tell me your safeword."

Sam quickly replies, "Zebra."

He clears his throat.

She seems nervous as she shuffles her feet and quickly says, "Zebra, Sir… Master, Sir."

The back of his fingers brushes down her cheek before he turns her so her ass faces him.

I thought she'd be afraid but when her eyes locked onto mine, I see a sexy, crooked smile beaming below eyes drowning in wicked lust. She's never looked sexier than right now, and my nipples stiffen at the thought of kissing her.

"Since you like to talk so much, I'll give you ten lashes and you'll count them out loud."

"Yes, Master JoeSmith," she replies with a moan that sounds like it came from a sex-craved whore.

His head tilts to the left and I wonder if he's disappointed that she isn't resisting.

Master raises the flogger and slaps it across her ass. His chest swells with excitement and her teeth clench but her jaw quickly opens so she can take a breath, only to close on her bottom lip. Her eyes slowly open and she blinks several times as her eyes search side to side in anticipation of the next swat.

"One," she sounds off. Again, he swats. "Two."

When it's over, she's left quivering from the adrenaline, the pain, and her heightened level of arousal. Her eyes open wide and meet mine. They're glassy as though she were fighting back tears, but she licks her lips and grins.

Holy shit! She loved it!

JoeSmith spins her to face him. He drops onto his knees, lifts her right thigh and rests it on his shoulder. He pushes two fingers into her dripping wet slit, lifts his mask slightly, and buries his mouth on her pussy.

I can barely see around her but when I lean to my left, the side of his head comes into view. I watch as he fucks her while orally pleasuring her and hope he'll pull his face back so I can see his lips and nose now that they aren't covered.

Her tummy muscles contort as her chest heaves. She lifts her head and her jaw widens and she sucks in a deep breath. She stiffens as euphoria overwhelms her mind and body. She jerks several times before coming to rest.

I'm not surprised at how quickly she orgasmed. It was obvious she was extremely aroused by her lashings. My vagina aches for attention. JoeSmith stands with his mask in place and pats her cheek before he unties her. He sets a chair at the end of the bed to face the mattress and has her sit. He binds her hands behind the chair and places a black hood over her head to blind her.

His gaze falls on me. I remain seated with my back against the headboard, legs slightly parted, and my hands resting palm down on my thighs.

"Are you enjoying yourself, today?" he asks.

I nod and fight back a smile.

JoeSmith takes the plug from me and sets it on the nightstand. He opens the drawer and collects a hot-pink cotton mask and places it over my eyes, blinding me. It's his turn to be mask-free.

I hear him walk to the end of the bed and the room fills with ear-ringing silence. Most likely, he's watching me. What's he thinking? I hear a condom package tear open. A few seconds later, his weight shifts the end of the bed as he slowly crawls up. He wraps an arm around my lower back and lifts enough that he can lay me out, flat on my back.

He eases himself down against my core. His weight feels like a warm hug as it holds me to the bed. His breath on my neck sends shivers throughout my whole body. Hot lips graze my jaw and glide toward my mouth, leaving a trail of tiny hairs lifted in their wake.

"May I kiss you?"

He's asking for my permission? What?

"Speak to me."

I whisper clearly so he won't question what's said. "Yes, please kiss me."

His plush lips press to mine and I eagerly kiss him back. Sam's scent is on his face and strangely, I like it. I want his kiss, his love; or at the very least, his acceptance. I crave the affection I've earned through the year and waited so patiently to receive. I feared I'd never experience this level of generous reward. He has never made love to me.

He guides my arms around his neck, which is something I've never been allowed to do unless it's to brace myself, and that's only at his guidance. But this is different. He's different.

I can't lose myself in the romantic fog. It isn't real. He doesn't love me the way this feels like he does.

Master desires a play toy, not a love interest. Lady Catherine's made that very clear. She warned me to keep my heart tucked away, but my heart is stronger than my will.

How can this be wrong when it feels so right?

With my face burrowed against his neck, I press my lips softly onto his skin. I catch a whiff of his cologne; another first, he usually smells of soap. It's intoxicating with its manly musk scent. I breathe him in and lose myself in the warmth of his embrace.

I want to stay like this forever; in this moment and in his arms. With ease, he slides into me in one smooth motion, stretching open my walls until his pelvis rests against me. His tongue caresses my lips with its warmth and gentle touch.

We move like a well-choreographed dance couple. I know how he fucks, so it's easy to predict his movements. I slide my hands down his body, another taboo. I grip his ass and lift my pelvis to meet his thrusts. He wraps one of his arms under my right thigh and lifts, pinning it to my side. It's as if his cock suddenly grew another inch and now reaches my core.

To brace himself, he rests his forearm by my shoulder and weaves his fingers in my hair to cradle my head. His lips feather mine and our quickening breaths blend as we breathe each other in.

This is perfect. Maybe having Sam join us will bring him and me closer.

Master's making love to me. Love. It feels like love. I'm sure it'll be short-lived and as soon as he leaves this bed, that, too, will end.

Sir's ass muscles flex in my hands with each thrust. My thoughts are fleeting.

I'm losing myself to him. An orgasm crashes through me. I hadn't even realized I was close to coming.

My cries of passion fill his mouth as I'm swept away with him holding me. JoeSmith soon copies my wail with his own and it clears the orgasmic fog in my mind.

"You're my favourite."

His whisper warms my ear seconds before his body spews his hot seed into the condom.

He brushes tiny kisses on my neck for a full minute until his breathing calms. I savour the moment and the quietness of our souls. Did he make love to me, or was this another of his fantasy scenarios? Perhaps he was simply too tired to fuck me hard and rough because he exhausted all his energy with Sam? All I know is I care for him more than I should.

JoeSmith kisses my lips once more and walks away. I hear him whisper something to Sam and then silence. A few seconds later, I hear a door open and close.

Chapter 15

JS

Let Me Taste You

I feel lonelier than ever. Tears drip from my eyes but I quickly wipe my face to destroy the evidence. Sam will assume it has something to do with her. I tried to keep my heart out of this, but he makes it so damn difficult. Maybe I should stop coming to see him.

No! I don't want that.

The door opens and we're given the all-clear by the peppy schoolgirl. I remove my mask and wipe my eyes once more. We follow her and another woman in a schoolgirl costume.

These showers are used by subs after a session. We aren't monitored here and we can take our time, talk amongst ourselves, and not be under the rule of our master or mistress.

"So, what did you think?" I ask Sam as the warm water flows over my body, bringing new energy with it.

She groans under the showerhead next to me as water flows over her welted backside.

"I loved it! My ass cheeks are still hot but that was fucking awesome. I don't think I have ever cum that hard and fast." She turns so the water runs over her chest and smiles at me. "I even enjoyed going down on you. Who knew I'd get off on licking a muff? Or that I could bring a woman to orgasm. I didn't. Have you ever done it?"

My cheeks flush as I recall how sexy she looked. "No, I haven't. Not yet, anyway. I'm sure he'll have me do you next time. It should be interesting." I tip my face under the water and reach for the soap. "Hopefully, I'll do it as well as you did. You were great. I didn't know your mouth was so soft."

I can't hold her gaze. I don't know why I'm so embarrassed; I wasn't at the time.

"Why wait?" she says. "I mean, we're still in the castle and I assume whatever happens here stays here, right?" She shrugs innocently.

Why do I suddenly feel so self-conscious? I can feel myself blushing and my fingers and toes feel numb.

"So, if you'd like to try it, you know, to see if you like it, I'm game." She bites her bottom lip and looks at me with wide eyes.

The water flows down my face as I try to look at her to determine whether she's serious. I wipe the water from my eyes and examine her expression closer. She's not kidding. As if I'm filled with newfound confidence, I shake off all my inhibitions.

I shut off my shower and step toward her. I push her against the wall and plant my lips on hers without pause. She wraps her arms around my waist and kisses me back, accepting my tongue in her mouth while she flicks it with hers, reminding me of how fantastic it felt on my clit.

I kiss down her body and she opens her stance to invite me in. Without hesitation, I bury my mouth on her womanhood just as she had done to me. The skin between her labia is unbelievably soft against my lips. Her flesh is silky and hotter than the water flowing down her body. My lips feel rough in comparison. I love how she feels in my mouth.

My tongue quickly finds her clitoris. I flick and spin it between my lips, and then stretch my tongue further between her folds and back to her clit. I suck, flick, and circle until she's panting wildly.

Her fingers entwine my wet hair so she can hold my head in place. As I press my lips around her clitoris and suck, she gasps and releases my hair to grab the shower spout above her head.

I push two arched fingers into her and bump short thrusts toward the spot that always drives me wild. In seconds, her legs jerk and she cries out. Superheated fluid sprays down my fingers, chin, and neck.

She's coming! Literally orgasming on my face! I made her cum with my mouth! This is so incredible!

Her body relaxes and her knees give way. She drops her ass to the shower floor and gazes at me with hooded eyes. We laugh like high school girls with an inside joke. I lean my back against the opposite wall and sit with my legs outstretched. Here we are, two grown women sitting on the floor of a shower, cackling like idiots.

I stand and offer her my hand. She struggles to get to her feet, then flings her arms around me and holds me tightly.

"Thank you for bringing me here and sharing this incredible experience with me," she whispers.

"Thank you for not judging me when I told you about it."

*****

The ride home is quiet except for the occasional snicker coming from Sam. She had a superb time, and so did I. Now she has her own white rose to set on her desk.

What bothers me is that I don't know why JoeSmith touched me with such endearment. During those moments, we weren't dominant and submissive; we were lovers.

He was making love. He never does that. I know he cares for my wellbeing but he's careful not to show his heart. Why did he this time? Am I reading too much into it because he only did it to prove he enjoys the company of his Pet more than his Slut?

No, he's too experienced at this to let himself fall for his submissive. I'm overthinking it, like I do most things.

Chapter 16

JS

Per His Instructions

Christmas vacation starts after the party tomorrow. Every year, we pick names for our Secret Santa Gift Exchange. I picked Lyndsay's name. She has a great sense of humour, so I bought her an ugly Christmas sweater.

Not everyone joins this activity. Some of our fellow workers are of different faiths so they don't celebrate in the Christmas-themed festivities. They do, however, partake in the lively *Year End Party*, as they call it. We all have a great time together and respect each other's faiths. There have been no issues; small companies are like that.

"So, why are you actually doing any work?" Sam snuck up behind me and jolted my thoughts from the tedious, mind-numbing work. "Seriously, nobody ever puts in this much effort in accomplishing anything on the second last day before a week's vacation."

She pushes some of my papers off to the side and sits on my desk while I shake my head and move those papers into the proper folder.

"So why are you working so hard? I mean, look around—everyone's daydreaming and pretending to work. Most are convincing, except for Jack." She looks his way, tilts her head, and scrunches her nose as if she smelled something bad. "He's not convincing anyone. He deserves to be reprimanded for the simple fact of being such a terrible actor."

I lean back in my chair and glare at her. "Why do you feel it necessary to creep up behind me and scare me at least once a day, every day?"

She laughs louder than she should and picks lint off her button-up dress shirt. "You were sleeping with your eyes open. I'm your rescuer. How humiliating would it have been if your head dropped and slammed off your desk? I mean, it would've been hilarious for everyone else." She pauses to take a breath and squares her shoulders, slams her hands on her waist, and turns her head with her chin raised. "You can call me Sam: Superhero Extraordinaire."

Sam's happier this week than I've seen her in a long time, and that's saying a lot because she's the peppiest person I've ever known. She seems calmer and more content with life and not as edgy. I think about Saturday night and grin. I can't possibly get angry at her. She's so happy.

"You thrive on the fact that you have a dirty little secret. It looks good on you." I wink as I spin my chair side to side and glance around for eager listeners. "So, do you still want to tag along if he wants you back?"

Her eyes widen and her arms flair for emphasis. "Duh! Of course, I want to come along. Beg him if you must. I had the best night of my life with you two. That was fucking amazing. I've read stories about this kind of lifestyle—and yes, they turned me on more than I'd care to admit to just anyone—but I never thought I'd experience it firsthand. I want more of what he's offering. And, I want more of you." She smiles wide, then bites her thumbnail. "Maybe we can have a sleepover tonight. It's not like we'll work hard tomorrow, so it won't matter if we're tired. What do you think?"

Sam looks at me with hopeful, puppy-dog eyes.

I smile and shrug. "I don't know. We didn't ask JoeSmith if we're allowed to play away from his presence." My arms cross over my chest and one side of my face scrunches. "Hmm, should I ask if I can have sex with someone outside the castle that I play with inside the castle? I'll write to ask if it's permitted."

Her face is contorted in an unappealing way. "Why would you have to ask his permission? Think about it; he's probably married or in a relationship and does this weird dominance thing on the side. She might not even know about it."

She picks up my stapler, pulls it open, and wiggles the row of staples before slamming it shut, sending a staple to the floor. She waves it around as she talks.

"Do you honestly think he's a single guy? He's so hot! Besides, if he isn't cheating on someone, why does he cover his face? What's he afraid of? It's not like we could find out who he is unless he's some famous guy." Her face lights up and she slams the stapler on the desk beside her. "Oh, my God! What if he's someone famous? That'd be so cool. Damn confidentiality contract! I don't have a lot of money, but what I have I'd like to keep. Besides, Lady Catherine would never allow us to come back if we shot our mouths off, and I *really* want to go back."

"I hear what you're saying, but he's our master and we have to ask his permission for certain things. I'm sorry if you don't agree, but I've been with him longer and I think it's right to ask." I shrug and put my hand out to her and she slaps her palm onto mine. "Very funny, Sam. Give me your cell phone so I can email him. I don't see Bossman anywhere."

"Now?" she asks. I nod and she slides off the desk. "Sure, I'll get it. I suppose it's better to ask than be punished worse than I was last weekend. Damn, that hurt, but it was sexy as sin."

Sam disappears and I rearrange my paperwork. She returns and hands me her phone after she unlocks it. She doesn't understand how much worse it can get and how much pleasure she'd get from it. But she'll know soon enough.

"Did you get your results from your screening?" I ask.

Sam had a physical, blood work drawn, and a vaginal exam to adhere to the castle rules. Everyone must go through this once a month in order to have a membership to Miss Catherine's house. We get it done right there in the mansion. She must pay that doctor well because he comes when requested and gets the results quickly.

"Yeah, they called today. Sorry, I forgot to tell you. I'm clean, safe, and healthy. Ever since I started having sex, I've made sure to get tested regularly. This just saved me the trip to the clinic."

She gives me an exaggerated wink because she's been sexually active since she was fourteen. It used to baffle me how much action she got in college. I was envious because I wasn't a free spirit like her.

"That's great. I would have been worried if something came back positive after we... you know."

I wink back at her and we giggle and then open my email and send off a quick message to ask if we need to ask his permission to play. I stare at my inbox. My tummy flutters. I'm not sure if it's because of the email or that I might be doing whatever with Sam later. What if I do something wrong or it's utterly awkward? This could be a terrible mistake.

I look up at her with my eyebrows lifted in the center. "I don't know what to do with a girl. I mean, not really. Aside from last weekend, I hadn't touched a woman sexually. They've touched me but I was bound at the time. This is all new to me. What if I don't do it right?"

Sam leans in closer. "Oh, trust me. You did it right." She bites her lip. "I'll tell you what, you do to me what you'd like to have done to you, and I'll do the same. This way, we'll learn what the other likes. Besides, we're friends first, lovers second. If it turns out to be weird, we'll just leave it for when we're with him."

I'm a little more at ease. She's right, we are friends above all else. Her phone pings.

"Oh, wow! That was fast. He wrote back."

Our eyes meet and we're both biting our lips. With her encouraging nod, she urges me to open it but then leans over my shoulder to read for herself. I read it aloud anyway in a whisper.

"He said: *Yes, you may play but before you do, I want you to buy a strap-on dildo. Be sure to get a cock with some girth to it. I want you to fuck each other until you're satisfied. NO TONGUES TO CLITS. You can wait. From now until I see you, no clitoral orgasms for either of you, and that includes masturbation. Save that for me.* Okay, so I guess we're going shopping after work."

I pout before I sign out and hand her the phone.

Sam pats my shoulder and slowly walks backward toward her cubicle. "Yup! We can take my car if you'd like. There's a place a few blocks from here. I've been there a few times."

She disappears and I spin my legs back under my desk with a quick glance around. Rick's at the water cooler holding a paper cup, deep in thought and staring at nothing in particular.

Could he be JoeSmith?

He has dark hair and a nice body, much like Sir. Rick's an extrovert and always joking around and making passes at the ladies. It gets on my nerves sometimes because he just seems so skeezy. I shake off the icky thought. I don't want to imagine Rick's cock down my throat. A shiver runs down my spine.

Every man in the office has similarities to JoeSmith, but could one of them be my weekly punisher/pleasurer? None of them look like a person who would get off on this type of play. They all seem rather general and not too driven in life.

I expect my master will be just as domineering and aggressive in his regular life as he is in the playrooms because that's not something anyone can fake their way through. I'm submissive and I couldn't successfully pretend otherwise. To most people, I must look like every other average woman. If my co-workers knew what turns me on, it would shock them.

I glance up at the boss's office. He's standing at the glass wall, looking at everything and nothing, as if he has a million things on his mind. That's standard for him but running a successful business at such a young age doesn't come without its burdens. I feel bad for him. Perhaps a hardy fuck on his desk will ease his woes. God, that'd be so hot!

His family has old money that's been passed down through the generations. He started this company about ten years ago after he graduated from university with a business degree—top of his class, or so I've heard. I'm sure this business has been very lucrative, not that he needs the money.

When I picture him naked, I see his body as being impeccable. Of course, I imagine he has a great cock that's thick and hard as steel, and always at the ready. On over one occasion, I've witnessed the defined bulge held prisoner behind the fabric of his well-tailored pants and it's impressive.

In the office, most of the single guys—and some married ones, too—have come onto me. I've turned every one of them down. None of those men do it for me. If Ben Manning asked me on a date, would I go?

He is a sexy, soft-spoken man who doesn't have a lot to say and those are all qualities I look for in a man, but if it were to end badly, our work relationship would suffer. I would have to leave my job and since I like being here, I'd hate that. I would have to turn down his proposition, as much as I'm sure I'd regret it the second after I did.

A paper ball lands on my desk and wakes me from my stare. Sam must've thrown it. I've been staring at the boss, and he's staring at me. I look over at her and she shakes her head.

"Stop daydreaming and pretend you're working," she mouths with a smirk. "If you keep this up, I'm going to deem you the slacker award of the day."

I glance up at the boss and he's still watching me with his hands in the pockets of his black dress pants that are snug in all the right places. I pick up the paper ball and shrug as I toss it in the recycle bin beside my desk. My face is hot. I must be as red as a cherry.

He nods and sports a grin he may not have meant to look sexy, but it is. I smile and force myself back to work.

Chapter 17

JS

Shopping for Toys

"Do you want the black harness or the red one?"

Sam holds up two boxes and waits for me to choose, as if it matters what colour we get. I haven't stopped giggling since we walked in.

I can picture JoeSmith using most of these on us; some of them he already has. He's used vibrators when I was well-behaved, and once he fitted me with a pig's tail butt plug for a touch of humiliation. That was the only time I've ever seen it. I'm not one for humiliation on that level, and I've never considered a barnyard fantasy as being something I'd go out of my way to experience.

"I don't care, Sam. Whatever you want. I just want to get the hell out of here before I soak through my panties." I set a string of anal beads back on its hook. "Are you as horny as I am?"

Sam puts the red harness back on the shelf and takes my hand. She quickly leads me toward the dildos. When we're in front of them, she chooses a large red one from the assortment and holds it up.

Too loudly for my comfort, she says, "I want to fuck you with this one. I'm going to stick it on the harness, lube it up, and ram your pussy until you scream. I want to pump in and out of you slow and easy until you can't take it anymore and you start fuck back on it and cum so hard that you squirt all over my thighs."

I've stopped breathing and my cheeks are hot. "Oh my God, Sam! Use your inside voice."

She shrugs without a care if someone hears her. My face must be red as a cherry. I refuse to look to see if anyone's staring. Why doesn't she have a filter?

"Nobody in here is virginal, trust me." She waves the dildo as if to ask if I want it. "Anyone here is just as perverted as we are."

My imagination is in full swing as I picture the steamy scenario she just described in vivid detail. I imagine her wearing the harness with the red silicone dildo protruding and my pussy clenches. But I burst into laughter when I picture her falling forward because the weight of the cock throws off her balance.

"Do you like this one?" she asks, but when I don't stop laughing, she purses her lips. "I'm trying to be sexy here."

I bend forward and place my hands on my knees, hoping to ease my spasming tummy muscles. When I point to her and erupt again, she laughs.

"You're so weird!" she says as she slaps the dildo on her palm to feel its weight. "Why are you laughing?"

My laughter slowly eases. "I can't help it! You're so funny!"

"Um, yeah," she says and scoffs. "Seriously. What's so damn funny?"

"You'd have to be in my head to understand." A deep breath ends the laughing fit. "I never thought we'd shop for a joint toy. Think about it. Two weeks ago, you were oblivious to my lifestyle, and now we're about to hump one another with a rather large dildo wedged on a harness."

I pick up an insanely huge red butt plug, show it to her, and set it down. We stare at it, meet eyes, and shake our heads. We continue picking up one after another to look at them.

I continue. "It's crazy... very arousing, but crazy."

She holds a dildo out to me and I take it to feel its weight. My fingers don't quite fit around it and I imagine how good it would feel sliding in and out of my pussy.

"It's fucking hot, that's what it is! There's no other way to describe it," she says, and picks up another dildo but frowns and sets it down almost immediately. "I'm about to go home with you, get naked, and then fuck you raw. You have to admit that's hot."

"We should find a way to thank our master for bringing us together… sexually, I mean."

She picks up a black dildo and admires it. "Do you like this one?"

"How big do you think it is?" I take it from her and try to judge its weight and circumference. "It's a lot heavier than it looks. I like it and I think our master would be pleased with its girth."

"Do you really think he cares?" she asks, squinting while her mouth twists.

I shrug and open my mouth like I'm going to suck on it and she laughs. In my peripheral, I see a man in a grey suit staring at me wide-eyed. My eyes instinctively drop and his dark blue sweatpants are tented at the crotch. My eyes quickly shift to Sam and she turns to see what has me looking so pale. She sees him and his crotch, turns back to me with a shocked expression, and we both burst into hearty laughter.

"I think we'll be pleased with it more than he will, though," I say and wave my eyebrows.

"I agree. So, it comes in a light flesh tone, dark flesh tone, and a rather funky purple." Her brows furrow and she shakes her head. "If purple's a flesh tone, the model needs serious medical attention."

"I think the lighter flesh tone is best because it matches our skin better. We can pretend that's a natural part of our bodies." My fingers graze the veins on the huge pink dildo. "Haven't you ever wanted to have a penis just for one day? It'd be exciting."

Sam pretends the fake dick is hers and holds it down at her crotch. She jerks it off while her face contorts to look like she's having an orgasm. I grab it from her and walk to the cashier while I laugh and she follows, pouting like a child who lost her toy.

"Hello, ladies. Did you find everything you were looking for?"

The beautiful cashier takes our harness out of the box and examines it for flaws. She stuffs it back in the box and scans the barcode. The code on the dildo's tag doesn't scan, so she flattens it while I stare at her tiny hand clutching the fake cock. I picture her on her back, looking up at me with her mysterious dark eyes and purple eye make-up while her pouty lips beg for more. I'm shaken, literally.

"Earth to Terri. Hello?"

"Oh, yeah, I'm sorry." I clear my throat and try not to look flustered. "Debit, please."

The cashier nods and winks at me as if she's read my thoughts. She says, in a rusty voice, "Sweetheart, you can use whatever you'd like."

Is she flirting with me?

Sam lifts a brow. "Well, honey, maybe after she's done fucking me, she can fuck you, too."

Flirting comes so naturally to her. When I try to do it, I usually sound like I'm trying too hard. I've never been good at presenting myself with a strong sense of confidence.

The dark-haired cashier gives Sam the once-over, then licks her lips slowly. She whispers, "*I'd* rather fuck *you* with it."

Sam leans her elbow on the counter, set to flirt hard-core. "Mmm, fun!"

The thickly thighed woman stares at Sam's pouty lips as she shakes open a black plastic bag.

Sam speaks slowly and sounds so fucking sexy. "I have no doubt we'd have a fucking amazing evening, but that's something we'll have to put on the back burner." She stands straight and feeds her arm around mine. "This woman has plans to exhaust me before the night's over. She's good like that… insatiable."

Sam hugs my arm and I nervously smile at her. Why did she tell that to a complete stranger, no matter how sexy she is or where she works?

Fuck it!

"We can't invite anyone into our bed without permission from our master," I say to Sam, and her nod seems to awaken my wild woman within me who has no filter. "We allow him to control our sex lives. I can't even touch this beauty unless he says so. Even though I'm sure you'd be a sweet morsel she and I would have fun tasting, we'll have to pass."

I'm shocked at how easy it was to say all that. Sam's rubbing off on me, literally. Does she think Sam and I have been lovers for a long time?

“Pity.” The cashier groans as her beautiful, full bottom lip protrudes.

I stifle a laugh when the image of JoeSmith biting that lip and her yelping has my nipples stiffening. She looks sexually warped enough to be a fun sex toy for him.

She bags our purchases, then hands me the receipt after she writes something on it.

“I’m Lana. If you ever get permission from your master, give me a call.” Her eyes shift from me to Sam. “I’m sure we’d have a lot of fun together.”

The moment we round the corner into the parking lot, we burst into laughter. Sam snorts and I have to cross my legs so I won’t pee my pants. She waits until she stops laughing before she drives us back to work so I can get my car. She’ll need to go home and pack an overnight bag before she comes over for the night.

We’re going to fuck each other with that big fake cock. I’m apprehensive that I’ll do something wrong or it’ll go badly. I’d rather do this with her before I’d consider fucking anyone else. I trust Sam and she trusts me, so who better to experiment with?

Chapter 18

Alone with Sam

By the time Sam arrives, I've baked chicken parmesan, steamed some vegetables and brown rice. I insisted on cooking because, well, she's a horrible cook! I'm no chef, but I can feed myself.

She hands me a bottle of a locally made Pinot Grigio. I pop the cork and pour us each a glass while she sets the table. We joke and laugh about our trip to the adult novelty store and discuss going back to buy a few things that looked interesting.

We eat dinner without saying much. I think we're both nervous about our plans.

"I ran the dildo through the dishwasher to kill off any germs or bacteria," I say, and she stops chewing and raises her eyebrows. "It's something I like to do with toys that can be washed in boiling water. Doctors recommend it to kill harmful bacteria."

I sound like an infomercial!

She nods slowly. "Hmm, I didn't know that, but I'm going to run my dildo through a cycle tomorrow."

She takes a bite and suddenly tips her head back and roars with laughter.

I laugh because she's laughing, but wish she'd explain.

She points to me and says, "Your mom!" Her eyes swim with tears and she laughs while she explains. "Can you imagine forgetting to take them out after you've run a cycle? No problem, right? But what if your mom stops in and offers to help you with the dishes?"

"No!" My palms press together in front of my gaping mouth. "Oh my God! Can you imagine?"

She laughs at my reaction and claps her hands. "You might die from embarrassment, but holy crap, that'd be a funny story to tell at parties!"

"That wouldn't be funny at all." I cover my mouth, then snicker. "Well, it *would* be funny if it happened to someone else, but it'd be a nightmare to me."

I can see my mom screaming like she saw a King Cobra set to leap out at her.

Sam wears a sexy grin and looks at me from behind hooded eyes. She's unflinching and a bit intimidating when she says, "So, what you're saying is that we're ready to go?"

I try to sound sexy, but my voice trembles. "Yes…" I pause to take a breath and gain my courage. "I'm ready whenever you want me."

"I wanted to use my showerhead before I came over but I followed our master's rule: no clitoral orgasms. This will be a near-impossible feat. You know that, right?" She squirms in her chair. "I don't know about you, but I'm ready to pop like a Jack-in-the-box. Promise me you won't even graze my clit because I'll probably go off with the slightest touch."

I empty my wine glass, open the dishwasher, and pick up the disinfected cock. I hold it up between us and wave my eyebrows. She takes it from me and pops the tip in her mouth as if giving it a blowjob. She laughs because she can't fit more than half of it in.

Sam once told me her gag reflex is quick to respond. JoeSmith will break her of that by teaching her how to open her throat, as he did me, and he'll punish her until she figures it out. Maybe I'll give her tips before we see him again.

If I wait any longer, I'll chicken out.

I grasp her hand and pull her to the bedroom and then stand like a statue, frozen with self-doubt. She slowly presses her lips on mine and kisses me with loving caresses from her tongue. As she steps back, her eyes don't leave mine.

She unhurriedly unbuttons her jeans and removes her shirt. Soon, she's standing before me, completely naked. Her skin is pale and I remember it being soft as silk. She steps forward and kisses me again, but with much more heated desire. I've lost all my apprehension and quickly shed my clothing while our soft lips and firm tongues dance.

Sam lies on the bed, and I hover above her. I crawl up between her legs and kiss her breasts before I suckle her nipples. Her fingers weave their way through my hair and then flips it to one side to get it out of my way. Her skin's velvety soft under my touch.

My lips graze down her alabaster tummy and press to her smooth mound. My tongue glides along her labia majora. The scent of her smouldering pussy doesn't disgust me. Quite the opposite. I want to taste the arousal of her folds and savour the silky smoothness of her stiffening clitoris.

But I can't, no matter how much I want her clit to swell between my lips while she writhes below me. Rules are rules.

My fingers spread and brush down her smooth, velvety folds until her vaginal depths beckon me. Two fingers slip into her and fit perfectly, as if they were meant to be there. I'm careful to avoid her clitoris as I kiss and lick all around it.

Her head tilts to the side as my digits bury into her, and she moans and slips two of her fingers in her mouth. With my fingers inside her, wiggling as they slowly fuck, I slide up her body. She grabs my head with both hands and forces me to kiss her.

Sam's moan warms my mouth and my pussy tightens. Her whimpers and heated breaths ignite my burning desire and I want to touch every inch of her, kiss her until our lips feel raw, and take her out of herself and into orgasmic bliss.

She's moaning because of me, because of what I'm doing. Christ, I love this!

She releases my head and I slide down her body and kiss just above her clit. Her hips lift and my finger slips deeper. I breathe in her musky scent and slowly drag my tongue between her folds along her outer labia, careful to avoid her clit. She's hot on my tongue.

Sam's breathing heavily and moans when I slip a third finger into her and suck her labia into my mouth. She slips the head of the dildo between her lips and sucks. I fuck her with my three fingers and lick all around her clit, but never touch it.

I suck the skin just above the fold of her pussy, right at the V. Her free arm flops over her head and grips the comforter. Her moans radiate about the room.

This is so exciting! She's ravenous with desire and writhing from aching need. If I suck her clit, she'll likely cum in seconds. But JoeSmith forbids it and will punish us for our disobedience. A few seconds of euphoria isn't worth it. Besides, this is the first time he's given an order that is to be carried out outside of the castle, and I want to obey it. He'll reward us for good behaviour, and it'll be awesome!

I reach for the dildo, but she resists. "No, I want to wear it first. Please, let me do you."

Sam wiggles out from below me to collect the harness from the nightstand and slips her legs into it. She hops onto her knees on the bed and I help her tighten the straps after we secure the dildo through the hole in the harness. She looks so tiny with the huge dong protruding from her.

Sam spins her hips and the dildo slaps from one thigh to the other. She bursts into laughter as it flings to her left and right thigh. I roll my eyes, but our laughter fills the room.

"Okay, knock it off," I say, and grab the dildo. "How am I supposed to find you sexy when you're doing that?"

"What? You don't think that's sexy?" she says as she slaps it off her thighs again and points at it. "You know what? I finally understand why men do this. It's funny!"

"Please, stop before I change my mind," I say, and grab the cock to stop her from swinging it.

She pushes her hips toward me and smiles widely. I slap it to watch it bounce and she buckles forward as a man would do under the same circumstances. She straightens her shoulders and shifts her weight from one knee to the other, laughing and pointing her skinny finger at me.

"You wait until you put it on. You're going to do the same thing!"

"Oh, I doubt it!" I snicker, and then shrug and nod with a tilt of my head to assure her I likely will. "So, how do you want me?"

It's her fantasy, so she can do the directing.

She hesitates for a moment, then spins her finger. I position myself on my hands and knees, facing away from her. Sam smothers her fake cock with lube, then guides the cool head against the opening of my eager pussy, separating my lips. I arch my back to give her better access.

Sam gradually pushes forward. The stretch is intoxicating. I push back onto the new toy and most of it sinks into me. A gentle moan caresses my breath.

Fingernails gently brush my ass cheeks as she holds steadfast. I think she's taking a moment to savour this as a favoured first moment. The scene must look incredible from her vantage point.

As if dancing the most seductive dance of her life, her hips roll back and forth. Shivers prickle my skin. I drop my head to the bed, reach back, and separate my ass cheeks to give her a better view. Her rhythm gradually increases and soft whimpers grace her heaving breaths. Is she about to cum, or quickly tiring from the exertion?

My body's growing need to orgasm has me fucking back against her thrusts while she grips my hips and slams forward with as much strength as she can muster, but she doesn't compare to the strength of a well-built man with a desire to bury himself deeper with every thrust.

My muscles tighten as I detach from reality and feel only the ravishing spasms my orgasm permits. Sam abruptly stops and I want to turn around and slap her or beg her to continue… just don't stop!

"What's… the matter? Are you… okay?" I say between quick breaths.

"I can't move or I'll cum. He said no clitoral orgasms, and I'm so close. If I move… Oh, my God! Wow! Wait until you see how fucking hot this is."

Sam pulls the cock from me and undoes the straps to release the harness. I had hoped for more, but I understand her need to stop. JoeSmith must have his reasons for wanting us to hold off and he had better make it up to us. I'm sure he has something special planned. It's that, or he selfishly wants to own our orgasms. I don't question him. I simply choose to obey.

I flop on my back so she can slip the harness up my legs and then roll onto my knees so she can help me secure it in place. My limbs are weak from thrusting back on her. Thankfully, she urges me onto my back. The dildo stands on end, thick and firm, and its positioning feels heavy on my clit. It feels good; maybe too good.

Sam straddles my torso and eases the dildo into herself. Her lips part and she tilts her head back as she settles and her weight presses my hips to the mattress. The light seeping in from the bathroom accentuates the crevasses her muscles allot. She's so beautiful.

She leans forward and rests one hand beside my head and the other cups my left breast. She kisses me with a fiery hunger. Her pillow-soft lips part, and her tongue darts into my mouth.

My fingertips lightly caress her small breasts and pinch her nipples how I would enjoy it.

Sam sits tall and rides the dildo slowly to start. She pushes down and swallows the entire cock as her hips tilt forward and back. Her moan fills the small bedroom. She leans her weight on her arms and slams herself onto me with a quickening need. I squeeze my ass muscles to lift my hips.

She cries out with every thrust. She sits straight again and digs her fingernails into her tits. Her head falls back, and the air vibrates with her raw, erotic wails.

Fuck, yes!

This is so fucking exciting. If only I could feel my clit inside her warm, snug pussy as her body engulfs my most sensitive body part, I would be in heaven. At this moment, I wish the cock was of my flesh.

She collapses forward and braces herself on her arms. With my arm around her waist, I urge her to roll until she's on her back and I'm at rest between her legs, the cock still connecting us.

I wave my hips above her while we kiss. She holds my ass and pulls me deeper. Her petite frame and the softness of her female flesh are so different from the intimate nature of a man. The scents of a woman—shampoo, perfume, deodorant, and yes, even vagina—are intoxicating.

I fuck her hard as she writhes and moans beneath me. Her legs wrap around my hips and pull me in, making it harder to lift. But I don't mind. I breathe heavily as my lips brush her neck. Her nails dig into my ass and the pain disorients me.

She screams as her orgasm ripples through her. Her pussy grips the cock, and the harness tugs just right. My breath hitches. Without warning, electricity resonates from my clitoris and flows to my belly button. Flickering lights fill my vision.

I can't make it stop, and I don't want to.

"I'm coming. I'm coming. Oh, fuck… Yes!"

I slam into her repeatedly until orgasmic convulsions overwhelm my existence and I'm locked in the most pleasurable pain known to women. My juices gush along my twitching clit and flow onto her to blend with her fluids on the pale blue comforter below.

I roll—more like fall—off her and rest my forearms on my forehead and fight to catch my breath. The dildo is still as ready to continue as ever. She sits up and pulls the straps to undo the harness, then flops back down.

"That was fucking incredible!" she declares in a husky voice. "Are you going to tell JoeSmith that you faltered?"

My lungs burn. "Yes, I have to." I groan. "Dammit! I broke a rule, *his* rule, and he'll punish me. But it was worth it," I say as my mental acuity becomes sharper.

That would be worth one hundred slaps from a paddle if that's to be my punishment. Sometimes, I think I enjoy being bad just to see the pleasure he gets from teaching me the error of my ways. His cock always gets so wet. Later, after he's pleasured me thoroughly, he will tell me how well I took his punishment.

"You don't have to tell him," she says.

Is it odd that I look forward to repenting?

I turn my head and smile. "What would be the fun in that?"

Chapter 19

Christmas/Year End Party

We don't work a full day, only until two o'clock, and no one is all that productive. Most of us check emails on our phones, try to bounce paper balls into a cup, or allow our thoughts to drift into pleasant daydreams. But then there are some others who flick small paper balls onto the desk next to them, like Sam and I and the four other cubicles closest to us—good ideas catch on quickly. The idea is to flick a paper ball across the aisle and through the unobstructed goal on the other desk. It's a fun time killer.

Now and then, I glance upstairs at Mr. Manning's office to see if he cares that his employees are blowing off a perfectly good workday, but his office has been dark since this morning, and his suit jacket doesn't hang on the hook by his desk like it usually does when he's here.

Maybe he isn't here, or he's in a meeting at the conference. I can't see that room from my desk. I wonder where he went.

I imagine him at some woman's house, having a torrid affair with his face buried between her thighs, granting her intense pleasure, and then fucking her hard while she's bent over the back of her sofa. I picture his strong thighs flexing, straining to hold his weight as he climaxes and wails in ecstasy.

"Hey!" Sam startles me. I jolt back to reality and she giggles.

"Why do you keep doing that?" I huff and glance back up at his dark office. "It was fun where I was. I wish you could have been there with me," I tease, with a glint in my eye.

She sits on my desk and fiddles with my stapler. "You have such a dirty mind!"

A staple flings to the floor and she closes one eye so she can aim, grips the stapler with both hands and squeezes. She pouts when the staple doesn't make it to Lucy's desk.

"You love my dirty mind."

"You know I do." Sam looks around the room, then up at Mr. Manning's office. "His lights are out. I wonder if he'll be back in time for the *party*." She drags out the word while her arms dance over her head. "It's almost two o'clock, and that means it's almost time to get our drinks on."

"Honey, try not to get too drunk this year. I don't want you puking in the cab on the way home. Do you know how furious last year's driver was? Of course not, you were too drunk. I thought the cabbie was going to drag you out by your hair."

For the past few years, she's gotten drunk at the Christmas parties and hurled before she passed out. It was hell trying to get her into the house.

Sam hops off my desk. In a whisper, she promises, "Oh, no! This year I want you to take me home and fuck me, and I want to remember it in the morning."

She makes her way to her desk while I watch her gorgeous ass as she dances and swings her hips.

As soon as the clock strikes two, everyone revives from their dreariness and heads to the lunchroom to get a glass of champagne and some treats. Someone cues an upbeat song over the loudspeaker while another turns off many of the overhead lights to create a better partying ambiance. I'm surprised to see how quickly six of the cubicles, desks, and chairs are slid out of the way to create a dance floor.

Sam emerges from the crowd gathered in the lunchroom, carrying two glasses of champagne and hands me one. She grabs my forearm and pulls me to the dance floor.

"Dance, woman!"

Her hips gyrate while she sings along to a popular song from the nineties.

I take a big swig from my flute to gain the courage to dance in front of my coworkers. Last year I danced, but I was quite tipsy. I'm not known for having the gracefulness of a dancer. You could say that my slick dance moves are comparable to a newly mobile toddler.

"Give me some time, okay?" I lift my glass. "I need lots of this."

"Then drink up, lady! Let's get this party started!" she yells over the music and bounces to the beat.

Everyone within earshot joins in her excitement and begins to bounce and sway along with her. Hips sway while off-key voices sing to the music. I notice Rick and Bob are watching me and talking amongst themselves. They tap the rims of their glasses together and look back at me, making me uncomfortable.

Mental note: steer clear of them tonight.

I gulp my champagne, then work my way through the crowd to get another. People are having a great time. When I finally get to the lunchroom, I'm laughing along with them. I fill my glass with more of the bubbly and then turn to rejoin the fun. Bob's so close I bumped into him.

"Hi." The edge of his skinny lips lifts, making him seem creepier than his usual self. "Are you having fun?"

"Ah, yeah. I'm starting to," I reply. "How about you?"

His smile fades as he closes the already too narrow gap between us. I smell whiskey on his breath.

He whispers, "You know, we could have a better time." His eyes drop to my cleavage. "We should dance and see where it leads us unless you'd like to skip the dance altogether."

His tongue juts along his bottom lip, leaving a thick coat of saliva. Eww!

"Um, maybe later," I say, and try to step around him. When he doesn't allow it, I shove him, hoping to push him off balance, but it fails. "I want to have fun with Sam for now."

"You ladies have been extra secretive lately." He leans in closer, and I turn my face away. "What's going on between you two?"

"What do you mean?" I ask, wondering if he may have overheard us talking. "She's my friend, my *best* friend, and doesn't always want people to know what we're talking about. There's no great secret conspiracy or anything."

He shakes his head and glares with resentment shaping his glassy eyes. His hand runs down my arm and stops at my elbow.

"Oh, come on. Admit it, you two are lovers. Everyone seems to think so." His eyes travel to the opening of my blouse while I shake my head. "So, are you two fucking each other? Come on, you can tell me. My inquiring mind wants to know."

I try to make my way around him, but his outstretched arm blocks my exit.

"Bob, move!"

He leans in until his face is mere inches from mine. I turn my face away again and ready myself to knee his crotch if he tries to kiss me. He's drunk, but it's no excuse for his behaviour.

"Just tell me. Are you two fucking each other, eating pussy, and sucking titties like two lesbians?"

The coffee mug in his hand is half full of golden liquid, and he smells like he's been drinking for days. Bob's typically a pleasant man, but it's becoming all too obvious that he's a spiteful drunk.

"Maybe your little cunts could use some real cock tonight."

I angrily hiss. "What the fu—"

"Is there a problem here?" Mr. Manning's calm voice sounds from behind Bob.

I didn't see him come in, but I'm glad he did.

"No, sir. I was just having a private conversation with Terri." He spins on his heel and offers his hand. "Merry Christmas, boss."

Bossman doesn't shake his hand. There's anger in his glaring eyes as he stands sturdy.

"I think maybe you should go home, Bob, before you say something you might regret when you've sobered up and find yourself standing before Carol in Human Resources."

Bob clears his throat and sets his mug on the counter.

"Yeah, I was leaving, anyway." He turns his face to look me up and down with disgust. "There's no reason for me to stick around when it's a taco fest and not a hotdog kind of night."

Bossman grips Bob's arm as he tries to walk past him. "I believe you owe Terri an apology."

"I'm sorry, Terri. I shouldn't have been so rude. Please, accept my apology," Bob declares with heavy sarcasm.

"Of course, Bob."

I forgive him even though I'd rather kick his shin.

Did Mr. Manning hear everything Bob was suggesting? Does he—as Bob claims others do—assume I'm in a sexual relationship with Sam? I wonder what he'd think if he knew the assumptions were true.

Bob leaves the break room with his head down. He looks defeated but glances at me before he allows the door to close.

"Are you all right?" Mr. Manning asks and tilts his head. His eyes have softened considerably.

He's my knight in shining armour; that's how the great romance novels would deem him. Who is better than him?

I imagine myself dropping to my knees to pay my gratitude for his heroic act by sucking his cock down my throat. I shake my head and clear my throat while I watch the bubbles rise in my glass.

"Thank you, but I had it handled. You'll have to forgive him. Bob isn't normally rude like that." I sip the champagne, then wave it in front of me. "He drank too much of this. Actually, I think it was whiskey. He'll apologize when he sobers up."

I often picture Bossman naked while he performs some naughty sexual act with me, and because of that, he intimidates me something fierce. His face drops to look at the floor but lifts just his eyes to look at me. My clit twitches and I'm sure my cheeks are hot pink.

The corner of his lips lifts but he clears his throat and lifts his face. Was he reading my thoughts?

"You can file a complaint with Carol if you'd like. I'll back you up."

He walks past me and picks up a glass of pre-poured bubbly and takes a sip. His eyebrows lift with approval.

"That's unnecessary. There's no harm done. Besides, Bob's a nice guy. I'd hate to let one drunken moment ruin his life. I have thick skin and have survived being called much worse than that." My voice cracked during that last sentence.

Mr. Manning refills his glass and holds it up to toast me. "Cheers to another year of success, future health, happiness," he pauses, "and to you; an intelligent and incredibly beautiful woman with thick skin."

His eyes lock onto mine and we clink glasses. Thankfully, the previous glass of courage I drank prevents me from saying something I might regret. He stops halfway to the door and turns. His eyes search the room before they meet mine.

"Save a dance for me, will you?"

I nod and grin like I just won a small lottery but hide it by tipping my glass to my lip.

An hour or so later, Sam, myself, and many others are shaking our asses all over the office. We laugh, sing poorly, and continue drinking. Aside from the champagne, I've had a few shots from the half-empty whiskey bottle Sam and I found in the bottom drawer of Bob's desk. I shouldn't drink whiskey; I gain fool's courage when I do.

Another hour passes, and the blurry room sways around me. I'm having a great time! Sam's drunk, too, but she's eased off since she realized I've been indulging more than I normally do.

When we go out, I'm usually the one to stay in control of my faculties. I look out for her to make sure she makes it home safely. Tonight, she'll be the responsible one and drag my drunk ass home.

I waltz myself to the break room for something to eat to soak up some of the alcohol. If I keep eating, I won't get sick. I learned that trick a few years ago.

While laughing, I fling open the break room door and enter with the grace of a newborn giraffe. Who's standing by the food and watching me stagger in? Ben Manning, of course.

Louder than I should, I say, "Hey, Bossman!" I giggle. "Are you having a good time?"

He's a little fuzzy, but still more gorgeous than any man I've ever known.

His eyebrows lift and with a deep voice, he says, "Bossman? I could get used to that." He leans his backside against the counter and grins. "And, yes, I'm having a great time. You look like you're having fun."

He's sober and still has his wits about him, so I'd better not say anything stupid. Does he even have alcohol in his glass?

I nod too much and talk too fast. "Oh, yeah! I should probably stop drinking now, but I don't want to. Instead, I'm going to eat. That might help absorb some of this champagne… and whiskey, thanks to Bob." I snicker and shove an olive in my mouth, but don't wait to swallow before I talk again. "And thank you for the yumm-ily bubb-ily."

"You're welcome," he says with a wide smile that shows off his gorgeous smile.

"Are you really having a good time?"

He laughs and sets his glass on the counter. "Yes, I am. You should eat more than just olives. Let me fix you a plate." He steps toward the food.

I move between him and the food and wave my hand dismissively. "No, I got it! I got it. I got it. Thanks, though."

He steps back and watches me. I can't seem to stop myself from talking, thanks to the liquid courage.

"So, what about that dance? You should dance with me before Sam takes me home. I *really* want to dance with you. I bet you're a great dancer. With those incredible thighs of yours… Mhmm."

With a tilted head, he looks down and points to his thighs with both palms facing me. "These thighs?"

"Oh, yeah!" I wave my index finger at them and think I'm talking in a sexy voice, but probably not. "I bet you can move in ways that would make any man jealous and every woman wishing she was next in line."

He looks at me with a funny smirk on his face. "So, you like my thighs?"

"You have great legs. Strong thighs are a huge turn-on for me. My mast…" I clamp my hand over my mouth, suddenly realizing that I almost disclosed I have a master, and he has great thighs, too. "You know what? I'm going to shut the hell up right about now before I find myself in Human Resources talking to Carol alongside Bob."

He steps closer to me. "Don't stop talking. I like it when you say what you think," he smiles, "especially when you'rc talking about my strong thighs and how thcy turn you on."

I scrunch my nose and shyly recoil. "I can't believe I said that to you. You're the *Bossman,* and I should behave myself."

"There's that word again." He licks his lips.

"What word?" I ask, and shove another olive in my mouth.

"Bossman," he replies and shoves one hand in his pocket, while his other hand nervously scratches the back of his head. "How about I confess something I probably shouldn't? Something I like about you. Would that make you feel better?"

I set my glass on the counter and stand tall in front of him with my fingers weaved together behind my back. "Give it your best shot. Let's see if you can match the strong thighs comment."

I look into his eyes, unblinking. He swallows hard and clears his throat. He glances at the door to ensure nobody's walking in.

"I think you're beautiful." He isn't smiling anymore.

I tilt my head and put my hands on my hips. "You said that in your toast to me earlier, so that doesn't count. Come on, you can do better than that!"

I fail to realize he's flirting. I slowly turn to give him a better view of my ass. His face loses all expression, and he looks away.

"You've been drinking, so I should walk away now. There are some things that an employer shouldn't say to an employee. I apologize if I've offended you."

He turns to leave.

"Wait a damn minute! You haven't offended me. You owe me a compliment, please." I stroke my finger between the folded-up sleeve of his crimson dress shirt and his strong forearm. "Sometimes women like to hear what men think about them. Don't you know that by now?"

"Hmm." His eyes lock on mine, and I think he's going to say something that will initiate a lustful evening. "I'll see you on the dancefloor, Terri."

He leaves the room while I smile like a smitten teenager, but it falls away quickly. Did he reciprocate my flirting or, in my drunken stupor, did I only imagine he did? I groan as I turn toward the counter and grab a piece of chocolate cherry cake and wedge the whole thing in my mouth.

It tastes so good I can't help but moan. I try to wipe the crumbs from my right breast, but the icing on my finger smears, and the more I swipe at it, the worse it looks.

"Fuck!"

"Hey, pretty lady! I was wondering where you ran off to." Sam dances as she makes her way across the room. "What the fuck did you do to your shirt?"

I laugh and flop my arms at my sides. "You can dress me up, but you can't take me anywhere."

"I'd much rather undress you." She moans and seductively licks the icing off my fingers. She waves her brows and then spins away from me like a ballerina. "I just saw our sexy boss leave this room. Tell me you two were just fucking like wild animals on this table?"

She grabs the corner edges of a table and humps it with an over-exaggerated orgasmic expression while flipping her hair side to side. I burst into a roaring laugh and tiny cake crumbs fly from my mouth. I nearly choke on the cake when I inhale

She drags me by my arm. "Come on, woman! Let's dance!"

Just as we get to the makeshift dance floor, the beat stops thumping, and the music slows to a belly-rubbing tempo and we pop our bottom lips out in a childlike pout.

"Will you dance with me, beautiful lady?" Sam says as she bows.

I curtsy and reply, "Absolutely, even-more-beautiful-lady-than-me."

She spins me and we laugh. She stops and her face lights up. I just know it's *him* standing behind me.

Loud enough to be heard over the music, I yell, "Why yes, Mr. Manning, I'll dance with you."

I turn to look at him and the pit of my stomach feels like it drops away, but I try to play it cool. He takes my hand, holds it to his upper chest, and gently holds my waist with his free hand. We sway to the music. We're close, but our bodies don't touch.

He and I danced last year, too, but so did most of the ladies and one flamboyantly homosexual man. Mr. Manning was kind enough to offer dances to everyone who requested one, no matter their sex or sexual orientation.

"You really are beautiful. I didn't tell you that for the sake of talking." His voice is loud to compensate for the music.

"Thank you," I say with a giggle and a flutter of my eyelashes. "And, just to clarify, I really do like your thighs."

He chuckles and leans his lips close to my ear. "You astonish me, Terri."

"I do? Why? I'm just a—"

He spins me, then grabs my waist and pulls me tight against his body. I rest my cheek against his chest and immediately feel comfort through his warmth. His hips sway with mine as he leads me around the dance floor with the grace of Fred Astaire.

Fuck! This man can move!

His body is warm, firm, and so strong that he easily controls my body when my drunken sways throw my balance off.

I can smell the mouth-watering scent of his cologne. I inhale and pretend that he's JoeSmith and we're dancing after one of our sessions. I wish he and I would dance like this, but that isn't the type of relationship we have. I've had too much alcohol, and I'm thinking too much.

Unfortunately, Bossman is too gentle-spirited and reserved to be a dominant. If he were, I might consider him to be a good option for a love interest. But I honestly don't think he even knows what a dominant is. So, I'll just pretend, for this dance, that this man who holds me is my private master. Who will it hurt if I fantasize?

I could take my mind off JoeSmith if I dropped my hand on the boss's ass to see if it is as tight as I believe it to be. I rethink that idea; drunken fog or not, it's not wise to sexually assault the boss. I might land myself in Human Resources.

Every few steps, his thigh presses against my mound and my pussy twinges in response. When I look up, he's looking down at me with seducing green eyes. He's panty-dampening handsome.

Please kiss me. Just tip your head forward and plant one on me. JoeSmith wouldn't like it, but I'll be punished for my clitoral orgasm anyway, so fucking kiss me!

The music stops and so does his swaying. The beat thumps again. He leans close to my ear.

"Thank you for the wonderful dance."

His hot breath on my cheek has a direct line to my clit.

"And, Bossman, I appreciate your very strong thighs."

He knows how its positioning affected me, and his sneaky grin proves it.

"I'm becoming very fond of that title," he says and winks before he walks away.

Chapter 20

JS

Pretend I'm Him

It's ten o'clock and most everyone's left the office party. Sam pours me into a taxi, then hops in beside me while some of our inebriated coworkers hoot and holler in the parking lot.

I can't wait to get home and let Sam fuck me with our new strap-on. If I can, I want to fantasize it's Mr. Manning fucking me. I know that's not fair to Sam, but I'd be okay with her fantasizing about someone else while I fuck her.

Once we're home, Sam helps me undress and we both stagger into the shower. The water runs down my face and helps sober me up a bit. She stands behind me as she soaps me up and kisses the back of my neck.

Her fingers slide between my ass crack and into my pussy. Her other squeezes my breast and pinches my nipple. It feels so fucking good. She gently twists until three fingers plunge into me.

With short bursts, she fucks me. I arch my back and open my legs for ease of access.

She abruptly stops, shuts off the water, and wraps a towel around me. Before I can finish drying off, she pulls me into the living room, and tells me to wait for her. A few seconds later, she returns carrying the bottle of lube.

Sam bends me over the back of the couch so my ass is in the air and my head rests on the cushions where our backs would rest if we sat properly. She tells me to spread my feet about shoulder-width apart.

"I remember you telling me about a fantasy you have of Ben Manning fucking you over the back of the sofa in his office." She giggles and slaps my ass. "You're going to pretend I'm him."

"I don't think our boss is into spanking." I giggle and play along, anyway.

"You don't know that!"

She slips three lubed-up fingers into my pussy and stretches me until she can work in a fourth. The alcohol has me so relaxed her hand up to her thumb is buried inside me. She waves her fingers and my head spins. I quickly open my eyes to stop the spinning. Her fingers feel so fucking good! I feel a pop and I jolt.

"Oh, my God!" she says excitedly. "My whole fucking hand is inside you. I didn't think it was possible, but… Fuck! Look at that!"

Sam gingerly glides her tiny fist until I buck for more. She fucks me fast. Her thigh pins mine to the back of the couch and her free hand grabs my hair and pulls back until my head is level with the backrest.

I fist the cushions and cry out. "Yes! Oh, my God! Fuck me, Ben! Yes!"

With every thrust of her fist, she slams her weight against me. I cum again and again as I imagine my boss ramming his huge cock into me. I cum hard and then sag limply.

Sam pulls her hand from my spent pussy and cracks my ass with it. The wetness accentuates the sound and the sting. I like it very much and thank her for it.

"Do you want to try to do that to me, too, or are you too drunk?" she asks as she leads me to the bedroom.

I grab her around her waist and pull her against me. I plant a kiss on her and try to continue kissing her as we walk to the bed. She lies back on the bed, and I don't take my eyes off hers.

"I would love to. I should warn you that it kind of hurts at first, but if you relax and let it happen, you'll fucking lose yourself."

"Well, you said JoeSmith will do it to me eventually, anyway. I want you to be my first." She runs her fingers through my hair and tucks it behind my ear. "Fist me, just please be gentle."

We kiss while I start with two fingers and gradually stretch her until she can accommodate four with little resistance. She moans while her hips lift off the bed to pull me in deeper. I bend my thumb in and apply gentle pressure. As if a barrier suddenly gives way, my thumb slips in. She gasps and digs her nails into my back.

I hold still and whisper, "Breathe, Sam."

I remember how painful my first time was. Although JocSmith's touch can bc vcry tcndcr and hc knows what he's doing, it still hurts to accommodate his manly hand.

She reaches down and feels my wrist. With her eyes wide, she whispers, "Holy shit! Your fucking hand is inside my body. Like, all the way inside me."

Her arms flop over her head, and her face falls to the side. Her slow breaths are laced with feminine moans. Her legs flop listlessly and her pelvis tilts. She's ready for my hand to move. I press more of my hand into her until her breath halts. I pause and wait. It's a slow process, and I'm in no hurry.

Ten minutes later, I'm fisting her pussy with gusto. She grabs my wrist and forces me to fuck faster and deeper.

I position myself between her legs, so my pelvis is level with my wrist. I fuck her with my hand while I lick and gently suck her nipples.

"It's your turn to imagine I'm Ben Manning and I'm fucking you on my desk with my huge cock."

She whispers between my gentle thrusts. "Yes… fuck me… Mr. Manning… Make me… cum on your… cock… Yes… Harder!"

Her arms stretch out from her sides, and she grips the comforter in her fists. She writhes and screams as a mind-altering orgasm shreds through her. Her breath holds, and she falls silent as euphoria steals her away from me.

Her vagina squeezes my hand with shocking strength. I fight to hold it inside and attempt to continue thrusting, but it isn't easy. As soon as she relaxes, I ease my hand free.

We slip under the comforter, and I pull her back against my chest and rest my arm over her waist. We're quick to drift into a much-needed slumber.

Tomorrow is Friday—our favourite day—the day we usually get an email from our master.

Chapter 21

A Promise of Punishment

I wake before Sam.

My sleep was restless, to say the very least. A large consumption of alcohol typically causes a person to pass out for hours. Not for me! I nodded off for only a few hours of broken sleep with intense dreams that were exhausting. Today I'll be drinking massive amounts of coffee just to survive.

I chew a few Acetaminophen tablets and sit at my computer with my first cup of Columbian brew, close my eyes and inhale the fumes to savour the joyful aroma. At least my sense of smell is fully awake.

After it loads, I open my email and scroll through the list. I delete messages I don't want from people I barely even like and wonder why I don't block them. I come to a new message from JoeSmith and my heart pounds.

I'm not even the slightest bit aware of my hangover anymore. My concern for my hangover has fallen to the wayside. My body is alive and aches for whatever he'll do to punish me for my disobedience.

I wonder if I should wait to open it with Sam, but she might sleep for a few more hours, and I don't think I can wait that long. I click on it.

Hello, Pet,

Tell me, did the two of you enjoy your new toy? Who fucked who first? Did either of you have a clitoral orgasm?

Tell me details so I can carry them in my mind until you grace me with your presence tomorrow evening.

Yours,
JoeSmith

Should I confess? Maybe Sam's right and I shouldn't tell him.

The punishment may be intense; like a spanking that will leave my ass purple and impossible to sit on for a few days or longer. Maybe he'll deny me his orgasm, which would be a huge disappointment. Allowing me his pleasure gives me great satisfaction. I want to take him to that sense of awe; to the floating euphoria of ultimate yen.

Hello, Sir,

Yes, Sam and I enjoyed the strap-on very much. Thank you for suggesting it.

She wore it first. I was on all fours on the bed while she penetrated me from behind. The dildo we chose was large and filled me completely. It was wonderful.

She told me she loved having that much control but she had to stop. Otherwise, she would've humped herself into a forbidden orgasm. It felt so good, I didn't want her to stop. She made me cum a few times.

I put it on, and she rode me while I was on my back. She fucked hard against me while I fondled her breasts and nipples. I have a new understanding of why men have such difficulty warding off their orgasms. Just to watch her writhe on my fake dick was almost more than I could bear. I can imagine how exciting it would be to feel her pussy clench on my real cock, if I had one.

I flipped her over and fucked her missionary style until she came again. She didn't have a clitoral orgasm; she was a good girl.

I did something unintentional. The harness rubbed my clitoris just right. With all the excitement of Sam losing control of herself at my doing, in combination with the stimulating harness, before I even knew it was happening, I lost control and had a brain-numbing, body-convulsing, clitoral orgasm.

I'm sure you're disappointed with my disobedience, and I'm sorry to have let you down. I accept any punishment you deem suitable.

Yours to do with as you wish,
Terri

I send the email and wonder if he'll be angry at me because I can't obey a simple request. He may not want to see me tomorrow.

Stupid email jokes fill my inbox daily and I hate it. The prime offenders are people I barely even like, but if I block them and they send me something they may ask about later, they'll know I blocked them. It's not the confrontation I care to have, so I'll continue deleting their many ridiculous emails and hope they bore of it and stop on their own.

His reply appears on the top of the list, and I don't hesitate to open it. What will my punishment be? Will he tell me now or make me wait until later?

Dearest Pet,

I understand how difficult it is not to lose yourself in the moment, especially while you're the hand granting someone else's pleasure. I wanted you to abstain because you need to know you can control yourself in any situation if you put your mind to it. And, selfishly, I want to watch you and Slut climax after waiting for it. You must work on your self-control.

You'll be punished for your disobedience, and Slut will be rewarded. Don't fear me as I'll never cause you detrimental suffering. I know your limits and how far to push you.

I want you to be strong in everything you do and push yourself beyond the lines you draw for yourself. You're capable of accomplishing great things and your confidence has grown considerably from the first time we met. You doubted you'd be a good submissive or that you could handle more than a few swats of a paddle. And yet here we are. You enjoy our time together, and I'm grateful to have you as my sub.

What I want is for you to take the strength you've awoken in yourself and use it in your daily life, in all situations. You're stronger than you think.

My goal is to help you believe in yourself so you can succeed at anything you set your sights on.

Your adoring master,
JoeSmith

The leather chair squeaks as I lean back and take a deep breath. I shake my head and rub my forehead, and then my hand slides down my face and comes to rest over my mouth.

He has a point. Since I met him, I've become more confident in myself. I don't hunch my shoulders like I used to. I look people in the eyes more often and hold their gaze no matter how uncomfortable the situation. That's something I couldn't do pre-JoeSmith.

When someone tries to intimidate me, I know they have nothing on my master. Because of my time spent with him and the challenges he's put in front of me, I'm able to stand up for myself more than ever.

Master,

Thank you for building me up and showing me my strength. I am forever grateful for the strength you've built within me.

I await your instruction.

Your grateful, adoring pet,
Terri

I close the computer and sigh heavily. My head aches too much to have an inner argument over whether telling him was a smart thing to do or if I should've lied.

After I collect two pills for Sam and fill two mugs with coffee, I head to the bedroom and sit on the bed.

She lies flat on her stomach with her arms and legs strewn across the bed. The sheet barely covers her abdomen. Her breaths are deep and relaxed. Even when she's asleep, she's adorable. I've been told I look like a hot mess when I'm asleep. I probably snore, too.

"Sam…" I run my fingers down her air-chilled skin and rest my hand on the arch of her back above the two tiny dimples above her bum cheeks. "Honey, do you want coffee and pills for the headache you undoubtedly have?"

I finger-brush her messy hair from her face and she squints from the bright sliver of sunlight dancing through a gap in the drapes. She groans for her hangover to fuck off, and her face scrunches unattractively.

She slowly rolls onto her back, stretches and yawns, and then hugs the sheet around her neck. Her slatted eyes meet mine and, as if she recalled the happenings of last night, a weak smile grows.

"Yes, please. Coffee… Must have coffee. Thank you, my beautiful friend."

Sam rolls to her side, lifts her head off the pillow and takes the mug. She breathes it in, sips it, and then holds the mug near her chest while she smiles and blinks too much. She hands the mug to me and flops onto her back for one more stretch.

Through a yawn, she asks, "How'd you sleep? When did you get up?"

I glance at the clock; it's 10:07. "I slept like crap. By 7:00, I gave up trying and just got up, ate some acetaminophen, and drank coffee."

"So, do we have any plans today?" she asks and swallows the pills with a slurp from her mug.

"We're probably going for our wax later; other than that, we're pretty much free and clear. We can go out for dinner after the salon if you'd like."

"Are you asking me on a date?" She chuckles, then winces from the pain shooting through her brain. "Judging by the hollow ringing in my head, I think I drank too much."

"Me, too. The pills will help."

She groans, tilts her head to the left and right to crack her neck. Every time she does that, I cringe. It's supposed to feel great, but if mine cracks when I turn my head, the little hairs all over my body stand at attention and my stomach twists.

"I almost forgot, it's Friday and we know what that means." Her eyebrows wave, but only for a second before she cradles her forehead in her palm. "Did he email yet or does that usually come later in the day?"

She sits up and hugs the sheet to her body. Her lip rests on the mug's rim and she blows the steam before she sips.

"We got an email from him, but it isn't about our waxing or tomorrow's adventure. He just wanted to know how everything went with the strap-on. So, I filled him in." I smile with a dirty grin.

"Did you tell him you came, or are we pretending that didn't happen?" She shrugs and raises her brows.

"I told him." I stand and open the drapes, temporarily blinding Sam. "If I'm going to be an excellent submissive, I need to learn to follow the rules exactly as he sets them. Maybe a punishment is warranted so I won't forget to stay in control."

"I get that, but shouldn't being in control be necessary when we're in his presence in a session?" she says as she tries to open her eyes wider than slits. "I don't know. I just… I don't think he should punish you for something you did at home. You shouldn't have told him."

"I don't know why I did. I want to please him. If that means I should do as he always says, I will." I tilt my head, cross my arms over my chest, and rest my weight on my left leg. "Is it weird that I'm looking forward to his punishment?"

She yawns as she says, "Well, if it is, then I'm just as weird as you are because I totally got off on that spanking." She bites her lip as she watches me round the bed. "Nobody grows up thinking they'd like someone to beat their ass and tell them what to do."

I pick up her bra and panties and set them on the dresser and make my way to my side of the bed.

She smiles widely and shakes her head. "As kids, we rebelled against our parents who did that exact same thing to us."

Sam sets her coffee down as she sits up and stretches her arms over her head until her face turns red. I pull the covers up and fold them over, and then fluff my pillows as I place them at the head of the bed. She looks at me and frowns. She doesn't want to get out of bed yet, even though I've made my side and want to fix hers.

She drops her legs over the side of the bed and the sheet falls to reveal her perfect breasts. With a grin and sexy, hooded eyes, she says, "JoeSmith is very good at what he does. There's truth to the saying there's a fine line between pain and pleasure. He blends that line very well."

She winks at me, then groans out a few orgasmic sounds and she swings her hips as she makes her way to the bathroom, bringing her coffee with her.

At three o'clock, he replies to the email. Sam left a few hours ago, and she made me promise to call her before I open it.

"He wrote to us!" I sing to her through the phone before she greets me.

"Yes! Okay, read it! Read it! Read it!"

She's way too excited for my lingering headache, and I wince in pain after holding the receiver away from my ear until she quiets. I love how thrilled she is about joining me in this adventure, but my head hurts!

"It reads:

Dear Pet and Slut,

You both must: Be at the pickup point by 5:30 Saturday evening. You're expected at the salon today for a waxing.

Hints for Saturday's session: Punishments will be applied deservedly and pleasure will be provided as a reward for good behaviour. I'll display you both while you silently endure.

Do you both accept?

Master of two,
JoeSmith."

I clear my throat and suck my lips into my mouth and bite them. "I'll admit that I'm a little nervous about my upcoming punishment. What will he do to me, I wonder?"

"I was a good girl, so I'll be getting pleasured. Thank you, JoeSmith," she says with an evil laugh. "Seriously, though; you'll be okay, right?"

I send off the acceptance reply.

"Yes, I'll be fine—I'll endure." I sit back in my chair and swing the chair side to side as I look at the crack in the ceiling and cringe because I keep forgetting to fix it. "He'll never, like, beat me with a bamboo whip to the point of splitting my skin and scarring me, or anything like that. At least, he hasn't so far."

"I don't want to watch you scream while someone beats the shit out of you. I'll throw the towel in first," she promises.

"Oh, God! No, he would never hurt me. Extreme punishment is a hard limit for me." I take a breath. "Listen, don't worry about it. I'll be fine. Besides, the pain he initiates arouses me."

"I hear that! Uh, uh, ooo ooo, yeah! Spank me, motherfucker! Yes! Yes!"

Judging by the way she's breathing, she's either dancing or humping the air. I titter and roll my eyes, even if she can't see.

"Yeah, something like that."

"So, should I just meet you at the salon?" she asks, and I hear dishes clink together.

"Sure, that sounds like a plan." A thought pops into my head. "Oh! Don't forget to bring your questionnaire with you. You filled it all in, right?"

"Oh, shit! No, I completely forgot. I meant to ask you if you'd help me with some of it, but I kept forgetting."

I hear paper rustling and then she grunts before something slams.

"You didn't lose it. Did you?" I ask, and lean back in my leather computer chair.

"No! It's here somewhere. It's fairly straightforward, but I don't want to regret okaying something that's really not okay. If you know what I mean," she says and sounds frustrated.

"You don't want that! Bring it with you and we'll go over it tonight. Are you feeling any better?" I say and groan. "I swear this headache is determined to split the left side of my skull."

I hear a drawer slam and another open, more shuffling papers, and finally a celebratory squeal.

"Woot woot! I got it!" I can tell she's dancing. "Yeah, my hangover finally fucked off about half an hour ago."

"Oh, good. You're lucky. I've been trying to clean but it's painful." I stretch my legs straight out and roll my ankles. She says nothing and I wonder if I lost the connection, but when her exhale sounds hollow, I ask, "What are you doing?"

"I'm going to do some laundry. It's the dreaded chore I've put off far too long. While I wait for that to cycle through, I'll clean; another chore I've been putting off."

I hear a ding and the dryer starts.

"I should probably do a load or two," I mumble, more to myself than her.

"Can you throw my blue t-shirt in with your load?" she asks. "I left it on the chair in your bedroom."

I get up to retrieve it, add it to my hamper, and grimace at how much my head will thump when I have to bend over to get the clothes at the bottom of it.

"So, shall we meet at 4:30 tonight?" she asks.

"That works for me. Okay, I'll see you then," I reply and hang up. I look at the laundry basket and huff. "Where are the magic fairies when you need them?"

Chapter 22

Setting Her Limits

I pull up at the salon next to Sam's red sedan. She looks up from her phone and smiles when she notices me. We hug at the door, then make our way inside. As usual, they lead us to the back room where the hair removal task begins. She looks nervous.

Sam yelps more this week than last. I tease her, of course; that's what friends do. I don't know how the technicians don't burst into laughter at the people who act like they're sawing off a leg. I couldn't do this job. Not only do I not want to touch all those genitals, but I'd crack up too much and humiliate the clients. They'd fire me for sure.

Even though it's chilly outside, wearing a skirt was a good idea. The cool air relieves my tender pussy lips. I wish I could sit outside with my legs wide open until the heat ebbs, but my bare, red pussy is sure to draw unwanted attention. Sam's gait isn't her usual sexy, peppy stride, and it has me laughing at her.

While we wait for our dinners to arrive, we review her contract and discuss a few items on the list she didn't know whether to check off. She wanted to know what I checked as being acceptable and what I said was a hard limit. I told her, but let her know it was up to her to set her limits.

Sam tucks the folded papers in her purse and zips it shut. She sighs heavily and rests her elbows on the table.

"I feel better now. It's done and I can stop stressing over it."

"It's hard to choose your limits when you aren't sure of what they are." I shrug and see the waitress walking toward us with two plates. "You can always change them later or ask him to push past your boundaries if he thinks you can handle it."

She lifts her right shoulder and chews the tough skin beside her baby fingernail. "I could do that."

I whisper as the server nears. "That's why we have safewords."

The waitress sets our plates in front of us and asks if we need anything else. We shake our heads. She smiles and tends to the couple at the table next to us. I take a bite of a carrot, then cover my mouth with my hand to ask Sam a question that I'm not so sure I want an answer to.

"So, at the party, did I act like a fool? I have some blank spots." I scrunch my face and look toward the heavens. "I remember dancing with Bossman and thinking he was so damn sexy—that man can really move his hips. I wanted to fuck him right there by the water cooler. I didn't though, right?"

My panicked eyes have her laughing.

"Well, you did this one thing…" She pauses and laughs when my eyes widen and the blood leaves my face. "You look so scared."

"You would be, too!"

She waves her fork. "You were fine."

I sigh with relief. "I remember he smelled clean and manly, and I so badly wanted to taste his skin. He held me just right, and *fuck me*, that man can dance!"

Her shoulders slump and her eyelids sag. "Just watching you two had my pussy dripping. I think everyone thought the same thing. Maybe there's some chemistry there."

"I'm sure there'd be some serious fucking going on if we could, but he's my boss and I'm with JoeSmith," I say, and she rolls her eyes. "Well, I am, sort of. So, did I say anything that'll get me fired?"

She laughs. "I don't think so. Bossman was a knight in shining armour when he saved you from Bob's advances."

I nod and roll my eyes as I recall the incident. "I remember."

"Bob was a dick to you. I can't believe he said that shit." She shakes her head and holds her arms out to her sides with her fork dangling from her fingertips. "I mean, curiosity is one thing, but holy crap. It's none of your business, nosy *motherfucker!"*

"He was drunk. The things he said he'd never say if he were sober. He'll apologize."

"Even so," she says and sips water from her glass, "he never should have said those things."

I swirl my fork around my plate while she shoves bite after bite in her mouth. She's thinking about something and I wish I could hop into her mind and see what has stolen her thoughts. I clear my throat and she looks up from her plate.

"Things got hazy by the end of the night. Was I acting like a needy whore? I mean, on the dance floor." I rub my forehead. "Did I do something regretful, like, with Bossman?"

"Not that I saw. I think he was flirting with you, but I couldn't hear the conversation. Do you remember it?"

One edge curls up on her parted lips while her eyes widen from curiosity. She stabs a chunk of chicken and lets it hang off her fork tines. I take my time chewing a mouthful of Romaine lettuce, which tests her patience, especially when I hold up a finger asking her to wait. She jams the bite in her mouth, then circles her fork in the air, urging me to hurry.

"I remember complimenting him on his strong thighs, several times." I drop my head into my hands and groan. "I can't believe I told him that."

Sam laughs so loud that people turn to look at her. Some people smile, but a few folks seem annoyed at her outburst. They must have miserable lives if they can't enjoy someone else's happy moment.

"You worry too much, Terri. He was obviously flirting with you, too. You looked down at his thigh at one point and he seemed amused when you said something and then laughed. In fact, he kept pulling you close to him."

I shrug. "Yeah, he had a good grip on me because I was drunk and swaying… you know, because of the mass consumption of alcohol."

"It looked like more than that. At one point, you two were chest to chest, dancing slowly and looking into each other's eyes." She moans, waves her brows, and points at me with a fork stabbed through a lettuce leaf. "You two look great together. I would probably spontaneously orgasm if I watched you two make love; not just fucking, but actual, romantic lovemaking. Fucking hot!"

"It'll never happen, but you can dream," I tease with a roll of my eyes.

She bites her bottom lip. "Oh, I will! I'm so excited, my pussy's smouldering." She shuffles in her seat as her eyes drift. "Wait! No, that's caused by the waxing."

I agree with her and we burst into laughter.

We eat in silence, and I lose myself in thought. I imagine Ben and me in a passionate embrace with his hard cock buried inside me as his hips slowly lift and lower above me, all while he kisses my lips with a gentleness that can't be matched.

"Hey! Earth to Terri." Her hand waves in front of my face. "You know you can't go there. If you do, JoeSmith will sever ties with you. You can't be sexual with someone else. It's in the contract. Besides—and this is completely selfish on my part—he wouldn't want me without you. We come as a package, and—"

"I'm sure he'd send you an invitation. He enjoyed playing with you."

"No, he liked how *you* reacted when he played with me." She shrugs and sips her coffee. "Promise me that if you decide to get it on with Bossman, you'll tell me first so I can enjoy a last tryst with our master before life goes back to the boring daily grind that once was my sad, pathetic life and would be again. Fuck me! I'm depressing myself!"

She glowers and stabs her fork at her plate. I shake my head.

"Oh, please! When did you have a sad, pathetic life? You've had more sexual rendezvous than anyone I know."

"Yeah, but they weren't this good!"

I take a breath and drop my eyes to my plate and push the remaining food around with my fork. I set it down and push the plate away from me.

"Don't worry, I'm not going there with Mr. Manning. He was probably just drunk and got lost at the moment. It's hard to hide your inhibitions when alcohol has been consumed. I'm sure he's already forgotten all about it." I lean forward on my elbows to stretch the aching muscles in my back. "He might be worried he said or did something that could land him in hot water with Human Resources, or worse, at the focus of a lawsuit."

"That would suck! I hope he knows you'd never do that," Sam says, then beats me to the bill and tosses a twenty on it before I can.

"Wasn't it my turn?" I ask, but she shrugs and blows me a kiss.

She holds the mug up to her mouth after the waitress tops it off.

"I hate to break this to you, but he wasn't drinking." She takes a sip while I stare at her, not sure I hear her correctly. "I mean, I only saw him with one glass of Champagne and that was only to make a toast. I didn't see him drink a sip out of the glass after that. He was stone-cold sober, my dear."

"So he remembers everything!" My head jerks to the side, and I clap lightly and let my sarcasm spew. "Great, that is so great! He'll remember all the dumb shit I did and said. Awesome!"

We hug in the parking lot before we drive our separate ways. I think I'll do some laundry before I go to bed. I really wish I could masturbate to ease my stress; it might help me sleep.

I'm anxious about tomorrow and what Master has planned. I'm horny and scared at the same time, but scared in a good way, like when you watch a movie knowing something is going to jump out at you, but you continue watching, anyway. I'm waiting for the impending *boo!*

Vibrating myself into euphoria would certainly tame my racing thoughts, but it's forbidden.

Rules are rules!

Chapter 23

JS

Love It or Hate It

I arrive at the corner to wait for the limo and wonder how I beat Sam here.

A bus pulls over a block down the street. Sam hops off and jogs toward me. She weaves and dodges the other pedestrians as she zips around them. Her cheeks are flushed, and she's breathless by the time she reaches me. I calmly sip my coffee and look at the imaginary watch on my wrist.

"You realize that you have over five minutes before the limo's expected to arrive, right?"

She holds her hand over her heart and slumps forward. "Yeah, I know, Miss *I run fifty kilometres a day*!"

"Fifty?" I jerk my head back and blow out my cheeks. "There's no way in hell I'd run fifty kilometres in a day. Yikes!"

"Whatever! I'm never late—*never*! To me, arriving less than ten minutes early is late. It's one of my phobias; allegrophobia. It's a recognized phobia. I can't help it." She points to her head with both hands, nearly dropping her purse. "It's, like, in my brain mechanisms or, you know, thingies. Let's change the topic. How are you doing?"

She steps closer and hugs me, then digs through her purse and pulls out a five-dollar bill.

"You're so weird. I'm just teasing you. I love all your quirks and phobias." I turn and glance down the street to see if the limo's coming early, but it's not as I had expected. "And I'm doing great today, thank you. I'm looking forward to my discipline," I say sarcastically as I rock back and forth from heel to toe.

"Yeah, that's going to suck. I'm glad I'm not you today." Her bottom lip pulls tight and her eyes open wide. "I'll be right back."

Sam runs into the coffee shop. Only a minute passes before she returns, clutching a large coffee. She points at it as she nears me, wearing a quirky grin.

"Necessary energy juice," she says and alternately bounces her shoulders as she pops the lid.

We tap our cups together and sip. She slips her fingers in the back pocket of her jeans and rocks from heel to toe, right along with me. We stare toward the expected limo. It's obvious that she's nervous, maybe even more than me.

I wrap my arm around her shoulders to stop her from rocking. I was a shaking mess the first dozen times I waited on the corner, just like she is now. But she has to stop swaying; she's making me dizzy.

I whisper, "Think about the pleasure he'll inflict upon you. He'll make you cum so hard you'll get lightheaded."

She slips her arm around my waist. "I know. I was a good girl, deserving of his just rewards. I'm worried about watching him punish you. I don't know if I can do it without protest. What if I yell at him or something?"

"Or something?" I try to meet her eyes, but she's looking at her cup. "Like what?"

"I don't know… charge him, maybe." She steps out of my hold and turns to look at me with worry darkening her pretty face. "If I do something stupid, he'll punish me or you even more intensely. Do us both a favour and don't fucking cry. If you do, I'll freak out on him. I swear to God. I can guarantee I won't be invited back."

My shoulders soften and I grip her shoulder. "Sam, that's why he gives us safewords. I'll use it if I need to. And trust me, JoeSmith cares more about our well-being than satisfying his need for sadistic pleasure. He would *never* injure us. Try to keep that in mind."

I smile to calm her but she still looks like a baby doe; wide eyes and standing on unsecure legs. She rakes her fingers through her hair and bites her lip.

"Besides, I love his punishments because I know an incredible amount of pleasure will follow, equal to or better than the punishments themselves, but only if I grant him my trust. I've been doing this longer than you have and I wouldn't lie to you."

We hug until the limo rounds the corner, cruises up, and stops in front of us. Sam steps forward toward the door handle, but I grab her arm and jerk her back quickly. With a shake of my head to gesture for her to wait for the driver, she spins her torso side to side with nervous energy.

"Good evening, ladies. How are you both this evening?" asks the stout, well-dressed man in his early fifties as he opens the door.

As Sam gets in, I smile at him. "We're having a great day, Jim. How's your day been so far?"

With a welcoming grin, he tips his hat and more of his salt and pepper hair pokes free. "Today is a glorious day filled with promise. Don't forget your hoods."

I sip my coffee from under my hood. Sam clears her throat and I hear her curse. She must have spilled her coffee on her shirt.

I snicker. "It takes some practice. I still splash it on myself more often than I care to admit."

A while later, the limo stops and the door opens. We remove our hoods and fight to condition our watering eyes to the sudden brightness of the blazing sun that has yet to set.

Greeting us at the car is a tiny woman who's not all that pretty. She has very short hair and wears no make-up. She wears a tight, one-piece red latex suit. The outfit doesn't suit her vanilla appearance.

Without a word, she walks us into the mansion and straight to the desk to sign the release papers. Sam hands her filled-out checklist and the woman in red lingerie is more than happy to take it. We're led to the locker room, to clean ourselves, and finally to the preparation room.

Sam and I sit in director-style chairs while the ladies apply our make-up and style our hair. By the time we're finished, Sam's wearing a cute baby doll white dress with patent leather, side-buckle shoes with a flat heel. Her make-up is soft to give her an innocent appearance. Two fancy braids trail down her back in a complicated style.

I'm dressed quite the opposite I'm outfitted in all black. Latex stockings don my legs and stop high on my thighs at the crease between my ass and legs. There are clips attached to the top of them that dangle between my legs.

I want to ask what the fuck those are for, but I don't dare speak without permission.

They tie me into a black leather corset so tightly that it takes me a minute before I can breathe easily. I pull at the corset and say nothing, but they're patient while I adjust myself to make it bearable. This is what JoeSmith requested, so my protest is futile. I stand in very high heels and wobble. I debate whether I'll be able to walk anywhere without tripping or spraining my ankle.

My breasts are squished in the corset and balloon over the top in an ill-fated attempt to escape. Leather patches over my nipples are removable. Black latex gloves line my arms.

My attire is completed with black latex gloves and a thick leather collar with four large metal loops I could probably fit three of my fingers through. They must be there so he can attach my neck to something, or perhaps he wants to leash me like Lady Catherine leashed the sexy blond Adonis.

I don't want them to parade me down the hall like a dog. That's too much humiliation for me. Besides, I don't think my knees can take it.

I don't recognize myself when I look in the mirror. This woman looks vicious. Her make-up is thick and dark, and her long hair extensions are gathered in a ponytail at the top of her head and flow down her back. This seductive dominatrix is beautiful in a terrifyingly wicked way.

Sam stares at me, and I see she's nervous. Maybe she thinks he'll have me dominate her. That's possible. I smile and she smiles back, but still looks concerned.

We're bent over and examined. The dresser's fingers pull at my ass until I'm relaxed enough to compensate for a medium-sized butt plug that, once inserted, leaves me trailing a long, dark horse's tail. I want to shake my ass at Sam and laugh like a wild-woman, but I'll be scolded if I do. She bites her lips together to restrain her laughter. And if I don't avert my eyes, I'll lose control.

The latex-clad, average-looking woman returns with two powerful men in tow. The two muscle-bound men have short, dark hair and wear snug blue jeans—that's it. They stand on either side of me, each holding an elbow. The delicious men balance me as she leads us to the toilet for a final pee before we continue down the corridor and into a room that looks like a stereotypical dungeon.

The walls are lined in old cobblestones, and the floor is a dirt-coloured laminate. It's not bright in here as only six candle sconces light the ten-metre square room. There are several bondage furniture items and a few chains dangling from the ceiling, ready to sustain a human's weight. Even the smell is dank like an old basement storage unit. How did they manage that? I can't imagine a candle with that scent would sell well.

Sam shakes as she looks at the apparatuses meant for bondage and torture more than pleasure. Her arms cross over her chest to warm herself. It's chilly here but it'll heat soon enough. She glances my way, so I flash her a wide smile. She nods and returns the gesture, signalling she's okay.

I'm led across the room to the St. Andrew's cross. The men assist me as I step onto a short platform in front of the thick wooden planks. JoeSmith tied me to one of these once before, but I didn't have to stand on a box before they affixed me to it.

The woman uses black latex tape to fix my arms to the top portion of the X while two chains spanning between the boards at head level are fastened to my collar to keep it in place.

She wraps the same wide latex tape around my waist and the wood to secure me to it. She removes the stool from under my feet, but I don't fall—I don't drop at all. She tapes my legs to the boards in three places and leaves my high-heeled feet to dangle.

At least I don't have to stand on these ridiculous shoes. I can't move at all, not even my head, but I can wiggle my fingers. I'd be lying if I said I wasn't nervous.

Sam's hands are bound in leather gloves that keep her hands fisted. One of the large men lifts her while the other secures the gloves to a chain dangling from the high ceiling. He sets her down, but her feet barely touch the floor. She looks horribly uncomfortable as she tries to balance herself on the toes of the patent leather shoes.

They leave the room and the flickering flames on the sconces fade to black as if someone blew them all out at once. A few seconds later, two bright spotlights illuminate us; one on Sam and the other on me. The rest of the room remains shrouded in infinite blackness.

This is sexy, dangerous, terrifying, and yet so damn arousing that my pussy is dripping wet from the thrill of it all.

Sam's nipples protrude beneath the thin fabric of her dress. She's breathing quickly while she struggles to still herself on the tips of her shoes and she giggles. She looks at me and is about to whisper, but the silence breaks with the creak of a heavy wooden door opening.

Chapter 24

JS

My Favourite Pet

A small crowd of eight people enters and whispers to each other as they make their way across the room, hidden by the shadows that surround them. I hear the brown leather shift as they sit on the sofas perched against the far wall behind Sam. The voyeurs are quiet when a man enters and closes the door behind him, once again darkening the room outside of the spotlights.

Shoes scuff the floor and I know it's JoeSmith by his gait. My pussy clenches as I mentally prepare to give myself to him and trust he'll protect me. He storms into the light, looking dangerous as fuck!

He wears a black hood that covers his head completely, having only eye holes and a slit for his mouth. He wears black leather pants so tight they outline his restrained, semi-erect penis as it hangs to the left, and a riveted leather harness that crisscrosses his chest.

Sam watches him as he approaches her. He circles her with his hands fisted, scanning up and down her body while she balances. Her quick breaths hold when he presses his chest against her back. She shivers and I'm sure it's because she can feel his scalding breath on her neck.

The hood muffles his whispers, but I hear. "Your safe word is zebra. It will always be zebra every time we meet. Do not forget it. Repeat the safe word."

"The safe word is zebra, Sir."

He reaches around her chest and grips the front of her dress with his fingerless leather gloved hands and rips the front enough to free her bra-covered breasts. He crosses his arm over her chest and gently cups her left breast in his right hand. His other hand glides down until it reaches between her legs. He pulls up, lifting her by her crotch until her feet are off the ground and then grinds his pelvis against her ass.

He suddenly lets her go as if he's bored with her. She swings and fights to regain her footing.

JoeSmith strides toward me. He examines my bindings and then grabs the sides of my jaw and applies pressure until I open my mouth as wide as I can.

His shrouded lips are so close to mine I can feel their heat. I'm shaking, but it's not from fear, but from excitement. I want him; I want his punishment; I want to please him, and I desperately want his bare lips on mine.

"If you're as good a submissive as you claim to be, you'll refrain from using the safeword unless absolutely necessary. I plan to test your devotion. I don't expect you to be a superstar, so if you need me to stop for whatever reason, I expect you'll say zebra." He takes a step back and speaks in a deeper and sexier tone than usual. "Repeat the safeword."

With my eyes focussed on his strong, leather-clad chest, I whisper, "The safe word is zebra, Master."

He steps to the side and I hear two clicks. With a *whoosh*, the X flips backward and I'm upside down. I scream as a wave of panic overwhelms me.

"What the fuck? Oh, my God!" I squeeze my lips to stop the word vomit and then take a breath in through my nose and release it through my parted lips. "I apologize, Master JoeSmith."

He slowly turns the X horizontally until I'm looking in Sam's direction, who looks like she's upside down and balancing on top of a chain. I don't like being upside down, so this will be a challenge.

He busies himself while I stare at his leather-outlined cock. Something cold that feels like metal slips into my pussy. Two wires hang down, but he gathers them and plugs them into an electronic unit topped with many dials and buttons.

I close my eyes and breathe in through my nose and out through my mouth. I gave myself to him because I trust him. He'll keep me safe and never harm me. I know this to be true. I open my eyes and imagine my tongue outlining his cock with saliva.

He attaches four sticky pads to the sides of my ass cheeks and plugs them into the unit. He pinches my nipples firmly and pulls until half of my breasts poke out from the holes in the corset and clips little metal pincers to them. They're tight and they hurt a great deal, which intensifies when he tugs them. It's not unbearable but my poor nipples will be sore as hell later.

Master pushes a button as the unit lights up. He turns a knob while he watches my face. I feel an acute sting on my nipples, and tears fill my eyes.

Electricity? This is new.

Is he going to zap me from inside my pussy? Oh, my God! No! This'll be so painful. Tears drip over my eyelashes and down my forehead. I've never cried upside down before. If I wasn't tied so tightly, I'd be shaking violently. Instead, my breaths are ragged and my chin quivers until my teeth chatter.

JoeSmith crouches and brushes the back of his fingers along my cheek. He whispers, "Just breathe. Calm yourself. Don't let your fear determine the outcome. Are you ready to continue?"

I nod and take as deep a breath as I can manage with the corset's restriction. I exhale slowly, and he wipes my forehead to dry my tears.

He returns to the control box and turns another dial. My ass cheeks tighten and loosen, only to repeat with a harder clench. Just when I think I might laugh from the awkwardness of my flexing ass, the tightening ceases but is quick to repeat. He turns another dial and the plug inside my pussy pulses in the most delicious way. My lungs deflate with a whimpered moan I couldn't have held back if it meant a million dollars.

I had imagined horrible pain, but it's quite the opposite. The thumping increases until I moan louder than I should, but I'm unable to control myself. I've felt nothing so magnificent in my whole life. But then the pain from my ass cheeks breaks through the bliss to inflict a cruel pain. It confuses my senses. Am I enjoying this or hating it?

Leather sings in the air with a *whoosh* as he swings the tassels of the heavy flogger against my latex covered leg. It has a heavy and quick impact but doesn't hurt. I open my eyes and see him swing it again. He strikes my legs until I'm sure they bear a pink or red hue. The sound of the leather slapping the latex is more intimidating than the contact itself.

Pleasure or pain?

I moan with delight and scream in pain all in the same breath when all the electrodes pique. I try but can't stop myself from being so verbal.

"Do not close your eyes," JoeSmith says just before he walks away from me.

I hadn't realized they were closed.

Master's boots stomp as he rushes toward Sam and abruptly grabs the edges of her torn dress and continues to tear it. Her ribs swell and contract quickly as he pulls at the fabric until it falls free of her body.

She looks sexy as fuck as she sways until she regains her balance. She wears only white stockings, a thong, and push-up bra that only shoves her breasts upward but leaves her nipples exposed.

He reaches down and slips his finger beneath the waistband of her frail thong. Her body jerks from the force as he rips it off.

She wobbles when he wraps his hands around her tiny waist and pulls her against him. He grips her jaw and kisses her with a roughness that screams his need to own her.

He cups her ass and lifts her until her thighs rest over his shoulders. He lifts his mask to bare his mouth, which I can't see, and buries his lips between the folds of her pussy. Her head tips back but, oddly, she emits no sound from her gaping mouth. She's obeying his rule to remain quiet, which I can't seem to manage through the squeezing and thumping.

She bends her knees and hooks her feet around to his chest at his armpits. Her back arches high in the air as his arms flex to brace the small of her back. The seams of his leather pants strain to maintain his bulging thighs. What a picture this would make!

Her body twists and her chest heaves. She's going to cum. He isn't stopping like he usually does to procrastinate an orgasm. Instead, he continues to lick and suck her clit until her body tenses and her breaths halt. She withers, but he doesn't let her down and continues to lick her pussy. Her expression tightens as he continues torturing her sensitive clit with his flicking tongue.

He unzips his pants but leaves the top button fastened and frees his steely erection through the open zipper. Using only one hand, he covers it with a condom. He swiftly pulls her thighs off his shoulders and drops her hips down, but pins her legs together and rests them against his chest, so her ankles remain at his right shoulder and her pussy is at his crotch.

Master grips her hips and slips his cock deep into her awaiting folds. Without hesitation, he pounds into her suspended body and holds her legs against him. He reaches around to the small of her back and nearly folds her in half while his hips thrust into her. She's incredibly flexible and somehow he knew this.

I want him to touch me and hold me in his arms. My ass muscles ache to a nearly unbearable point. My vagina is soaked and so aroused by the pulses. It feels like I'm being fucked by a ghost. But every time he thrusts into me, his cock thickens. It's so fast; nearly twice the rhythm of my heartbeat.

My body is being put through a test of endurance with simultaneous pleasure and pain. I love this and yet hate it. I hang on the teeter on the edge of orgasm but can't quite get there.

JoeSmith eases Sam down until she's dangling by her arms, and she looks totally spent. He pulls off the condom and disappears into the darkness between her and me. He enters the light as he nears me while his cock sways with each step as it juts from the open zipper of his tight leather pants.

He fiddles with the electronic machine and increases the thumping in my vagina until my mind whirls. I want to cum so badly, but I can't get over that edge. That's a good thing since he didn't grant me permission.

As he rests on one knee, I see the layer of sweat that lines his flesh. His eyes look dark through the mask and I can see some of his bottom lip, but not enough to see its true shape. He leans in, covers my eyes with his palm, and kisses me hard with bare, hot lips.

Pain!

The left nipple clamp is removed, and the pain has a scream wedged in my throat. He continues to kiss me but his breath quickens; my pain excites him. I whimper, almost begging him not to release the right clamp, but he isn't sympathetic, and my whimpers lodge in my throat with my breath.

I'd hoped the release would be the worst pain, but I know better. He pinches and rolls them between his fingers, and my breath catches.

"Breathe, my beautiful pet."

He stands and his cock's so close to my mouth. He touches my vagina and then I feel pressure, a lot of pressure. Soon, I feel it on both of my labia. The clamp attachments hold my lips open on my stockings. The cool air stings my clit now that the sheathing hood is pulled back.

I hear a buzz, then something cold presses between my labia. My entire pussy simultaneously vibrates, thumps, pulses, and tenses. This is euphoric, but I can't cum. Maybe the pain overshadows my pleasure.

"Open your mouth," he says, but in my confusion, it doesn't register. He lifts the vibration and repeats himself. "Open."

I obey, and the tip of his penis pushes past my parted lips. He slides farther into my throat, nearly causing me to gag.

He holds himself there and says, "My cock was just inside Slut."

I try to breathe through my nose, but he's too far down my throat. I gag. He yanks from my throat and my face is slapped, but not hard enough to hurt more than my ego.

Harshly, he warns, "I'm going to fuck your face and you will not gag. Tell me you understand."

I sharply say, "I'll try not to gag, Sir."

His cock enters my mouth again, and with a slow, steady motion, fucks my throat. As he recedes, the tip of his cock rests on my upper lip. While he pauses, I take a breath. He suddenly takes a few steps back and rests his hands on his hips as his masked face tips toward the ceiling. I watch him take several slow and deep breaths before he moves.

JoeSmith lowers the chain connected to Sam until her feet rest flat on the floor. She looks relieved. He switches his leather gloves for a pair of black latex and picks up a bottle of lube.

Through hooded eyes, I watch Master cup both breasts and suck a nipple in his mouth. I think he bit because she winces and sharply retracts.

He drops to one knee and rests her left thigh on his right shoulder. Two of his gloved fingers slip into her pussy and he looks up at her face, which is tilted down so she can watch him. He fucks and diddles her folds for what seems like a long time, but that's only because I'm desperate to cum and I might literally lose my mind soon if I don't.

As he carefully pushes three fingers in and gently twists his wrist, he watches her facial reactions. Her eyes are closed as she fights not to cry out. She's enjoying the pressure. Her head drops back and the hint of a soft moan rides her breaths.

He plants his mouth on her clit and fucks his fingers into her pussy unhurriedly.

Her head drops forward and her abdominal muscles flex uncontrollably as she reaches orgasm. His fingers flap inside her as her excitement drips down his forearm and off his elbow. He stands and walks away, abandoning her while she squeezes her quivering thighs together.

Master rubs Sam's cum all over my face, smearing my heavy make-up even more than my tears had. It's a good thing her scent turns me on. The thumping and muscle tensing suddenly stops, and I can't decide if I'm relieved or disappointed.

I hear a click and I'm slowly flipped upright. I breathe as deeply as I can to help my brain right itself. He sets my legs free and removes my shoes before placing my feet on the stool, and then he frees my neck, then my waist. My hands are freed but immediately bound in front of me, using the latex tape that bound them to the X.

He carries me over his shoulder to another apparatus. I'm grateful he doesn't make me walk because I'm still dizzy and my legs are so weak I'd undoubtedly fall.

"Get on your knees and bend over this bar."

I comply, and he fastens my thighs to the cold metal base and stretches my arms above my head, attaching them to a metal hook on the floor. He re-affixes the electrifying nipple clamps, much to my chagrin, and attaches their wires to a small hook beneath me. He pulls to stretch my aching tits downward.

I breathe through the pain and discomfort but soon don't care about it because the delirium of pulsation in my vagina begins.

JoeSmith spanks my bare ass with his latex-covered hand, which heats my skin quickly. Each whack jolts through my body, which pulls my nipples. I'm not sure which hurts more. Every time his hand lands at the same time my ass muscles are being electrified, the pain hinges on being too much, but my clit is aching to be touched. I could cum in an instant.

I consider saying mercy, but I won't break. I'm stronger than my body's frailty. I disobeyed an order and deserve his punishment. If he wants to beat the hell out of my ass, I'll obediently let him. I want to please him so I can forgive myself.

The flesh on my ass is red hot when he's satisfied and stops spanking me. I'm shaking, and watching my tears drop to the floor distracts me from the pain. Either his cheek or his lips press to my aching ass cheek while his fingertips caress the other. He's pleased.

He removes the metal electrode from my vagina. His fingers circle my ass as cold fluid drips to coat them. He slips one in and then two, and fucks and stretches. I'm relaxed and my ass is eager for attention. He glides something much bigger into my butt. It isn't until his pelvis rests against my ass that I realize it's his cock.

He escalates his rhythm until he's bucking me with hard thrusts, fast enough that my breast jerk and one of the nipple leads is yanked off. The zap is intense but it only hurts for a second and the sensation shoots to my needy clit, pushing me closer and closer to orgasm.

The other clamp follows suit on the next hard thrust and an orgasm erupts so fast I can't restrain it.

"I'm sorry! I'm comi—" I yell and my mind sinks into blackness.

The delicious tickle ripples through my body, becoming increasingly glorious until I'm floating. I can feel him fucking me and I can hear him talking, but nothing is clear.

The brightness of the two spotlights slaps my retinas, and my mind rouses back to reality. He's still fucking me, and my clit is throbbing.

"—could cum," he scolds through panting breaths. "I didn't permit it and you didn't ask."

My ponytail is grabbed and used to pull my head back. His other hand covers my mouth and pinches my nose to prevent me from breathing to instill fear. He lifts his palm and I quickly take in a breath because I know this privilege is earned. He does this several more times, holding longer each time. My lungs burn.

His hand leaves my face, much to my relief, and he steps away. He pulls off the condom as he struts toward Sam. I'm left panting wildly, but thrilled he forgave me. If he hadn't, he wouldn't have fucked me.

He kisses her tenderly as his hand reaches around her head and holds her face to his. Three of his fingers slip between her thighs and she spreads her legs just enough to give him easier access. I have no doubt he's waving his fingers as he fucks her.

She gasps for air around his lips as they press hard to hers. Her body jerks and her muscles tighten. She stills and cum pours over his hand and down her legs to the floor. His kisses soften, as if he treasures her, and she is no longer his thing there for his pleasure.

Is he developing feelings for Sam? Is that why the kiss is so gentle, almost romantic?

He releases me from my confinement and lays me on the cold floor, spread out like a starfish, and then clips my wrists, ankles, and collar to braces in the floor using ropes and C-clamps. I open my mouth so he can place a bulb there and wrap the strap around my head to hold it in place. A dildo protrudes. I can only breathe through my nose and I look ridiculous, like a confused unicorn.

He lifts my head and slips a small pillow beneath as he whispers, "Since you can't say the safeword, wave your hands and I'll release you."

I nod and he leaves me to free Sam's hands from the gloves. He carries her to me and sets her down on her patent leather shoes. He stands in front of her and gently brushes his hands down her ponytail as his hooded face hovers above hers.

It's a tender moment and my tummy twinges from jealousy. I want him to be gentle with me today. He's mine, not hers, and he should touch *me* like that, not her. She hasn't earned his affection yet. I've worked hard to earn it.

Wait a minute! What the fuck am I saying? I love Sam, and I care deeply for JoeSmith. Yes, I want him, but I want her, too, and if they want each other, that's great. Right?

He whispers to her, "Squat over her face and take your pleasure."

Sam has her whole bottom lip pinched between her teeth, and she's looking into my eyes. She's happy. That makes me happy.

She kneels beside my head and inserts the dildo into her vagina. She smiles, but it's weak and she looks tired. As she slides nearly to my nose, I can smell her sweet, well-used pussy.

He stands in front of her face and says, "Open your mouth. I'm going to fuck your throat. If you stop fucking her, I choke you. Got it?"

She nods, opens her mouth and takes most of his girthy cock with little effort. He strokes her head appreciatively as I watch from below. He tilts his head like he's looking past her and down at me. He holds her head against his groin and she gags. He releases her head, and she swallows the saliva pooled in her mouth.

"I'll continue to choke you with my cock until you ride her face like I told you to do." He pushes her face into him until her nose meets his tight abs. "You'd better start fucking that cock."

She doesn't hesitate to fuck the dildo. He releases her head and she gasps and burps. I fear she may vomit on me if she stops again.

Sam collects herself and opens her mouth. She takes as much of him as she comfortably can and doesn't forget to multitask. His breaths quicken as his orgasm nears.

After a dozen more deep throat fucks, he pulls out of her mouth and lifts her to her feet. He unfastens me and helps me up before he removes the strapped dildo from my mouth. It's humiliating and I don't like it. I mean, watching Sam fuck it from such close proximity was interesting, but having it jutting from my face like that is embarrassing.

He attaches a leash to my collar, then leads me over to the table, where he hands me a condom and tells me to put it on him. He doesn't flinch as I gently roll the sheath onto his rock-hard cock. I want to drop onto my knees and take him down my throat and fuck my face with his cock. I want him to cum in my mouth so I can taste his pleasure. But it's not his desire.

He takes Sam's hand, and he walks us to an armless metal chair. He sits at the edge and pulls Sam between his spread knees. With his hands on her hips, he turns her to face away from him while I stand looking at her and holding my leash.

Well, he ironically calls me Pet, so it's suitable. I curl my lips between my teeth so I won't laugh.

"Bend over and put your hands on the floor."

Sam sticks her tongue at me and crosses her eyes, then smiles as she bends forward. I clear my throat to hide the laugh that slipped free.

I can't be sure, but I think he's manipulating her asshole until he's sure he can enter with little resistance. Sam's legs are shaking, so she won't be able to hold the position much longer.

He guides her ass onto his lap until he buries his cock all the way into her. He leans around her, grips under her knees, and lifts and spreads her legs and rests them over each of his widespread thighs. It's an incredibly delicious view of her entire pussy, his cock deep in her ass, and his testicles dangling below.

With his hand outstretched, palm raised, he waves his fingers at me. I step closer and hand him the end of my leash, which has me hunched over. He weaves his fingers through the leather handle and cups her breast with that hand. He leans back in the chair and pulls her back against his chest. His other hand glides over her tummy and down between her thighs. A single digit twiddles her swollen clitoris. Her head relaxes against his shoulder, and he kisses her neck through his mask.

He pulls on the leash until I'm on my hands and knees with my mouth pressed to Sam's pussy.

"Make her cum," he whispers, and it's the sweetest words I've heard all day.

This is so fucking hot!

My pussy's dripping wet, and my clitoris twitches with excitement. I can only imagine how she must feel. This entire session is about her pleasure and my grovelling, and I'm thrilled about it.

While his hips slowly lift and lower, my tongue circles her clit while I suck it firmly. I flatten my tongue and run it the entire length of her pussy from asshole to clit. Over and over, I lick and slurp, pausing only to flick wildly at her stiff button. Each time I pause, she tenses. She doesn't want me to stop, but I don't want her to cum yet. I want her to enjoy as much pleasure as possible before it ends.

JoeSmith rocks his hips. He grips under her thighs, and she grabs onto his muscular forearms. He lifts her up and down the full length of his engorged shaft. He pants and groans like a man filled with raging desire.

It's more difficult to aim my tongue where I want it to be until he finds his steady rhythm. I suck her clit and flick my tongue frantically. She's crying out as if on the verge of coming but doesn't. JoeSmith isn't punishing her for her moans. I wonder why not?

"Suck my balls," he says, and I comply. "You're my favourite pet."

He moans when I engulf each one gently.

"Suck her clit and don't stop. Make her cum," he groans, and it sounds like his teeth are clenched. "Slut, cum on her face while I fuck your filthy ass."

He speaks louder than a whisper, but it still isn't his full voice.

She cries out and bucks wildly against us as our master tries to hang onto her. The moment she collapses back on him, he drops my leash, and I sit back on my heels with my palms resting on my thighs.

As he lifts Sam, he stands and then sits her on the chair. As he walks past me, he pats my head, and I smile.

"Well done, Pet," he whispers and continues toward the table.

He removes the condom, puts on another, and picks up a hood, quickly slipping it over Sam's head and putting her in darkness. He orders her to put her hands under her thighs and not move. She complies and leans against the back of the chair.

Master takes my hand and leads me to a mattress on the floor covered in a leather-like sheet. He unties my corset, and it drops it to the floor. I take a deep breath now that I can. He instructs me to lie face down with a pillow under my hips. I do as he asks and rest my arms up by my head and rest my cheek on the sheet.

The voyeurs I had forgotten were watching us in the cover of shadow leave with little noise other than the occasional scuffle from a shoe.

He sets his mask on the bed. I can't turn my head enough to see his face, but if I flip over, the mystery will be solved, and I'll finally have my answer to what he looks like. But at this very moment, I don't want to know. I crave his pleasure. I did everything he asked of me tonight, and now he'll reward me.

He straddles my thighs and slips his steely, hard cock easily into my eager pussy. A soft moan escapes me, and I don't regret it. I've patiently waited for his gentle touch all night, and I'll savour every second of it.

His forearms rest along mine, and his fingers weave into mine. His super-heated chest rests against my back while his arms support most of his weight. His bare cheek presses against my neck. I can see the tip of his nose when I strain my eyes, but it's blurry.

He's tender with me, almost loving as his hips move with gentle aggression. He kisses my shoulder as he makes love to me. Is that what he's doing? I feel a connection and it's more than just physical. Tears drip from my eyes and onto the sheet. He lies still and pulls his hand from mine to wipe a falling tear off my nose.

"Why do you cry?" he whispers.

With my congested nose, I sound like I have a cold. "Because I'm enjoying this too much."

His forehead rests on my shoulder, and he shakes his head once but says nothing. Instead, he resumes fucking me. I swallow down my tears and feel like an idiot for letting myself think for even a moment that he cares for me deeply. I'm his Pet. If he cared at all, he would have said something.

"You've pleased me today, as you always do. Never forget that you'll always be my favourite pet. You make me very happy, even when you disobey me." He kisses my cheek. "You're beautiful, sexy, and mine. Merry Christmas, Terri."

He used my real name, a genuine gift more precious than diamonds. Great! I'm welling up in tears again!

His fingers slip beneath me and between my thighs. A finger slithers between my folds and steadily circles my clit with the pad of his index finger. His hips gyrate at a steady pace and my need to cry is gone.

His face is naked behind me. His cheek presses to mine. He must care for me at least some.

"Close your eyes and don't open them," he whispers, and I close them tightly.

He shifts slightly and his hand slips between the sheet and my cheek and he lifts my head. His lips press to mine, and I'm shocked he's willing to risk his anonymity by entrusting me not to open my eyes, even though he knows I'm desperate to know his identity.

Perhaps this is the ultimate test of my will. Just a flutter of my eyelashes and the secrecy ends. Slivered eyelids would be so easy to do and he wouldn't even know because he's kissing me. He may have his eyes closed, too.

No, I won't open my eyes and ruin the fantasy for him. For whatever reason, anonymity is his desire and perhaps his fetish. Maybe one day I'll learn his true identity, but I'll do it on his terms.

My little button swells under the delicate dance of his finger. In seconds, my orgasm builds to such monstrous proportions that I wail in his mouth. It rips through me with such force that my mind falls into blackness.

His primal grunts sing in my ear and its music vibrates my soul. With only a few more thrusts, his body tenses above me and his breath holds. His tiny whimper brushes past my ear and we both shudder as reality yanks us back from the delicious fantasies that filled our minds.

Did he feel the heartfelt connection the same as me, or did I create the fantasy in my mind, and I simply lost him in the pure lust of it all?

His weight sags against my back and presses me to the mattress.

"You didn't look?" he says that more as a question.

Was he hoping I would? Should I have taken the risk? Does he want me to look now?

He kisses my neck, takes a deep breath and whispers, "Don't open your eyes and don't move."

He stands and leaves the room while I lie breathless, alone and missing the heat of his flesh.

The room brightens and the two muscle men enter and lead Sam and me to the showers so we can clean up and be driven home.

We're so tired we barely speak in the showers, aside from simple formalities. On the drive home, we sleep. Sam spends the night at my place and passes out immediately after she strips and falls into bed.

I lie beside her, deep in thought. The way he said I was beautiful, sexy, and his plagues me. Those words, and the sincere way he said them, replay over and over in my thoughts. He claimed me as *his*.

Does he have deeper feelings for me than he should? I hope so. He addressed me by my real name and not as his pet. I loved hearing my name in his whisper.

A toothy smile grows as I hear his words in my memory one more time before I drift off.

"You've pleased me today, as you always do. Never forget that you'll always be my favourite pet. You make me very happy, even when you disobey me. You're beautiful, sexy and mine. Merry Christmas, Terri."

I'm falling in love with him, despite my efforts to separate the physical from the emotional, and I can't resist his charms.

Chapter 25

Home for The Holidays

We had a freak snowstorm last night and a light dusting of large flakes still floated down and melted on my windshield. The odd and sudden drop in temperature through the night shifted the rain to ice and snow, coating us in a few inches of slushy mess. The further east I drive, the deeper the snow becomes. The plows and salt trucks haven't hit all the streets yet, making my car swerve in the tire ruts of the cars that passed before me.

I park in front of my mother's house and still myself to calm my nerves before I get out of the car.

Having driven for an hour through snow-covered back roads and heavily salted highways, my anxiety's high and my knuckles ache from clenching the steering wheel so tightly.

If it were still coming down heavily when I woke this morning, I would've called to cancel and it wouldn't have broken my heart! It'll have melted by tomorrow night.

My stepfather's great, and I love him so much. He's been my dad for most of my life. I'd never admit it to my mother, but I like him a lot more than her. I love my mom because she's my mom, but she's quick to critique me and she's very pushy. It wears on me.

Robert married Mom when I was eight years old. I couldn't have been happier to have a father again. He's a kind man, unlike my angry-at-life mother who can't see past life's disappointments to see the positive, including her daughters' achievements. Until she gets her way, she makes sure we're all miserable.

My birth father—A.K.A. the sperm donor—packed his things and left us when I was five. He crushed my mother's spirit, and I don't think she ever fully recovered.

He claimed the love of his life was an exotic dancer at the local strip joint and that he never really loved my mother. He quickly realized the woman wasn't the love of his life, either, and he treated her like a possession he didn't want. I don't know why she stayed with him as long as she did.

I met her when I was fifteen and set out to rebel against my mother. I thought a reconnection with my father would piss her off. It did, but he turned out to be so much more horrible than Mom, and it hurt me more than her.

I wanted to go home, but he refused to drive me. He said he had to bring *the whore*—his words, not mine—to work. Since my mom's house was in the opposite direction, I had to walk twelve miles. What a loser!

I ran into him at a grocery store about five years ago. He looked twenty years older than his age, miserable and rather pathetic. He asked how I was. I wanted to tell him off, but he looked like he was barely hanging onto life, and I couldn't be so cruel as to crush the spirit of a wounded dog. I was polite but cut the conversation short.

He died six months later with no money, no girlfriend, and no family. I think loneliness and regret killed him; not a stroke, as the doctor claimed. I went to his simple burial that the city paid for. It didn't surprise me to see that I was the only person to show up. Nobody mourned him, not even me. I only went because he named me as a contact and I felt obligated.

I shake away my thoughts and get out of the car. I trudge through the snow-covered walkway and the snow topples over the rim of my mid-calf boots—*cold!*

Just before I extend my gloved hand to knock, the door bursts open and Robert extends his arms to take the gifts from me. I turn to view my path to see if I dropped anything. I'm impressed I hadn't, unless what I dropped fell into the deeper snow. In that case, they'll find it when it melts.

"Merry Christmas, Robert," I say with a toothy smile as I hand over the last bag.

As I step inside, I kick the packed snow from my boots and the melting clump that fell inside begins to melt and soaks the left side of my sock.

"Hello, young lady!" he says and kisses my cheek before arranging the presents under the beautifully decorated tree.

The house looks the same as it did when I left for college and that was years ago. As I hang my scarf and unzip my coat, I have an overwhelming urge to peel the curling edge of the fifteen-year-old wallpaper that lines the entryway. It could use some paint instead.

The old wood floors would benefit from a refinish, but Mom refuses because she thinks it *gives them character.*

Robert yells, "Lena! Honey! Terri's here."

"Hey, Dad, you need to shovel the walkway," I say as my boot slips off my foot. I shake my leg to rid my pants of snow. "The snow's higher than my boots."

"Yeah, yeah, I'll get to it." He rubs his forehead as he narrows the distance between us. His arm flails. "I keep forgetting."

My lips quirk and my hands rise at my sides. "Well, you know… age." I snicker, and he teasingly shakes his fist at me with pursed lips. I ask, "Where's the shovel? I'll do it right now. It'll only take a minute." I pause before hanging my coat in the closet.

Robert waves his finger. "You absolutely will not. Get in here and warm up."

I pick up my purse and follow him into the den. "You could tell Christy to do it. It wouldn't kill her to lift a finger once in a while."

He scowls and his lips form a hard line. He shakes his head as if fed up. "I'd have a better chance of maintaining an ice rink in hell," his eyes widen, "in the dead of summer."

We both hush our laughs.

"Nah, I can't see that ever happening. She'd complain to mother, and she'd defend her—" He groans and changes the subject. "You must be tired from the drive. How was it?"

I set my purse on the end table and tuck my hair behind my ear. "I white-knuckled it the whole way."

He shakes his head and flashes a sympathetic smile just as Mom scurries around the corner. She looks a little plumper than the last time I saw her a few months ago. She smiles as she wipes her hands on her apron.

"Homemade cranberry sauce?" I question with hopeful eyes, and she shrugs with raised eyebrows but doesn't answer.

I've begged her for the recipe, but she refuses to hand it over. She says I can have it when she's dead, but until then, I must visit to get some. That's her way of getting me home more often. I'll need a better reason than that.

"Hello, sweetheart." Mom hugs me and kisses my cheek. "Let me look at you. Oh. my, you're so skinny. Let's see if we can fatten you up a bit before you go home."

"I'm not too skinny. I look fine." One minute in and she's already dancing around my big red irritation button. "What about you? Did you lose a few pounds?"

I lied, but if I tell her she looks chubbier, I might get glass in my mashed potatoes. No, not really. But I'd get the corner-eyed leers and the cold shoulder until I left.

"Oh," she says and tsks. "Don't lie, Terri. It's rude. We all know I've gained a few pounds."

Oy Vey!

She's been on a yo-yo weight cycle since as far back as I can remember. She's always fought hard to keep her weight down, but she gets depressed and eats her feelings instead of getting help from a doctor.

I work out every day and try to eat healthy because I don't want to become like her. I've seen her struggles and want no part of it. She can be spiteful toward me because of it.

Aside from my existence, the only good thing my father ever gave me was his awesome metabolism. Being healthy is most important to me, not someone's size, and Mom's healthy enough, just heavy. She goes to the local indoor pool and swims three times a week with her friend of forty-two years.

"Would you like a glass of wine?" Without giving me the option to opt-out—not that I'd turn it down—she asks, "White or red?"

She knows I prefer white, so I just nod as she takes the Pinot Grigio from the fridge and pours me a glass. I utter a thank you and suck back nearly half the glass. That'll help me get through this.

"So, how're things going for you, Mom?"

"Oh, you know… Same ole, same ole. But enough about me. How are you?" She leans in toward me with hope in her eyes. "Have you met your special someone?"

Here we go!

I take another gulp and shrug. Can opener… can of worms… open.

"I met someone."

Mom halts, stirring a wooden spoon in the pot and leans her elbows on the island across from me to give me her full attention. The thrill in her eyes has me wishing I'd just said I hadn't.

"Don't get too excited." I finger the wineglass to wipe the drip left from my lip. "As you can see, I didn't bring anyone with me, so that tells you it's not all that serious, yet, and it may never be. It's sort of new… so, take a breath."

She's optimistic. "Well, you never know, honey. Maybe it'll bloom into an incredible romance. Just think, next year you could be engaged to him, or married!" She smirks, then returns to the pot to continue stirring with newfound hope glinting her eyes. "I might have a grandchild for Christmas next year."

Grandchild? I clutch my chest and clear my throat. My brows furrow and I shake the thought from my head.

"Don't count my chickens before they hatch, Mom. Grandchildren? Um, no!"

She glowers, then smugly lifts her shoulder and turns her attention to the pot.

"A mother can hope."

"You can keep hoping because it's not going to happen!" I hiss.

I refill my glass and join Robert, who's watching a football game in the living room. I have no idea what game or who's playing, but being here is better than being drilled about my love life. I learned a long time ago to feign interest in sports to avoid her intrusiveness.

With my wineglass spinning in my hand to swirl the golden liquid, I bite my lip to hold back a laugh. If she only knew what happens when I take my clothes off, she'd disown me. At least, very least, she'd pummel me with a million questions, and then cringe and tell me how disgusting I am and how abusive JoeSmith is when I answer.

Christy, my lazy, spoiled, dreadful half-sister, flops down in the love seat. She didn't bother to dress appropriately for Christmas dinner. Instead, she's donned an oversized sweatshirt and baggy jeans with a rip in the knee. She infuriates me, but I always try to keep the peace for the benefit of my parents.

"Hi, Christy." I smile and keep my eyes on hers so as not to look at her clothing with a scowl.

She crosses her arms over her chest and smirks without uttering a word. She's such an awful person. My parents let her walk all over them, so she respects nobody. From the moment she was born, they catered to her and made her the center of their attention.

Just being in the same room with her makes the tension in my stomach worsen. Coming home wouldn't be such a stressful event if she'd just move away and not come back. My parents would be better off, too.

Christy is in her second year of university, studying psychology. I think she's too judgmental for that career choice. It's not just me she's bitchy toward; she treats everyone poorly. I'm just her focus. She seems to hate me the most, and I don't know why.

She's never had a job that lasted more than a week; she either gets fired or quits, claiming they demand too much from her. She expects Mom and Robert to pay for everything. The worst part is they allow it, and that drives me crazy.

I was expected to have a job when I turned sixteen, so I got one and rode my bicycle to and from. I also paid for most of my schooling. I haven't been without a job for more than a few weeks at a time. She and I are complete opposites.

Christy's quick to point out my flaws and blame me for all her emotional woes. I punched her in the mouth when I was seventeen; she was eight. I knocked out her baby tooth. It felt so good to do it, too. She took all of my photos and shredded them when I was at work. She even tore up my yearbooks and then cut up my clothes. She was never punished for it, aside from losing a tooth, thanks to my fist. I don't regret it!

She does and says whatever she wants with no repercussions. They created a self-entitled monster.

Mom and Robert were furious with me for assaulting her, but I didn't care. She had it coming. In my mind, the sucker punch was not enough. She's been horrible to me since she learned to speak. I have no idea why and will never ask her.

When Mom and Robert pass away, she and I will go our separate ways, never speaking to each other again. If we can't find peace between us, I'll welcome that day; not the passing of my parents, but the parting of ways from the bitch.

We take our usual seats around the festively decorated table and Mom recites a prayer before we pass the bowls of food from one person to the next.

"So, what's he like, Terri?" Mom asks.

"Who, Mom?"

I know exactly who she's referring to but why not play with her a little? She picks up her fork and scowls.

"You know who. You said you have a man in your life." She stabs her fork into a slab of turkey and slices through it with her knife. "What's he like?"

Time to make the conversation more interesting!

"What makes you think it's a man?"

I shove a lettuce spine in my mouth and shred it with my molars while her eyes burn into me. The clock ticks loudly in the next room while Mom's face loses colour and the air in the room thickens.

Robert clears his throat but doesn't follow up with words. "Ah. Um. Ah." He's winded.

Christy shouts, "I knew it! You're a lesbian." She titters. "That explains a lot."

"What does it explain?" Robert asks and glares at her while Mom remains frozen with her knife and fork buried in the meat, eyes locked on me.

Christy says, "Like why she's never brought a man home." She hoods her eyes and twists her lips. "So, why'd you leave your bitch at home instead of bringing her here to meet your family? Are you ashamed of her? You're such a twat. I can't believe she takes your shit! You're so self-absorbed!"

Robert's face flushes a bright crimson. He points his finger at her and yells louder than he ever has. "Christy, that's enough. Shut your damn mouth!"

I'm shocked to hear Robert talk to his daughter that way. I've never heard him raise his voice to her, and I can't help but taunt her more with a wink and an air kiss. Her lip purse while her arms hug her chest. She's such a child.

If she knew she could get away with leaving the celebratory dinner table, she'd slam her bedroom door to make a statement. Our mother would never allow us to degrade the sanctity of Christmas dinner by leaving the table, and Christy knows it. So, to avoid further humiliation, she remains in her seat with her face scrunched.

"I'm kidding," I say in a soft voice, but Mom still stares at me. "Mom, he's a man. It's too early to discuss our future. Can we leave that topic for now, please?"

"I think that's best," she snaps and continues to saw at the meat. "I swear you girls have always been at each other's throats. I was hoping, at some point, the two of you'd mature and become civil toward one another, but that doesn't seem to be in the cards."

Before my sister argues that it's all my fault, Mom points her index finger at her and huffs, stopping her before she starts.

Mom's quiet through most of the dinner and I know she's overthinking what I said. I put my foot in it this time by ruining dinner with a joke I thought would be funny. I don't know what the big deal is about who I love, but to her, that means no grandchildren and she desperately wants them.

If she only knew it was partly true…

"So, Terri," Robert will change the subject. I can always count on him to come to my rescue. "How's your career going? Are you still happy there?"

I nod and swallow a lump of mashed potatoes and wish I'd used more gravy. "Yeah, I'm happy. I mean, it's a job and some days just going in seems like a heavy burden. But yeah, I'm pleased with where I'm at."

"That's wonderful, sweetheart!" He smiles and pats my hand. "Is there a chance for advancement?"

I set my fork on my plate and rest my forearms on the edge of the table. "Since you brought it up, I just got an opportunity for a promotion. Bossman," I shake my head, "Ben Manning—sorry, I'm so used to calling him Bossman. Anyway, he pulled me in on a big account that just came in. I'm excited to tackle it." And him, if the opportunity presents. "It'll be an interesting challenge. If I do well, he said I might get a pay raise."

"What's the name of the firm you're being assigned to and are they foreclosing?" Robert asks with great interest while my mom and Christy pretend to ignore us.

I sip my wine and set the glass down while I watch Mom pull a steamed carrot off her fork with her teeth and not touch the tines. A lady doesn't smear lipstick onto utensils.

I remember a woman who wore dark red lipstick that ended up smeared all over my body by the time she was done with me. A fork offers nothing in comparison. I stifle a laugh and wonder what Mom would say about that.

I reply, "Because of the confidentiality clause, I'm not allowed to discuss the case. I can say the company believes they have an employee or feeder company that's corrupt. By going through their books, we can usually find them."

I sip the wine again while Robert chews. His focus is still on me.

"Sometimes they hire us to save them money by using cheaper supply companies or letting useless employees go. We usually get a hefty bonus if we find a scumbag that's been ripping off the CEOs. They love their money, so if there's a thief in the midst and we find them—" I shrug and pick up my fork. "Well, let's just say the owners are often very grateful."

"And you enjoy it?" Robert asks, and covers his mouth to hide a wad of food stuffed in his cheek.

I smile and stab at some stuffing smothered in gravy. "It's fun. I feel like a detective following the money trail to catch a crook."

My sister pipes up. "So, why don't they do their own investigation instead of paying someone like you to do it for them? That makes little sense." She scrunches one side of her face.

"Because, sometimes the person doing the stealing is the person who does their books. If the person says they didn't find any abnormalities and the company heads trust them, they won't look further. By hiring us, we're independent and we don't know the employees so we won't overlook anyone."

"All right, *sis*. If they know they're going to get caught by your company, wouldn't the thief cover his or her tracks so you don't figure it out?" she asks with attitude. "Criminals aren't stupid, you know."

My fists clench below the table. "No, they're not, *sis*. Other than the CEO, nobody at the company knows we're snooping around. And, we're great at what we do." I sit straighter. "Finding hidden clues is our specialty. If money leaks out of the company, it's rarely hidden well enough where we can't find it. It's why we're a booming company."

With an eyebrow raised and her chin lifted, she stuffs a carrot in her mouth and flicks her wrist to lift the tines in the air. "Whatever!"

It's her turn to be in the hot-seat.

"So, what are you doing for money these days?" I ask, and sip my wine innocently.

She huffs. "I'm going to school. You know that!"

"Just say it like it is. You're lazy, and Mom and Dad are paying you to go to school."

"I hate you."

Her words are followed by an attempt to kick my shins under the table, but my legs are wrapped around the chair legs and she's kicking at air. I know her tactics.

"Are you serious?" I yell, and the screech of my chair legs on the floor echoes off the walls. "Why won't you grow up? God, you're such a bitch! Everyone thinks so, but nobody wants to say anything to you because they don't want to hurt your feelings. But, I don't give a shit, because at the rate you're going, you'll never succeed at life." I stand tall and press my hand to my chest. "I will. I am, and you're so jealous of me you can't stand it, can you?"

She jolts to her feet and aims her finger at me, rage seething out her pores. She begins her rant, but she's quickly shut down.

"Enough!" Mom yells and slams her palm on the table.

Robert yells, too. "Christy, Terri, that's enough!"

He pounds his fists on either side of his plate and bolts to his feet, nearly knocking over his wooden high-back chair. His angered eyes glare at the daughter who shares his DNA.

Calmer than I thought possible at this moment, he says, "She's right, Christy! You need a job. Terri worked while she went to college, and so can you. Immediately after the holidays, you can get a goddamn job!" His head drops. "I'm *so* tired of your lazy ways. We've spoiled you, and if this keeps up, I'll never be able to retire."

I want to run to him, hug him, and tell him I'm proud of him for finding his balls, but I pick up my napkin and sit instead.

He squares his shoulders and breathes in a calm breath before he sits. "I've had enough. If you don't get and keep a job, I'm not paying for your next semester, and if you aren't going to school and aren't working, you'll need to move out."

Mom's jaw hangs, shocked by his outburst. I half expect her to throw the turkey carcass at him. Her eyes dart around the table but don't focus on anything.

"Robert, this is not the time for that conversation." Her blink is long, and she slowly shakes her head. "This is our family Christmas dinner and we're damn well going to have a happy, loving family dinner if it kills us. I worked hard on this food, *by myself*." She glares at a shrinking Christy and then aims her next comment at me. "I'm sure you can manage to be nice to one another for one hour. That's all I ask. Now, let's eat and be merry."

She picks up her fork and stabs at her potatoes, then jams it in her mouth and chews as if angry at the vegetable.

My inner goddess is dancing a happy jig, but if I show my enthusiasm I'll be the bad daughter, again. I take pleasure in knowing I've won the battle my sister started.

How would JoeSmith react to this situation if he were listening in? He'd be upset with me. I wasn't in control of myself and because of that, my mother's upset. I'm suddenly disappointed by the way I handled the situation. I let my emotions rule over reason.

I help Mom tidy up while Robert and Christy watch the end of the game in the living room. I'd probably fall on the floor dead if she offered to help with the dishes. Her laziness is her trademark, and I highly doubt she'll ever change as long as Mom continues to make excuses for her.

Mom shatters the fragile silence I was comfortable in. "Terri, are you a lesbian?"

I wrap my arms around her and give her a long hug. "If I were a lesbian, would it be such a bad thing?"

"No, I suppose not." She hugs me tighter. "You can tell me, you know. You'll always be my daughter, no matter what."

I release her from the hug and lean on the counter. "Mom, there *is* a man in my life. I like him and I think he feels the same way, but it's complicated. We're not getting married or shacking up anytime soon."

She offers me tea and I nod.

"I have a best friend, a girl named Sam. You've met her. And despite our excellent friendship, she and I are not getting married." I chuckle.

I didn't lie to her. I just didn't tell her the whole truth.

"Are you and Sam..." she asks.

Dammit! My stomach drops out. Avoidance!

"Mom, really?"

She leans in and whispers. "Are you two… you know, exploring?"

I roll my eyes and scoff. "You know what, Mom? I've explained my relationship status repeatedly, and I'm not doing it again. Maybe one day I'll bring someone home to meet you. Until then, please stop asking about my love life." I take her hand and I plaster on a loving smile. "My intention is not to be disrespectful, and I love you, but butt out of my love life."

Mom clears her throat and slides her hand from mine. "Okay, Terri. I'll butt out. Just know that you can talk to me about anything. I'll do my best not to judge you even if I don't completely agree." She hangs the dishtowel on the oven handle, leans on the island and takes my hand. "It's hard for me to see you as an adult. To me, you'll always be my little girl. One day, if you have a daughter, you'll understand. I want what's best for you. I want to be included in your life." She smiles and pats my hand.

It's time to include her, sort of. I will ease her worry.

"I love you, Mom. But there's nothing to tell you at this point. I work, I go out with my friends, and occasionally I go on dates. When I find the right person, you'll be the first to know, I promise. Okay? For now, my career comes first, love life second."

She frowns. "Sweetheart, don't wait too long. You won't be fertile forever and I'd love to have a few grandchildren." She unties her apron and folds it even though it's headed for the laundry hamper. "God knows if your sister has children I'll be the one to raise them and I'm getting too old to chase children around."

"You aren't old," I say and then look to the ceiling and purse my lips. "But, yeah, you'd be raising those kids."

I don't know if I want children, but I don't dare tell her that.

After we exchange the gifts, I drive home and sing off-key to '80s rock songs while wearing the purple knit hat and gloves my mom made for me. I have a full tummy. Christy got put in her place, and the roads are in better condition. Life is good!

Chapter 26

JS

A Tight Schedule

I slept in until 10:00, but it was a restless night.

In one dream, my mother walked in on a bondage session. JoeSmith had me bent over and someone's fist was in my pussy while he fucked my ass. He kept fucking me. I screamed the safeword, but he didn't stop. My mother stood there screeching bloodcurdling wails and I could do nothing.

I woke up with a tear-soaked face. It wasn't the only nightmare I had last night, but it sure was the ugliest.

After making a coffee, I open my work email. We're allowed to share work-appropriate funnies as long as they're politically correct. Mr. Manning, A.K.A. Bossman, sent a message addressed to me only. Maybe it's about the fresh case.

It reads:

Hello, Terri,

I hope you enjoyed the holidays. I know it's short notice, but if you're in town around six o'clock tonight, I'd like to meet at the office to go over some time-sensitive material. I'm aware that you may already have plans, but if there's any way you can cancel or push them until after our meeting, I'd be grateful.

Your job status does not rely on your attendance.

I apologize for the short notice.

Ben Manning

I don't have any plans, aside from picking up some groceries, but I can do that on the way home from the office. I write back that I'll be there at six o'clock.

There are no emails from JoeSmith. He's likely busy celebrating the holidays with his family. Hmm, wife? Kids? What would they look like? Do they wear masks, too? I snicker to myself.

It's Friday, and I was hoping he'd have written to proposition us by asking for a Saturday meet-up. Then again, I rarely receive his email until later in the afternoon. I hoped we'd get together during the holidays, but he could be out of town or have other commitments. If he's married with a family, I'm sure he'd rather be home with them.

The idea that he might have a family and I'm his side piece pangs an ice pick in my side. Am I the other woman? How would she not know about his dominant nature? Surely he's been aggressive when they're having sex. Can he hide that side of himself well enough to keep it a secret? If it's not a secret, does she know about Sam and me?

And why am I jealous of a woman that may not even exist?

I finish my coffee, walk on my treadmill, and shower. A pair of yoga pants and an oversized t-shirt will do just fine today. After pouring myself another cup of coffee, I make my bed and then settle in front of my computer to check my personal email and eat a piece of toast with avocado spread.

I'm excited to see a note from my master.

My Pet,

I just got back into town and am itching to spank you. There must have been something you did to warrant a punishment. I want you to tell me what it is.

JoeSmith

I sit back in my chair and chew my fingernail. How does he know I did something deserving of punishment? He doesn't. He's guessing.

Hello, Sir,

Why do you assume I did something spank-worthy? Do you know me that well?

I argued with my sister even though I could have just let it go. My mother and I always get into it about my relationship status or lack thereof.

Were you well-behaved, Sir?

Curiously,
Pet

His reply comes quickly.

Beautiful Pet,

Family is forever, and sometimes we need to bite our tongues instead of allowing a situation to progress in a negative direction. Always remember that you have complete control over yourself and your reactions, and nobody can take that away from you.

Have I not taught you anything?

Your disappointed master

"Oh, my God! Is he serious?" I take a bite of toast and chew as if I'm set on punishing the avocado. "If he were there…"

I groan and quickly reply.

Sir,

Respectfully, you haven't met my family. My mother is pushy and my sister is spoiled. I cannot control what they say.

Annoyed,
Pet

I stand and pace while I chomp on the toast until it's gone. More food! I peel an orange and realize that my lips are pursed because I'm angry. Am I angry at him or myself because he's right?

Before I open his reply email, I take a calming breath and sip my coffee.

Beautiful woman,

You cannot control what they say or do, but you can control what you say and how you react to situations in order to abate the crisis. You're a strong, intellectual woman and arguing is beneath you.

When you're bound and forbidden to speak, you're still in control of the situation. At any point in time, you can stop everything or choose not to.

The same concept applies to life outside the playrooms. You can take charge of your life with that same strong-mindedness. Nobody can truly demean you unless you allow them to.

Your friend,

JoeSmith

My *"friend?"*

I never thought of him as being my friend. His lover, sure… plaything, of course… sexy woman he can't stop thinking about, hopefully! But a friend, really? Is that what I am to him; a friend?

Sir,

Thank you for your guidance. Our time together has taught me I'm strong, both physically and mentally. You have shown me I can endure great suffering to gain an incredible reward. You have pushed me until I thought I'd break, but I didn't. Instead, I overcame it and I'm stronger for it. I'll forever be grateful to you for that lesson.

Yours,
Terri

I debate on whether I should change *"Yours"* to something less ownership-like, since I'm only his friend. Friends can't be owned. Fuck it! I send it as is.

His response is almost immediate.

My precious Pet,

Join me tonight, so I can remind you of your strength. The car will arrive at seven o'clock. I hope you'll be waiting.

Your adoring master

Well, fuck me sideways! Now he adores me? What happened to friendship?

I push back from the desk, tip my head back on the headrest, and spin the chair while I stare at the cobweb over my head.

Ben's expecting me at the office at six, but JoeSmith wants me for seven. There won't be enough time unless Ben only needs me for a few minutes, but I doubt it.

This is a dilemma. On one hand, I committed to Ben, and he's offering me a chance to advance my career, so cancelling won't make a good impression. But I could use a good spanking by Master's hand and the intense sexual release… Well, I always crave it.

Dear Sir,

Regretfully, I can't come to you this evening. There's a work commitment I prefer not to cancel. A later time would be better, but if you can't manage that and need someone, perhaps Slut will be a suitable substitute.

Your regretful friend,
Pet

The inside of my cheek is sore from chewing on it. My chair spins until I'm nauseous. Nothing. No response, and it's been ten minutes.

I'll make a tea but leave the sound on so I'll hear a ping when he writes, if he writes. Is he upset because I refused him and that's why he's not writing back? I've never denied him before. No, he has to know I have a life outside of him.

The kettle's whistle eases when I lift it off the burner. I fill my mug and dunk the tea bag a few times. I toss it in the trash and hear the ping and rush to read it, careful not to spill on my hand.

My driven Pet,

Your commitment is admirable.

I did not *ask for Slut. I asked for you.*

The car will arrive at eight o'clock and I hope you'll be waiting.

I look forward to our time together tonight. I'm eager to satisfy my need to spank your ass and ravish your body.

Impatient and hopeful,
JoeSmith

I snicker and sip my tea before I reply.

Dear Impatient and Hopeful,

We shall see if I'm as eager to be spanked as you are to spank me.

Sincerely,
Workaholic Pet

I squeeze my thighs together because my clit aches for attention. As much as I'd rather vibrate myself until I pass out, I'll restrain from satisfaction until Sir deems me worthy.

This may prove to be a mistake since I'll be sitting alone in a room with the sexy as sin Bossman while I'm wound this tight. Is there such a thing as self-masochistic behaviour?

At a quarter to five, I drive to the salon to get waxed. Unfortunately, I've been waiting thirty-five minutes already because the woman ahead of me is freaking out. She screams like her arm's being ripped off. I feel bad for the beautician.

The owner's standing outside the door trying to get the woman to give up and leave, but she refuses to quit. She says she's getting married Saturday and wants to surprise her husband on their honeymoon. If it hurts her that much, it's not worth it.

I want to kick open the door, grab her by her hair, and toss her ass out. I don't have time for this snowflake bitch!

To occupy my mind, I imagine her strapped to a pole, being whipped and ass fucked, but it always ends with her on the floor, curled in the fetal position and crying like a little girl while she threatens to press charges.

Some of the other patrons must think I'm cruel because I'm laughing so hard tears spill from the corners of my eyes. What's even funnier to me is that nobody else seems to see the humour in this woman's misery. If I had a dollar for every evil glare, I'd be able to fill my gas tank.

I'm finally out of there at ten minutes to six.

Chapter 27

Alone with the Boss

I race to the office as quickly as I can and park next to the boss's car. I rush inside and look up toward the glass wall of his office. He stands when he sees me and waves for me to come to his office. I quickly make my way up the stairs, where he takes my jacket and hangs it next to his on the line of hooks beside his private bathroom door.

"I appreciate you coming in. Hopefully, you didn't cancel any plans to be here."

If he only knew.

"I had no better offers when I read the email." I smile and tuck my hair behind my ear and flatten my shirt on my tummy.

As I set my purse on the chair opposite the desk, he holds up a bottle of whiskey and offers to make me a drink, but I decline. A drink? Aren't we here to work?

He sits on the black leather sofa and leans toward the long coffee table with folders and papers scattered about. He glances up at me and offers me the empty cushion a foot away from him.

"I wanted to get started on this as soon as possible," he says and smiles, but it doesn't reach his eyes. He clears his throat. "Your holidays were good?"

"Um, yeah. Yours?" I ask and round the table.

"Yes, but I'm happier when I'm working."

Just as I suspected, he's a workaholic and not relationship material. Maybe he doesn't get along well with his family. That's something we'd have in common.

As I sit, the soft, manly scent of his woodsy cologne brushes my nostrils and awakens my naughty fantasies of him and me on this couch getting it on, tearing at each other's clothes and fucking like wild beasts. I breathe him in, trying not to be obvious about it and cross my legs to hold pressure on my needy pussy to keep her from invading my thoughts.

My mind flashes to the faint scent I picked up from my master that one day. I remember how his cologne was intoxicating. I swear they made both scents from the pheromones of a sexy god.

"What kind of cologne are you wearing?"

Ben's emerald-coloured eyes meet mine and my clit twitches, reminding me of how needy she is.

"Why do you ask? Does it bother you?"

His deep voice is smooth but riddled with concern. His eyes could steal my soul if I dared stare into them for too long.

"No, it's quite pleasant. It just reminds me of a friend of mine. He smelled a lot like yours, but with a bit more musk mixed with a slight hint of leather."

I titter when I remember he wore leather at the time, so that would cause the scent.

Hoping I'll elaborate, he asks, "Leather?"

I wave my hand. “Um… never mind, it’s not important.” I avert my eyes to the papers he has on the table and bite my lip to suppress my smile. “So, why did you ask me here?”

Does he want to have sex with me? Steamy sex that turns into a relationship, maybe.

His arm reaches across in front of me as he shifts some papers. Sculpted muscles ripple beneath his fitted dress shirt, the sleeve rolled halfway up his arm. But my breath catches when he leans forward to open another folder, and his strong back muscles flex.

I regret not masturbating earlier.

JoeSmith doesn’t permit me to have a sexual relationship with anyone outside of the castle unless I inform him previous to the following session.

Could I give up my master for a shot at my devilishly handsome boss? Would it be worth it? Probably not. We humans build people up in our minds, but they rarely live up to our expectations. But it’d be fun to take him for a test drive, so to speak.

He flips open the thick folder on the coffee table in front of us and shows me a list of investors.

“I need you to go through this list of companies affiliated with our client. If you can save him money, that’d be great.” He turns several more pages. “These are the financials. I’ve been going through this to see if everything is on the up-and-up, but something’s off.”

I lean in toward the paper. “Is someone stealing, do you think?”

“I’m not sure, but we’re going to find out.” His deep voice is thick with curiosity. “I can’t wait to delve into it further. I’ll follow the money, but if I can’t find anything, maybe you'll have better luck. For now, see if you can help them save on expenses."

"Saving companies money is what I'm good at," I say without thinking as I flip a few pages.

"That's why *you're* here and not someone else." He quietly sifts through some papers and stuffs them into the different folders.

Ben slides the folder closer to me and sits back on the sofa and bends one leg at the knee so he can face me easier. "If we work together, I think we can finish this on time. He set a ridiculous timeframe, and he's agreed to a hefty fee." He rests his arm over the backrest. "There's a bonus in it for you."

"A bonus? That's an excellent incentive but…"

How about we skip chatting about my financial bonus? Instead, you can fuck me over this sofa like I've pictured us doing from the first day I showed up for an interview with you.

"… it's the challenge that excites me. When do you need this finished?"

Ben wakes from his thoughts and finds me staring at him. His eyes widen and he clears his throat while his fingers comb through his perfectly styled, lush black hair.

"He's hoping for a, ah…" He clears his throat again and fusses with his watchband. "A two-week turnaround. I'm sure we can do it if we both play our roles."

It's my turn to lose myself in thought. Our roles? Like, will he play the role of sexy Bossman, and I'll be the secretary that can't do her job well so he has to bend me over the desk and spank me? He'll have to fuck me, too, of course.

I tuck my hair behind my ears and lean forward to open the top folder he set in front of me. There's a lot of information to go through. It'll be a time-consuming job that'll require plenty of overtime, but I'm intrigued. Ben's great at sniffing out embezzlers and thieves, so if he finds himself at a loss and I discover the inconsistency, it'll do wonders for my standing with him and likely lead to career advancement.

We bounce a few ideas off one another, but our conversation drifts to our holiday celebrations with our families. I'd like to get to know Mr. Manning better than just as my exceptionally delicious boss that I fantasize about consuming more often than what's probably healthy.

"Did you go to see your parents? Do they live around here?" I bend my leg to rest my calf on the cushion to better face him.

He shakes his head. "They don't, but I got to spend a few days with them."

His dreamy eyes bore into me and he smiles shyly, but spins his face to look over the backrest and through the glass wall overlooking the cubicles where I spend my workdays.

He rubs his chin and meets my eyes now and then. "I don't know about you but for me, going home and sleeping in my childhood bedroom brings back all the feelings of fear and ridiculous anxieties I had when I was growing up." He laughs while he watches me nod with wide, rolling eyes because I understand. "Only now, it all seems so silly and immature. My parents will always have a way of making me feel like a child again. Whether or not that's a good thing, I don't know. But, aside from all of that, it was a pleasant visit."

Wow! He just offered an in-depth look into the inner workings of Ben Manning's mind. I like it.

I agree with him completely, except that my old bedroom is filled with crap Christy's collected over the years. These items are supposed to be things she'll need when she moves out, but I don't think she ever will. Needless to say, I couldn't stay there if I wanted to.

"What about you? Did you visit family?" he asks.

"Yes, I drove there and stayed for the day. My family gets on my nerves, something fierce sometimes." I sigh and pick a tiny piece of lint off the back of the sofa. "My sister is a real piece of work who does everything she can to make my visits miserable."

"Older or younger?"

"Younger. She's always been a terror for me." I groan and feel his eyes burning into me as he listens. "I don't know why. She's just… horrible!" I wave my arms mockingly and say, "And then there's my mother who wants me married, barefoot, and pregnant." I scoff and roll my eyes.

"You don't want children?" His brows nearly meet but quickly relax when I open my lips but say nothing. "It's okay if you don't. I'm all for choices and think women should have the right to do what they want without judgement."

"I might want kids. I–I don't know. Maybe in the future sometime, but definitely not now."

His eyes drift down to my breasts, pause, and then quickly shift to an imaginary piece of lint on his pants. "I've always believed women are stronger than men. We may act tough and impenetrable, but we're actually weak and vulnerable under the right circumstances. In my opinion, women hold all the cards."

I jest, "Oh, I don't know about all that—"

"It's how I was raised." He clears his throat and shifts between his body and the subject. "So, your mom wants grandchildren and your sister is a real piece of work… Do you have a male figurehead in your family?"

"My stepdad. He's awesome. I'm closer to him than my mom. I can talk to him about pretty much anything and he doesn't judge me or make me feel like I'm a disappointment. He's happy if I'm happy." I tilt my head to the side and run my fingers through my hair before tucking it behind my ear. "It's odd that he's not my blood relative because I'm more like him than my birth parents."

"You're lucky to have him," he says with raised brows and returns his arm to the backrest after having removed the non-existent lint.

Ben's easy to open up to and I'm enjoying our time together, but when he looks at me with his seductive green eyes, my body reacts favourably, especially between my legs.

"We had little money growing up, so I worked hard and put myself through college. Robert did his best to help me when I was desperate and I'll forever be indebted to him for that. I wouldn't have made it through college had he not been there," I confess.

"He sounds like a kind soul," he says and lifts the corners of his thin lips.

"Yes, Mr. Manning, he's nothing shy of a saint."

He groans. "Oh, please. Call me Ben. I feel so old when people call me Mr. Manning, especially when those people are close to my age. My father is Mr. Manning." He shrugs one shoulder and smirks. "You can call me Ben or Bossman. I'm growing fond of that name."

"I can't believe I called you that." My cheeks flush, and I cover my mouth with my hand.

"Is that how you reference me to people?" he says with a hint of humour in his deep voice.

"Just Sam," I say and drop my hand away from my face and try to reign in my embarrassment.

If he only knew how I fantasize about calling him Bossman when he fucks me hard, he wouldn't think it was so funny.

"Ben, now that I've told you about my crazy family, tell me about yours."

"My mother's fun, exciting, and always doing silly things to make people laugh. When I was a kid, I thought she was the best bed sheet fort builder in the world."

His eyes drift to the right as the memory has him flashing a toothy smile.

As he talks, he stares out over the cubicles, but he envisions his mother, not desks. I memorize the shape of his hooded green eyes and then drop my gaze to his lips. How would they feel against mine? How soft are they? Are his kisses tender or does he command ownership of his partner's lips?

"She'd set up a play area under the dining room table and then make us lunch. We'd eat while we rested on a pile of pillows and blankets. Sometimes she'd put a television in there so we could watch cartoons in our fort. I usually fell asleep beside her. Most often, she'd still be there when I woke, no matter how long I slept."

I can't help but envy his childhood. "Your mom sounds like fun. I think I'd like her."

"Mom's always been there for us." He looks past my head for a moment and smiles at a memory before he looks at me, still holding the smile. "I'm sure she'd like you, too."

I tilt my head and shrug. "My mom was not the fort-building type. In fact, she'd probably have gotten upset because I messed up the room. I'll admit I'm a bit jealous."

"Don't be!" he says and his smile fades. "She made up for my father's stinginess. He was unbearably strict. Children had to be polite, quiet, and respectful toward their elders."

He shifts and puts both feet on the floor and pulls at the buttons on his dress shirt to straighten it.

"He's nineteen years older than my mother but he always seemed old, even when I was a child."

A muscle in his jaw clenches, proving his memory of his father isn't favourable. Instinct is to rub his back to comfort him, and I *really* want to so I can feel the muscles under his strained shirt, but I squeeze my hands tighter together to prevent it.

"He was always on my case to get excellent grades and to not be immature. I suppose the best thing he taught me was how to keep my emotions out of anything pertaining to my life decisions, especially where business is concerned."

Ben gets up and offers me a coffee instead of whiskey, and I accept.

I stand, cross my arms over my chest, and stroll to the glass wall overlooking the first floor. He stands here often, usually holding a coffee mug in one hand with the other tucked in his front pants pocket. How many times have I stared up here and peeled off his clothes with my eyes?

I clear my throat and snicker as I turn to look at him. "You let me complain about my mother when your father was… well, worse."

While he's distracted, I allow my eyes to drink him in. His ass is tight and when he moves, deep pockets form on each cheek. He's fit and looks strong. Strong enough to make me be his slut.

Oh my God, Terri! Stop!

I turn and look down at the vacant room below; the bullpen, as we call it.

He sets two mugs side by side and says, "Your mother was there daily. My father wasn't home much, and when he was, he spent most of his time arguing with my mother or the staff. The rest of his time was spent hidden in his office, and he was not to be disturbed. I didn't see him much, which was fine with me." He pours the coffee and asks, "Just milk; no sugar, right?"

I spin and look at him. "You know what I take in my coffee?"

"Yes, I pay attention. I have an uncanny ability to remember little details about people. It comes in handy sometimes. Like right now, making your coffee." He glances at me as I sit on the sofa. "I remember you saying that I have great thighs."

"Oh, crap!" Where did I toss that piece of lint so I can hide under it? "I'm so sorry. I was out of line."

He shakes a sugar packet. "No, you weren't. I paid you a compliment, too, or have you forgotten?" He pours the sugar into one mug and stirs with a shiny spoon.

My shoulders sag as my hands glide down my calves. "You said I was beautiful."

"Mhm, and I meant it."

Our eyes meet from across his office and he continues stirring the coffee longer than necessary. Am I imagining the heat he's radiating from that far away, or am I acting like a lovesick schoolgirl?

A hot breath fills my lungs, and I avert my eyes to the paperwork. As I move the folders out of the way so he can set the coffees down, the nervous tightening in my tummy has me swallowing a lot.

If JoeSmith has taught me anything, it's how to remain calm, even in the most gruelling situations. If I allow my desires to rule my reactions, I'm no longer in control of the situation. I clear my throat and lift my chin with confidence.

I am strong. I am smart. I am in control!

"But, as I recall, I asked you to give me a different compliment because you said the same thing earlier in the night, so it didn't count. You often tell people they're beautiful or handsome, so your compliment doesn't hold much water because it's not personal."

Come on, tell me you want to ravish me with your tongue. Tell me I make your cock hard or you want to taste me. Something… say something that'll make my pussy wet.

Ben crosses the room in silence and hands me a coffee. He sits beside me and turns to face me. I shift to face him and pull one calf onto the cushion. I patiently wait as we sip our coffees and set them on the table.

He clears his throat and quickly licks his lips. "All right. Here goes nothing."

He takes a breath and clenches his jaw as he swallows. His eyebrows meet in the middle, but only for a second.

In a deep, smooth tone, he slowly says, "When I get this close to you," his hand references that our faces are only a few feet apart, "all I want to do is kiss you, and it takes every ounce of strength I have to hold back that urge."

What?

My heart pounds loudly in my ears and my mouth is suddenly so dry that my swallow is almost painful. As if not in control of my body, I lean forward and plant my lips on his. He doesn't push me away when my arms wrap around his neck and my fingers mesh into his thick hair.

He grips my waist, pulls me against him, and leans back until we're belly to belly and I'm on top and in control. We kiss like two sex-starved adolescents.

Is this really happening or am I dreaming?

Oh, my God, he kisses so well! His lips are soft, but his kisses have purpose.

His right palm glides over my bicep while the other presses to my lower back to hold me against him. His cock is hard enough that I can feel it with my thigh.

Our tongues dance as my mind swoons. His body's hot and his abs are firmer than I'd imagined.

His fingers slip beneath the hem of my shirt and glide up my ribs. It tickles but there's nothing funny about this situation. With a quick tug of my bra, he frees my left breast, cups it gently, and brushes his thumb over my nipple, sending heat directly to my clit.

His other hand grips my ass cheek as his hips lift his impressive erection against my thigh.

Ben bends his leg up between my thighs. The only thing preventing my freshly waxed, bare pussy from rubbing on his dress pants is my floppy skirt. His hip slowly lifts and lowers. My clit twitches against his thigh and I moan in his mouth. My quickening breaths are met with his.

This is happening!

His restrained erection presses firmly against my thigh. I reach down to feel its size, but by the time my hand reaches his belt, reality crashes to the forefront of my mind.

I lift my lips from his and he lifts his head to kiss my neck and quickly lifts his thigh to move me higher, hoping to taste my nipple. I slam my hand on his chest, push him down, and peer into his emerald eyes that look so fucking sexy I debate whether to ignore my mind's urging for me to stop.

What have I done? Master will be so angry. I don't want to stop, but if I continue, JoeSmith may cast me aside. I can't let this go any further, but fuck, I want to!

I whisper, "I can't do this. I'm dating someone, sort of… well, not a dictionary's description of dating, but… Trust me, I *really* don't want to stop, but I…" My body screams at me to shut the fuck up, but I can't listen. He drops his leg and I slide to my knees between his knees. "I have to stop."

His cock is putting the seam of his pants to the test and I'm impressed by its size, but he quickly sits up, and I look away. I stand and tug my bra back in position.

I've wanted to do this with Bossman from the moment I met him, so what am I doing? Why am I stopping?

Ben sits properly with his feet firmly on the floor and lifts his hips as he pulls at his dress pants to rearrange his bent penis. He fixes the collar on his dress shirt while he looks at me with dreamy, hooded eyes and his delicious lips that are puffy and still glistening with our saliva…

I hop on him with my legs straddled over his thighs. My skirt lifts, and my naked pussy presses against his swollen crotch. My palms sprawl on the sides of his head and I mash my lips to his.

He grabs my bare ass and moans as he pulls me down onto him. His lips leave my mouth and find their way to my neck. Fervent kisses heat my skin and the tiny hairs all over my body rise at attention as if I were being electrocuted.

My head tips back as his lips trail to my clavicle. His hand shoots under my shirt and caresses my breast over my bra, but he quickly lifts my shirt so he can kiss the tender, bare skin between my breasts. He grips my ass cheek firmly and pulls and pushes, urging me to rock my hips.

Oh, my God! He's a sexually wild man! I thought he wouldn't be good at the art of seduction because he always seems so strait-laced and proper, and yet his physique screams man built for sex, and here he is, rocking my world and we aren't even naked.

He lifts my bra until my breast drops from underneath. He gently sucks my nipple into his mouth and rolls it between his lips. As if he's tapped on a direct line to my pussy, it tightens and I shudder.

I want him inside of me.

The cloud lifts and reality slaps me once again.

"No, no, no, no, no!"

I climb off and rush away from him as I fix my clothes for the second time. Confusion warps his sexy face and I don't like the change. *Fuck!*

I pace and confess. "I can't do this. Shit! I want to…" My arms flop at my sides.

He leans his elbows on his spread knees and looks up at me as if wondering if I've lost my mind. His fingers weave together and he looks calm aside from his white knuckles.

"Believe me, I want to. I'd give almost anything to continue, but please, please help me stop. You're my boss, and I'm with someone…" I stop pacing while my hands alternate up and down, as if weighing something on a scale. "Sort of with someone. Whether it flourishes into something great is debatable."

His voice is shakier than it had been. "You don't have to do that; tell me you have someone important in your life as an excuse to stop. You're right, I'm your boss and this shouldn't happen."

He stands and smooths his hair as he jiggles the waistband of his pants to shift his impressive erection. I jerk my head away to force my gaze off his glorious crotch.

"Yes, you're my boss, but there *is* someone else; two people, if I'm being completely honest." I can't stop pacing while my fists clench. "One of them would be very disappointed in me but the other would be thrilled for us. Not that there is an *us*. I mean…" My hand waves dismissively. "You know what I mean."

Why did I tell him that I have two lovers? He's going to think I'm a tramp. I halt in place with my hands on my hips and look him up and down. A pang of lust sweeps me, again, but I slap my forehead and pace to work off the endorphins.

He's so calm and in control, which irritates me since I'm a complete mess.

His voice is deep as his words flow slowly. "You don't have to tell anyone about this. We can keep it between us or pretend it never happened. I won't tell if you don't. It's probably wise not to since you're hoping to advance your career on your work ethic and not because you almost banged the boss on his sofa."

He snickers but I can't see the humour at the moment.

"I'm not like that. I'm way too honest and a shitty liar, just ask Sam. I'll tell him what almost happened here and accept my pun—" I meet his eyes and swallow. "I'll see what happens after that."

He picks up the mugs, stands, and carries them to the tray beside the coffeemaker. "Okay. I'll await a punch in the face by a brooding stranger."

I can't tell if that was a joke or if he's worried about getting jumped.

"I'm not going to tell him who you are. He doesn't need to know and I doubt he'll ask."

He offers me another coffee, but I shake my head. I smile and twirl a stray lock of hair.

"No punches in the face for you. Besides, he's always in control and would never let jealousy get the best of him."

The way he's looking at me—eyes hooded, cheeks flushed, lips puffy and slightly parted—has me reconsidering. I want to take off my clothes and envelop this man in all of my orifices. My glance meets the clock, and I gasp. It's seven-thirty! I'd forgotten all about my meeting with JoeSmith.

"Oh, shit! I absolutely must go! Speaking about that important person in my life, I'm supposed to be somewhere at eight and…" I groan and rush to get my purse. "If I hurry, I just might make it there on time."

I fling the purse strap over my shoulder and recheck my tit is in my bra, and then turn to look at him standing with his mug held in both hands. He looks so damn sexy, maybe more than ever now that I have a good sense of how skilled a lover he might be.

"In case I forgot to mention it… thank you for the work opportunity, and I won't let you down. I shouldn't have attacked you," my head bobs left to right, "twice. I'm not saying that wasn't hot as fuck, because goddamn! Sorry, shit! I have to go right now."

"I enjoyed it, too, very much." He licks his lips. "If your situation changes, let me know." Ben looks at his watch. "It is getting late. I should probably go, too. I'll follow you out."

We race to the door and say our quick goodbyes as we're both sliding into our cars. My slick pussy makes it difficult to concentrate on the road.

At this very moment, I could be bent over the desk and getting plowed hard from behind by Ben Manning, but I chickened out.

I didn't chicken out. I made a commitment to JoeSmith and my conscience won't allow me to lie about breaking it. He's been an important part of my life for over a year now, and I want to keep it that way. He's very important to me. I think I'm in love with him or, at least, the idea of him.

I'm afraid to tell him. What if I lose him?

Chapter 28

Keep Me or Don't

I park in my driveway and run down the street toward Jim, who's standing beside the limo and looking around with concern on his gentle face. He looks up from his watch and sees me running full out toward him. He's happy to see me and waves for me to stop running, so I happily slow my pace. What would happen if I wasn't in the car when he returned to the house?

He opens the back door and I slide in, breathless, not so much from the run but the anxiousness that urged me forward.

Jim waits for me to put on my hood, which I almost forgot to do. He drives off but stops after about ten minutes. We've never stopped on the way.

"Is everything okay?" I ask.

"Yes, ma'am. What do you take in your coffee?" he asks from the driver's seat.

"Just milk, thank you," I replied.

I feel the car shift as he exits and debate whether I should lift my hood to see where we are so I'll have a better idea of which direction the castle is. But I think I'm in enough trouble already.

Several minutes pass before my door opens, startling me.

His gentle voice calls to me. "Put your hand out. I have a coffee for you. This java is from my favourite coffee shop. If you prefer this coffee over the one you normally get, we'll make a detour each time I pick you up." I reach for the cup and he holds my wrist to steady it before slipping it into my hand. "Be careful now, it's piping hot."

I happily accept. "Thank you so much. What do I owe you?" I unzip my purse and blindly dig for my wallet.

"This one's on me. I'm a bear if I don't have a caffeine fix when I need it. You usually have coffee during the trip." He shuts the door and returns to the driver's seat. "Enjoy the drive, ma'am."

I wish he would call me Terri more often than he calls me ma'am, but he's all about being polite and gentlemanly.

*****

My leader has platinum blonde hair and most of it tucked into a big hat covered in red feathers, with only a few stray tresses poking free. Her fluffy coat matches the hat and hangs to her hips. Her sexy thigh-high, red leather boots have a three-inch spiked heel.

She looks posh and elegant with just a light dusting of make-up, except for her pronounced cherry red lips.

Nearly everyone who works for Miss Catherine is utterly gorgeous. I'm hideous in comparison. But for some reason, JoeSmith wants *me*, so I must have something going for me.

I sign the papers before I'm led to the locker room. An escort is unnecessary at this point. I've been here enough times to find it on my own, but rules are rules.

The way my body felt with Bossman's mouth on my nipple and his powerful hand guiding my ass while I ground my pussy against his crotch…

I have to stop thinking about him, but the entire scene was so fucking hot! My pussy lips slip against each other with each step, reminding me of how exciting it was.

My leader stops and turns to look at me with scrutinizing eyes. "Are you all right?"

"Yes, I'm fine. Why?"

"You gasped."

She waits, perhaps for me to explain, but I clutch my purse strap and shake my head with a shrug.

"I'm sure I'll be doing a lot more of that soon enough." I lift my brows and bite my lip.

She tilts her head, grins, and winks before turning and continues leading me.

I shower and do the preparation ritual while my inner battle between wishing I'd stayed with Ben and being thankful I didn't wear on.

My hair's left to hang long with fat flowing curls and my make-up is applied sparingly. They dress me in a light and airy white lace summer dress. White cotton panties, no bra, and a pair of fluffy slippers finish my look. The mirror reveals a woman ready to go grocery shopping and yet suitable for a fancy outdoor party, aside from the slippers.

I'm dumbfounded by the beauty of the dark-skinned woman who comes to collect me. She's absolutely stunning. Her long calves blend into thick thighs and wide hips that fade below her tiny waist and chest to match.

She wears a hip-length, skin-tight, hot pink dress that reveals the bottom of her perfectly round butt cheeks and small breasts. Her hair is neatly shaved and her make-up gives her cheeks a shiny, golden appearance. With her hand on her waist and a leg jutted to the side, she could easily pose for a magazine photoshoot. She very well could be a model for all I know.

This playroom is one I'm familiar with. The dimly lit black-walled room has a king-size bed fitted with a silky white bedsheet. The last time I was here, it donned a red sheet. The room's otherwise empty aside from a nightstand on either side at the head of the bed.

I'm told to wait inside beside the door and to remove my slippers. I wait with my bare feet chilling on the hardwood floor for what seems like ten minutes before a hidden door on the other side of the room pushes open and JoeSmith strolls in at his leisure.

My heart thumps hard in my chest. I should tell him about Ben before he touches me. But do I have to? We didn't fuck or have oral sex. We kissed, that's all.

His bare feet make no sound as he approaches. He's wearing a white t-shirt and a pair of blue jeans ripped at both knees. A plain white mask covers his face, bearing tiny holes for his eyes. It covers his head and stops at his chin. If he tilts his head back, I'll be able to see his bottom lip. But he's careful not to do that unless he's too far away for me to see any of his defining features.

As he approaches, I break a hard rule by speaking out. "I have a confes—" My voice cuts out, so I clear my throat and swallow. "A confession."

He stops twenty feet from me and stands with his legs shoulder-width apart, arms crossed over his chest. When I look at his mask, I feel small and insignificant.

"A confession," he whispers, lets out a long breath and tilts his head. "Tell me, Pet. What do you want to confess?"

How do I word this? I had a few passionate moments with my boss and desperately wanted to fuck him, and I sort of wish I was there in his arms right now. But I chose to be here, with you, confessing, even though I know there'll be consequences.

"I kissed someone tonight; a man. I came to my senses and stopped it, but I resumed and didn't stop until he had my breast in his mouth."

I think he's stopped breathing. He's as still as a statue. I clear my arid throat and wonder if I swallowed a cotton ball.

My voice is no stronger than a whisper. "I think it's important that you know."

He's calm, too calm. Will he walk away and tell me to go home? At least he's breathing again.

"Did you enjoy your time with him?" he asks.

My sights lock onto his eye holes and I don't look away, which is breaking another of his rules. My arms feel awkward as I move them from my sides, around to my back, and back to the front before I weave my fingers together to hold at my waist to hold them still.

"Yes, very much so," I confess, and expect him to rush me, but he doesn't.

Without emotion in his tone, he asks, "Did you want him to stop?"

Is he toying with me? Why isn't he angry? He should be spanking me or something. Shouldn't he?

"Absolutely not."

He looks down to adjust the black latex glove on his left hand. "Why didn't you have sex with him?"

I'm confused. Does he wish I had sex with the man? If only I could see his face, I'd know if he were angry or aroused by the idea of me entangled in a sweaty, hot embrace in another man's arms.

I whisper, "Because I belong to you."

I shake when he rushes up to me and stops when his face inches from mine. His fingers gently glide from my temple, down to my jaw. He lifts my chin and his mask and kisses me with incredible tenderness.

Does he forgive me or is this our last kiss goodbye? Tears leak from the outer corners of my eyes.

Please don't leave me.

Our lips separate but remain so close his breath caresses my chin. His mask lowers to shroud his mouth.

"Do you want a relationship with this man, or did you just want to fuck him?"

"What does it matter? I'm yours." My forehead creases and I can see through his eyeholes, but his eyes are closed and it's so dark I can't determine their shape. "Sir, I belong to you. Whether I want a relationship with the man is irrelevant. And no, he could never just be a quick fuck, which is another reason I had to walk away."

His palm brushes down my neck and rests at my clavicle. "If he were your boyfriend, would you still come to me?"

I hesitate and turn my face away. His fingers lift my chin and he leans forward, lifts his mask enough to brush his smooth lips along mine. But it's not a kiss, it's more intimate.

He whispers, "Speak freely, my pet."

My head sags forward, coming to rest on his warm neck. "How do I answer that? I don't want to be shared by both of you because living between two men would be too hard, and he'd never understand my desire for punishment. He wouldn't."

I lift my eyes and look at the holes and I see a hint of colour, but it's gone too soon to determine the colour. His fingers weave together behind my neck and his wrists rest on my shoulders. He nods ever so slightly.

"I could lie and say I don't want him, but I do, and I want you, too. Not just here at the castle, but in my regular life, as well. We could be a normal couple who happen to do bizarre things. But I know you don't want that." I place my hands on his thick forearms. My forehead crinkles and I stutter. "But I… I'm falling in love with you and… and I don't even know who you are."

He speaks matter-of-fact and shows no emotion, making it impossible for me to read him.

"You signed a contract stating that if you become emotionally involved with your master, he has the right to terminate the relationship." He wipes the tears that steadily spill down my cheeks. "Do you remember signing that?"

He's going to leave me.

"I remember, and it's been an ongoing inner battle between my head and my heart," I beg between tearful gasps. "Please, don't cast me away. I'm so sorry. I'll try to shut off my emotional connection to you. I can do it. I can. Just… please…"

He steps away and paces near the foot of the bed I wish we were in instead of having this conversation. He stops and sags his weight on one leg and rests his hands on his hips.

"I said you're my favourite, and I mean that. I treasure you, but you know nothing about me outside of this castle. And for that reason alone, you can't possibly be in love with me." He stands several feet from me and tips his head. "Why do you think you love me?"

At the moment and for the first time in a long time, I'm embarrassed and uncomfortable in his presence, but my tears have stopped spilling. Have I built a wall around my heart as I said I would do? I wipe my face dry and hold a long blink.

"You're a strong person who gets what he wants but you're also kind-hearted. You've taught me to control myself even in tough situations and because of that, I'm stronger than I've ever been or ever thought I could be." I take a step toward him and cross my arms over my chest. "If you don't care deeply for me because this is just heartless bondage and sex, why are you so sensitive and gentle with me, sometimes?"

"I reward you for good behaviour." He's so clinical. "I'll make a mental note not to do that anymore. I apologize if I've led you to believe this is more than what it's meant to be."

Running out of here and curling up in the showers to cry my soul to sleep sounds great right about now. With one arm still hugging my chest, the other slides down my forehead, coming to rest over my mouth. I turn and take a few steps toward the door.

He doesn't love me. I'm his sex toy; a mere plaything for his fetish games. I mean nothing to him. How have I been so foolish to have believed it could ever be anything more?

I stop and turn to face him, but I don't meet his eyes. His chest rises and falls quickly and his arms hang straight at his sides, fists clenched.

A calm-numbness washes over me as I expect my dismissal. Where this goes from here is out of my control now. It's in his hands.

"JoeSmith, should I go? The rules state that this contractual arrangement has to end. If you'd be so kind as to permit me to take my leave, we can get on with our lives."

Even though I'm dying inside, my tears don't fall. This is a time to be strong and think, not feel my way through it because that's what he taught me to do.

As if assessing me, he slowly and silently steps closer. My eyes don't lift to meet his, but my jaw remains clenched. I hold strong in the torturous silence, hoping he'll say or do something to end this moment.

"No. Go to the bed and take off your dress," he demands.

In my confusion, my questioning eyes shoot to his eye holes, then skirt about the room. I'm frozen in place, unsure of what to do. Did I hear him right?

My hesitation has him tilting his head and deepening his voice.

"I gave you a command."

Chapter 29

JS

Our First Real Conversation

I'm numb as my cold feet slowly carry me to the side of the bed. I pull the dress over my head and face the bed with my back to him, wearing only white panties. I wait for his next instruction.

He's my master; nothing more, nothing less. He's made that clear, and I'd be wise to keep that in mind. He'll play with my body and we'll satisfy each other's fucked up needs, but before we do, we'll leave our hearts at the door. I can do that. If I want him as my master, I'll have to.

I don't hear him walk up, but he stands so close behind me that I feel the heat radiating from his body. He takes the dress from me and drops it at our feet. He reaches up to my left ear and removes the diamond earring I must have forgotten to take off. I was distracted thinking about Ben.

JoeSmith sets the earring on the nightstand and then sits on the bed. He directs me to lie across his thighs. I follow his instruction and await the punishing spanking he's about to give me. If my assumption is right, it'll be the most intense one yet.

His right hand spans my upper back while the other caresses my ass over my cotton panties.

I expect the pain and hope it'll distract me from my thoughts. Emotional pain is so much worse than physical pain.

His hand comes down hard on my right ass cheek. I don't cry out or even flinch. He cracks me again in the same spot. It stings more the second time, but again, I don't react. More slaps, one after another, and I remain quiet.

If I give into the pain, it'll compile with the unbearable emotional ache I'm fighting to suppress, and I'll break. So, I'll hold fast and accept his punishment with grace and respect; he is my master. I've wronged him, and for that, I shall pay with my pain.

If he refuses to be in my heart, I'll take him any way I can, even if it blackens my heart. I need him in my life.

My left ass cheek is untouched while the right one burns hot. I bite my lips between my teeth until I'm sure they'll bleed. I can't take much more. My skin will surely split if he continues. Master knows what I can handle.

He tenderly caresses my un-spanked cheek while he slows his ragged breaths. He grabs my waist and lifts me to my feet. His head tilts when he sees my face is unmarred by tears.

He speaks slowly. "I didn't spank you because of what you did with the man. Your punishment was earned for fighting with your family." He stands and caresses my arms while I look down at the mound in his jeans. "Family is important, and that bond should be respected."

He picks strands of hair from my face and tucks them behind my ears. Through his mask, he pecks a kiss on my forehead and holds my jaw in one hand.

"I always want to know what you're thinking and feeling. It's important to maintain open communication. Keeping secrets only gets people hurt physically or emotionally. Now, slip off your panties and lie on the bed, face up."

I do as he says. He opens the drawer on the nightstand and picks up something black. I lie flat and stare up at the black ceiling and wonder why the colour makes the ceiling look infinitely distant. He walks silently to the door he entered from.

Is he leaving?

The light evaporates into darkness and I'm blind until a soft beam of light brightens the floor as it leads JoeSmith safely to me.

He shuts it off, and I hear it come to rest on the nightstand. I hear his clothing hit the floor, and then the rattle of what I assume to be a condom wrapper. The bed shifts under his weight.

Master's knees rest between my legs to open them wide enough for him to sink his very warm, naked body between them. The urge to wrap my arms and legs around him is powerful. I fist the sheet instead.

His whisper breaks the silence. "Take off my mask."

We'll be face to face, with nothing preventing our faces from touching or our cheeks from resting together. I can stare into his unshrouded eyes. Even if I can't see his face, I know it's right.

My chest flutters. Why is he doing this? He doesn't want emotional involvement, yet this—what he's doing—will have my heart front and center. Should I stop this? Should I say it…

Zebra?

I reach into the darkness and follow his biceps up toward his neck and further. My fingers shake as they grip the stiff material separating our faces and slowly lift it away. I lay it on the bed an arm's length away, but can't seem to let it go.

It's so dark I don't see his lips come toward me. They press into mine and my breath catches. I invite his tongue into my mouth. It feels right, freer than ever before. We're face to face with no barrier, and the heat of his face ignites my fire within.

But why is he making love to me? Is this his way of toughening me up? Why is he so gentle with his kisses? Is this his way to teach me how to enjoy someone's body at the moment?

Why is he trying to hurt me?

Spank me again. Don't do this… not this. He can't make love to me and walk away, leaving me to wallow in the unknown. I want this, but please don't hurt me.

The man kissing me could be anyone and not JoeSmith at all. This man above me doesn't have a face. He isn't a real person attached to a mind and has no thoughts or feelings that I need to concern myself with. I'll enjoy the feeling of a human man loving my body, but not my heart and mind.

This man is faceless, soulless, and heartless.

He combs his finger in my hair and rests his hand atop my head. He pecks my cheek and whispers in my ear. "Take me as you will."

It's a huge compliment for him to give me free rein to use him for my pleasures. Why? I didn't earn this great reward.

I roll with him, straddle his hips, and kiss him passionately while he holds my waist. I place my palm against his cheek and try to feel his features. He quickly grabs my hand and pulls it away from his face.

His whisper is stern. "Do not touch my face and don't leave marks."

Without pause, my lips press to his while I push my pussy against his manhood. He releases my hand and I rest it beside his head. I sink, enveloping his full length completely.

I don't know, nor do I care, if he's thinking about me or another woman. I'm not here with JoeSmith in the absence of all things rational. He may as well be a robot for all I care.

Our lips part and we sigh as if being in this moment is something we've yearned for our entire lives. My hands find his chest to keep my balance as I sit up. I rock my hips forward and back, dragging my clitoris on his tight, strong abdomen. But the absence of light has my equilibrium off and I waver.

The man beneath me takes my hands in his and weaves our fingers together. He helps balance me. My hips rock at a fast, steady pace, and my clitoris twitches. I fuck and grind against him, taking what I want.

My thoughts are of my clit and how fucking close I am to coming. My feet slide beneath his thighs to prevent me from floating away, and I grip his hands with an unbreakable force.

Three more bucks and red light floods my eyes. Not blackness, as per usual. My wail echoes through the ebony soup and fades into the corners. I've fallen into the abyss of nothingness where only orgasms can take me. I weigh nothing and yet a thousand pounds. My body slowly sags as my mind gradually eases awake. I'm here, back with the nobody-man.

He sits up, wraps one arm around my waist, and swiftly flips me onto my back. He sinks into me and immediately pounds hard and fast. I'm soon close to coming again, but he slows his rhythm. I squirm underneath him as his entire length glides from tip to base.

His forearms press into the bed on either side of my shoulders and I clutch onto his solid biceps. I'm holding on to the edge of climax but can't get there. His pace remains torturously slow, drawing the progression of the orgasm to a snail's pace.

Oh my God! This is fantastic! I've never been so close for so long. I don't want to cum yet. This is fabulous, like nothing I've experienced before. Once again, he's taught me something new about my body.

His mouth captivates mine. Without thinking, I grab his cheeks in my palms. He grabs my wrists and holds them to the bed on either side of my head. In my confusion, I don't know why he won't let me touch his face.

"I said no!" he growls.

My head spins, and I can't understand why he's upset.

"I wa… didn't—"

I do my best to apologize but I can't find any words that make sense. His cheek rests against mine.

"What am I going to do with you?" he whispers seductively.

I'm with JoeSmith. He's not nobody and I feel him. Yes, I feel him.

I whisper, without thinking. "I'm yours."

He suddenly kneels and flips me onto my knees and presses my upper back so my cheek is on the bed. He grabs my waist, and I arch my back to grant him full access to my backside.

His tongue glides up and down from my clitoris to my asshole. It's a bizarre feeling; very soft, wet, and delicate yet firm. His tongue slips into the pucker, and I moan.

"Oh… Oh, God! Yes!"

"Press your right cheek to the bed," he whispers.

The bed shakes when he leans to the right side of the bed. My eyes are closed when the flashlight flips on for only a few seconds before the darkness returns and he rejoins me.

Two of his lubricated fingers slip into my ass and gently stretch me. I want him in every orifice.

He straddles and kneels outside of my legs and pushes the tip of his erection into my lubricated butt. I don't complain even though it's uncomfortable and a little painful. He holds still to allow my ass to stretch, to compensate for his size.

"You're mine," he whispers.

"Yes," I reply, but my voice is mute.

The tenderness of his touch, mixed with the naughtiness of the act, toys with my mind. I love it. He fills me, and it's breathtakingly erotic.

Master wraps his arm around my chest beneath my breasts and lifts me onto my knees. His right forearm rests diagonally between my breasts, and his hand grips my left shoulder. He holds my back firmly against his muscular chest. I reach back and clutch at his sides, hoping to hold myself to him.

Something cool touches my clit and begins to vibrate. My body stiffens, but my mind whirls like I'm on a teacup ride at a fair, and a sadistic teenager is at the wheel.

My muscles can no longer hold me and feel like I'm falling, but never land on the bed. My thoughts melted away.

I just… *am*.

My existence explodes into a trillion pieces as I come apart at his hand. I gasp and moan as my body writhes. He holds me against him as I melt, jolt, and shake. My fingernails dig into his thighs. If he lets go, I'll shatter into a heap of flesh and bone.

Everything suddenly stills. Neither of us moves. We hold in place as if glued together. Did he cum? I didn't feel him swell in my ass. Then again, I wasn't here.

He loosens his grip, and I fall away. He reaches for my arm but misses, and his cock slides from my ass and I can't keep myself from landing on my face with my arms. I grab his forearm for support and turn so we're face to face, both still on our knees.

I follow the sound of his heavy breaths and press my lips to his. We shuffle until our bodies press together. He wraps his right arm around me, leans back on his other arm, and slides his legs out from beneath him. I straddle him and glide him into my pussy.

He grabs my hips in protest. "You could get an infection. Let me change the condom."

I know I'm not supposed to go from asshole to vagina but at this moment, I don't care. It'll be worth it. He sinks into me and my arms wrap around his head. Even after my thighs spasm, I continue to ride him.

He sits up tall when his moans sound like he's in horrible pain. His forehead rests in the crook of my neck and his arms grip me tightly around my back. He bounces me on his cock with such force that it takes the wind out of my lungs.

With each slam into me, his exhales are met with loud grunts. If he speaks, he won't be able to mask his real voice; he's too detached from thought.

He slams me down a final time and holds me so tightly I can't breathe. His shaft thickens and spasms as he unloads his seed into the condom. His breath holds as his abs flex and relax several times. A heavy exhale is the first of many.

I remain still, not wanting this moment to end.

He pulls back, cups my cheek, and kisses me lovingly. His face drops until his forehead comes to rest against my collarbone. I grip the back of his neck and hold his head against me while my other drops to feel the muscles in his back flex as he battles to calm his breathing.

JoeSmith lies me back on the bed, removes the condom, and rolls onto his back beside me. He reaches for me and urges me to rest my head on his chest. Finally, he breaks the silence.

"I always enjoy you and you enjoy me, too. I probably shouldn't tell you this, but I think of you throughout the day. I wonder what you're thinking about at that exact moment." He sighs. "Because of the legality of things, I have a discussion to have with Miss Catherine." His finger traces my shoulder blade.

"I'm not going to sue the castle if I don't like your face." I laugh, but when he doesn't, I bite the inside of my cheek. "I won't sue, and I don't care if you're ugly as sin."

"That's not it," he says with a throaty chuckle. "I'll talk to my confidants about their experiences, but I don't expect much. I doubt they'll think it's a good idea for us to… date."

He says it as if it'd be a burden to be with me outside the castle.

"I have a question," I whisper.

"You may speak freely."

"Are you doing this so you won't lose me to another man or because you actually want me?" I ask, not sure I care to hear his answer.

"You can't deny you're forcing my hand. But I'm drawn to you. I've never felt like this with any of my submissives. You're different." He sighs. "I may want you, but Miss Catherine may have something to say about it."

He kisses the top of my head.

I want to scream that she has nothing to do with anything. Unless…

"Are you in a relationship with Miss Catherine? Is that why you need her permission?" I wonder who'd be the top in that scenario. "Is she your mistress?"

"Definitely not my mistress." He suppresses a laugh. "We don't have a sexual relationship. She and I are friends, but we have a legally binding contract with obligations and expectations I'm to adhere to in order to maintain," he pauses, "membership privileges."

"Oh, so you pay, like, what? A membership fee?"

Even without seeing his face, I can tell he's smiling.

"Something like that. When it comes to who I entertain, I don't have to ask her permission, per se. It's more of a discussion about our thoughts and concerns. She's my friend, and she's the person who makes the whole place run smoothly. Her opinion is important to me because I trust her."

"I understand." My finger circles his nipple until he pins my hand to his chest to make me stop. "I was wondering who'd be the master and who'd be the submissive in that scenario," I add with a giggle.

He chuckles. "I would certainly be the submissive."

I'm shocked. "Why so sure?"

"Because she's not one to give up control."

"Neither have you."

"You couldn't be more wrong, my pet. I've lost control of myself with you, so many times and in so many ways. Tonight is a prime example." He kisses my forehead and slides out from under me. He gets to his feet and walks around the bed to pick up the flashlight. "Thank you for coming on such short notice. I'll see you soon."

The tiny light illuminates his feet as it lights the way to the door. JoeSmith opens it. I can see his outline with the aid of the bright light that silhouettes his body, but it's so bright I can't distinguish his features. He pauses and I wait to hear him speak, but the room remains silent, and the door closes behind him. It feels so empty and cold in this room.

A few seconds later, a man enters and, in a voice deeper than any I've heard, warns me. "Close your eyes."

I follow his orders immediately and the lights explode about the room, blinding me, even through my closed eyelids. I place my hand over my eyes to cast a shadow before I stand. When I reach for the earring, it's gone. He must have taken it with him. Maybe that's my punishment for forgetting to remove it. I'll miss it because it's part of my favourite set.

I turn to see Lady Catherine's dog-man standing a few feet from me. He has to be around six-feet, four-inches tall and his shoulders are so wide I'm sure I couldn't get my arms around them.

My eyes scan down his physique to admire the chiselled form before me, but when I see the size of the package hidden behind his shiny gold shorts, my face flushes red hot and I can't look away. He's definitely proportionate to his height, if not even more blessed. He snickers and leans closer, so I'll hear his whisper.

"Don't be embarrassed, I get that reaction a lot."

I lower my hand from my brow, meet his sky-blue eyes for a brief second, and whisper, "Sorry."

He tilts his head as his shoulders rise. "Don't be sorry. You can look all you want."

He stands tall, and my face flushes hotter than lava when my eyes are drawn to the golden bulge below his washboard abs. He offers me his massive hand and I reach for it and we walk me, hand-in-hand, to the showers while I try to catch glimpses of his face and body without him noticing. I'm pretty sure he noticed.

He looks like the stereotypical California surfer-boy, only much taller and ripped with muscle. His beautiful, long blond hair that's just messy enough to be perfectly suited to his appearance would be perfect for a master or mistress to weave their fingers into. With eyes bluer than Caribbean waters and his full, pouty lips, he'd make a cover model green with envy.

I stand beneath the water that isn't quite hot enough. I could kick myself for not asking my master for his real name. But I take comfort that JoeSmith wants me, too. Maybe this can work.

After I'm dressed with my beautiful white rose in hand, and led to the front door by the same scrumptious man, I slip into the limo and we drive into the darkness of night while my hood reminds me of tonight's loving moments shared in the cover of blackness. Sadly, I'm expected at work in the morning. It's back to the normal daily grind now that the holidays have ended. But how thick will the tension be between Ben and me?

It is nearly midnight when I arrive home. I'll be tired at work, but I don't care one bit. I'd gladly stay up all night for a repeat performance.

He's going to think about having a relationship with me, a real one; or at least, as real and normal as we can have.

Ben… shit! What did I do? He's going to want a relationship, or sex, or… I don't know.

Will he be too friendly with me tomorrow and the water cooler gossip crew will pick up on it and start a vicious rumour that I'll have to quickly quash? Dammit, I hope not! But what if he acts like nothing's happened, or worse, ignores me?

What the fuck have I started? I want them both.

I'm flustered and sleep is unlikely to come easily. It's after two-thirty before my brain slows enough where I drift off to sleep. Seven o'clock will arrive too quickly.

Chapter 30

JS

Restaurant Fantasies

My eyelids are puffy and lined with a purple hue, but worse are the veins that feel like gritty sandpaper each time I blink. I've been fighting to hold my heavy lids open ever since my alarm screamed at me, waking me from my peaceful but short slumber.

I rolled over and called Sam before my feet slipped into my slippers. She was so turned on by the exciting make-out session I had with Bossman, but seemed preoccupied when I told her about my evening with JoeSmith.

I told her everything about my conversation with him, but she had little opinion about it when I tried to analyze each sentence, which is something we often do. Is she upset that she wasn't invited to join in?

Ben's in his office and all I have to do is lift my face to see him, but if I do and we meet eyes, it'll be awkward. And yet, I want to gauge his reaction to me. The indecision is making it difficult to sink my mind into my work. Well, that and I'm tired as hell. I will not look up.

Two hours into the workday, my cell phone vibrates in my purse. I dig for it and punch in my code. Hmm, unknown number.

"Are you okay?"

My heart pounds a little faster when I look up and see Bossman peering through the glass wall. The corners of my lips lift and I nod. He looks sharp in his dark grey dress pants, burgundy dress shirt rolled to his elbows, and a silk tie hanging loosely below an unbuttoned neckline.

He looks at his phone, and his fingers tap the screen. He looks at me and my phone vibrates in my hand.

"You're sure?"

When my eyes meet his, my cheeks flush, and a grin overwhelms my face. My fingers press to my lips and my eyes scan to see if anyone noticed our silent conversation. Without looking at him, I nod and hold up a thumb. As I tuck hair behind my ear, I gaze up at him. He's trying to restrain a smile and looking everywhere but at me.

My smile fades quickly as I stare at nothing and remember that JoeSmith may agree to start a relationship with me. If that happens, I can't be with Ben. But if he doesn't want more, do I give him up so I can be with Ben? Juggling two men would be a nightmare!

Dammit!

When I look up and he's looking at me with concerned eyes, I smile and lift the file he gave me containing the fresh case. I was going to start on it last night if I had gotten home earlier.

On our way to the restaurant for our Friday luncheon, Sam whispers, "Why didn't Master want me there last night?" She glances behind her. "Does he still like me?"

"What? Of course, he does! He enjoys you very much. Don't you remember him saying that there'll be times he won't invite you?" I shrug. "This was one of those times. If he hadn't enjoyed you, he'd have told you not to come back and since he didn't, you're in good standing."

She scrunches her nose. "Yeah, I suppose you're right. Sorry, I over-thought it."

"It's what we do," I say with a smirk, and put my arm around her shoulder as we continue walking. "When I get home, I'll check for his email. I'm sure he has something in the works." I wink, and she waves her brows.

Sam pulls open the door to the restaurant, and she walks through first. As I follow, I hold the door and turn to see if anyone's following. Ben's so close to me I can feel his breath on my neck. I'm instantly weak in the knees.

"Oh, you startled me," I blurt out in a higher voice than usual.

"How was your date last night?" he asks as he follows me to the table.

I turn my face to reply over my shoulder. "It was good. Great, in fact."

"I suppose that's good."

He doesn't sound convinced.

"Umm," I pause a few feet from my chair, turn, and tuck hair behind my ear, "in some ways; bad in others."

Our eyes meet, but mine slowly sink to his chest.

"Yeah, bad in—"

Mack slaps him on the shoulder as he walks up and apologizes for interrupting and begins talking to him.

Sam's chatting with her arm flailing to emphasize what she's talking about, but I'm not listening. My thoughts are on how soft Ben's lips were and how he held my ass and ground his thigh against my pussy.

He sits across the table from me and I can feel the electricity in his stare, but I choose to look at the menu, even if I'm too preoccupied to read it. I'm swarmed with guilt but the desire I feel for both men can't be denied.

We place our food orders after we receive our drinks. The waitress laughed when I asked for a bottomless mug of coffee.

Sam's hand rests on my thigh. She knows that nobody can see because of the tablecloth. I feel like everyone is watching and they all know what she's doing. It's intriguing, scandalous, almost, but scary at the same time. Inch by inch, she slides her hand up along my jeans and slips her fingers between my thighs and against my hotspot.

I reach down and push her hand away, but she puts it back and pinches my inner thigh, making me jolt and wince.

Ben's eyes shoot up just as I look up from my lap, and Sam smiles at me with one raised brow. He squints with pinched brows, but when I meet his eyes and flash a smile with flushed cheeks, his lips part and his eyes dart between Sam and me. As if he suddenly understands Sam as being one of the people I'm with, he nods and swallows, and then drops his gaze to the knife he's been rolling between his fingers.

What's he thinking?

Sam continues gabbing with Randy, who sits kitty-corner to her and is oblivious to her attempt at pussy-play beneath the table. How she can rub my crotch and be able to hold up her end of the conversation without getting flustered is beyond me.

I lean close to Sam and whisper, "You have to stop because Bossman knows what you're doing, and if he knows, others will also pick up on it."

She stops talking to Randy and turns her face to me. Her face is so close to mine. "Is that so?"

Her devilishly sexy eyes dart to Ben's and she holds his stare as if to stake her claim on me. Both are unblinking.

The outer edges of his lips quirk, and I wonder what he's thinking. Is he picturing her and me having sex? Probably.

I look at Ben and wish I could slide under the table, unzip his pants, and suck his cock until he unloads in my mouth. I imagine him trying to orgasm without letting any of his employees in on the secret. Could he do it? Could he be that nonchalant?

With Sam rubbing between my legs and my imagination running wild, I'm getting very horny. I grasp her wrist and squeeze, not to hurt her but to inflict a little punishment.

"Stop. Sam, you have to behave at work. If anyone were to find out, we'll never live it down. We'll be the talk of the office for months, if not longer. Please, everyone already suspects we're lovers."

She pulls her hand away but continues staring him down while she leans close and whispers in my ear. "I want to kiss you right now. Just think about how hot it would be to lie on this table and have mind-blowing sex with each other while *Mr. Bossman* watches. Could he keep his hands to himself?" She leans away, and I meet her eyes. "I think not."

"Funny you say that," I whisper in a barely audible tone, and she leans closer. "I was imagining myself sucking his cock under the table and him trying to act normal when he cums."

Her eyebrows rise as she pictures it. "Oh, yeah! That'd be fucking hot." She pulls her hand from my groin and sits back in her chair, only to lean toward me again. "Mhmm, I'm going to picture that the next time I finger my clit."

"Yeah. Me, too." I keep my voice at my normal tone because nobody knows what I'm referring to. "That'll get the job done."

Ben's still looking at us, but he's breathing quicker and his face is slightly flushed. I don't think he's embarrassed, more likely aroused. What's he thinking?

So, now he knows Sam and I are in a sexual relationship. The way he's looking at us, it seems his imagination's driving him crazy. Later tonight, will he stroke his cock to the thought of us? Why wouldn't he? Watching two women sexually please each other is erotic.

Sam jokes with everyone and laughs like she hasn't a care in the world. She's so fun to be around and exquisitely beautiful. Some people thrive in a crowd, and she's one of them.

She'll befriend everyone until they cross her, and then she'll plot to make their life miserable until they apologize and beg for forgiveness. She's quick to forgive, even when she doesn't want to. Sam thinks that if she dies without forgiving someone who asked for it, she's giving them a life sentence of guilt and she wants no part of that.

I do my best to avoid Ben's eyes while we dine. Each time I look up, he's looking at me and I worry our coworkers will notice.

After lunch, we walk the two blocks back to the office. The intense summer heat and humidity will soon end, and I'm happy about it. I don't like when I feel like I'm breathing through a pancake. Today the weather is warm with a gentle breeze and sunny, making everything seem crisp.

Sam leads the crowd while she tells one of her ridiculous stories. She takes huge steps and then dances some weird jig while her arms swing. The three people directly behind her burst into hysterical laughter. I love her so much. Ben appears beside me and takes me off my guard.

"That wasn't fair."

I startle and skip a step in my stride and nearly trip. He reaches for my arm, but I recover before he grabs it. Well, that wasn't embarrassing at all!

He asks, "Are you okay?"

"You startled me." I flatten the tummy of my blouse and clear my throat. "What's not fair?"

He complains in a deep voice while smirking. "Sam and you… under the table… that wasn't fair."

He's not angry. He's horny.

I lick my lips and lift my shoulders. "Take it up with Sam. I wasn't doing anything. I told her to stop."

"I kind of thought Sam might be one of the two lovers you mentioned. Is she your main love or is it someone else? And are they a man or a woman?" he asks, as if he's entitled to my answer.

I tip my head and look at him as if to suggest he has no right to be. "Are you jealous?"

"Of course, I am. I wanted to be the one fondling you under the table." He looks behind us, then rubs his chin. "What man wouldn't want to touch you all the time?"

I look to the sky and jest, "A gay man probably wouldn't."

"Touché!" He stuffs his hands in his pants pockets and lowers his face. "You should have a talk with her about not doing things like that around your coworkers. If people think there's a sexual relationship between you and Sam, it'll be hell. You know some men here will be all over you, trying to get a piece of the action. It's not right, I know, but that's how some men think."

"Before I told you I was involved with someone, you hadn't picked up on her and I and we've been flirting for some time. If you still didn't know, you wouldn't have known what she was doing." I take a breath and glance behind before saying, "I'll talk to her. So, do you think like the *men* to which you referred?"

He chuckles as he watches the city bus drive past. He rubs his chin again, then sinks his hand back in his front pocket.

"I've wanted a piece of *your* action for a long time. The fact that you're with Sam changes nothing. I still want you."

"A long time?" I ask and snag my heel on a crack in the pavement. "Stupid sidewalk! Um, so, how long have you wanted me?"

We're walking slower than the work crowd, which Sam has blended into and is listening to Cheryl say something as her hands wave to add emphasis to her words. We're nearly back at the office and I hope nobody notices him and I arrive later than them. Will rumours begin? I'm not sure how good I'll be at denying gossip involving truths.

He looks at me and smirks. "A while."

"Did you like what you saw?" I ask as shyness intervenes, and I lower my voice to a near whisper. "Were you aroused?"

He stops walking and so do I, and then he looks at me with squinted eyes, as if trying to read my thoughts.

"You want to know what I thought?"

My face scrunches. "I wouldn't have posed the question if I didn't."

He looks around to ensure nobody's listening in. His weight shifts from foot to foot as if he's nervous, but the way his shoulders square shows confidence. His eyes trail down my body, and heat flashes through me. I could jump him right here and not care who saw, but I would surely regret the public display when the rumours spread.

"I wanted the two of you on the table pleasuring each other while I took off my clothes. I'd watch for a bit and then fuck the hell out of you in front of everyone." He looks at my gaping mouth and the corner of his lip lifts into a sexy grin. "So, to answer your question, it's a resounding *yes*. I may be a gentleman, but I'm also a sexually frustrated, red-blooded man."

"Sam pictured a scenario very much the same." I resume walking so we don't draw attention, and tease, "I pictured something slightly different."

He takes two long strides to catch up. "What were you picturing?

"Oh, I can't tell you that!" I tease, shake my head, and clutch my hands behind my back.

Two women walk toward us. Both scan Ben's face and body quickly before they pass by, surely turning to check him out from behind. That makes me giggle. We stop for the red light and I turn to look at them. I was right; they're looking at his ass but scurry away when I see them.

"Why not?" he asks as he turns to face me and tips his head to a man who tipped first as he rushed past us to cross the street on the green light to our left.

I own him right now.

"Fine. You tell me if you were hard when you watched us while imagining your scenario, and I'll tell you what I imagined."

He squints and smirks. "I was so hard I had to shift the position of my erection without being obvious, which isn't easy to do at a restaurant with a table of our peers." We watch a very loud car drive past and smell the burning oil in its wake. "Is that what you wanted to hear? That you have an incredible influence over me?"

I like having power. I can see the draw toward dominance. It feels good to own this much control. I turn toward him and he watches my lips.

"I pictured myself under the table and sucking your cock while you tried to act like nothing was happening. Just think about how exciting it would be to orgasm in public with no one knowing any different." My gaze drops to his crotch. "Are you hard now?"

His voice is deep and breathy. "Growing by the second! That'd be an interesting challenge." He takes a breath and clears his throat. "In your scenario, I'm not sure I could hide it very well. I'd get caught because I'd want to watch your mouth on me. Surely someone would wonder why I was looking down at my groin and grinning like a fool." His smile is wickedly sexy.

The light changes and I step off the curb, leaving him standing with his hands on his hips and his eyes following me. I hear him exhale heavily before he rushes to catch up.

Ben heads back to his office and me to my desk as if nothing sexual was discussed. Just as I get myself situated, Sam wheels her chair into my cubicle.

"So, what were you and big Bossman chatting about? You looked like you were having a captivating conversation."

She wears a sexy expression that always turns me on, even when we weren't fucking each other.

I feign innocence. "He wanted to know what I was thinking during lunch, so I told him, but only after I made him tell me what he was envisioning."

"Oh, goodie!" With enthusiasm, she leans closer and rests an elbow on my desk. "Do tell! Curiosity's killing this pussy." Her eyes are wide while she holds her bottom lip prisoner between her teeth.

I lean on my forearms and whisper, "He had the same idea as you but he said he'd fuck the hell out of me in front of everyone."

Her eyes squint and she speaks so fast I can barely keep up. "Oh, yeah! That's hot! He and I think a lot alike and that makes him okay in my book. Fuck! I'm so horny." She shakes her head and blows out a breath. "You should totally get with that hottie, and later, after you've corrupted him, we can tag team him. Wouldn't that be awesome? That poor guy would cum before we even touched him."

She tips her head back and laughs evilly as she wheels herself back to her cubicle, keeping her wide eyes on mine. I wheel my chair to follow her and lean around the partition.

"You're probably right, but it'd be fun."

Her eyebrows wave and so do I before wheeling back.

About an hour later, Sam bumps me with her hip, waking me from the blankness that my mind has drifted into. I think I was asleep with my eyes open. It's very possible since I'm so damn tired.

"I brought you an espresso. You look like you need caffeine. Are you hanging in there?" Sam hands me the small cup and answers her own question when I roll my eyes and sag my shoulders. "You will not make it. You're falling asleep at your desk. Maybe you should punch out early. I'm sure *Bossman* would let you slide," she leans in close, "on his cock!"

I hold the espresso under my nose and breathe in its aromatic scent. "I'm okay, I think. I don't know. I'm so tired I can't concentrate on anything. Sitting still at this desk makes it so much worse."

I set the coffee down and stretch my arms over my head and can't be bothered to stifle a yawn. She hands me her phone.

"Check the email. I'll go bonkers if I don't find out if he wants me tomorrow. Please, please, please!"

"He doesn't usually write for another hour or so."

She pouts, so I take her phone and hold it under my desk. Bossman's busy at his desk, so he probably won't look out and see me. Sam keeps watch for snoopy coworkers as I enter my password.

I'm surprised to see his email. I quietly read it to her.

Dearest Pet,

I expect Slut to go to the salon today because tomorrow you'll give yourselves to me to do with as I desire. I will lift you to a new adventure. The sky's the limit to what you'll endure and you'll be shared with many.

The car will be there at five o'clock, and I expect you both will be waiting.

Do you accept?

Always,
JoeSmith

Sam stops biting her fingernail to ask what I can't possibly answer. "What does he mean by the sky's the limit and shared by many?"

I shrug and frown. "Hmm, sky's the limit… I don't know, but I can't wait to find out." I smile widely and wave my eyebrows. "Shared by many is self-explanatory. He's going to bring in other people."

I don't ask if she's game to come along. I hit reply and confirmed. She drops her forehead on the desk.

"I hate the clues because it's never enough, and it drives me crazy." She lifts her face. "Shared… like a gang bang?"

Again, I shrug and she frowns.

"So, do you want to hit the salon with me right after work? I can go alone if you have something else to do… like *Bossman*."

I groan and pout. “You know I can’t be with him. I’d be honoured to escort you to the salon.”

She looks relieved. “Okay, it’ll be fun.”

“Even though I’m exhausted…” I yawn and glance at the listeners. “I’ve been so turned on all day.”

Sam crinkles her nose. “Yeah, me, too. I’m sure things aren’t summer breeze fresh down there,” she points at her pussy, “but I have baby wipes in my purse I can use to freshen up before I go.”

A memo from Ben pops up on my computer screen:

Terri, can you come to my office, please?

She looks at me and bites her bottom lip while her eyes grow wide.

“Oh, yeah, baby! Give it to me, Bossman. Fuck me good, Bossman. Oh, yeah! Make me cum!”

“Stop that!” I hiss and threaten to hit her, but she laughs and rolls her chair around the partition while still making sexy faces.

Chapter 31

Propositions and Apologies

I glance up at his office and see Ben standing at the window wall, looking down at me with his hands in his front pockets. Why does him doing that excite me so much?

I push back my chair and head to his office with the espresso in hand. There's no way I'm leaving it behind. After knocking, I push open the door. His desk is covered in paperwork and he's leaning over it with the sleeves of his pale green dress shirt rolled up to his elbows.

"Come over here." He taps his pen on one of the papers. "This doesn't add up. Have you found any inconsistencies?"

I groan as I set the tiny mug on his desk and try to avoid his eyes, even though he seems to want me to look at him.

"No, not yet. So far, everything seems to check out, but I haven't gotten as far into it as you obviously have. You've gone through all of this already? You're quick, that's for sure."

I pick up the page and run my eyes over it.

"Oh, I assure you, Terri, I'm only quick at my job. I like to take my time with the more intimate aspects of life."

I take a step away from him while still holding the page and ask, "What are you doing?"

"I don't follow?"

While sporting a sexy grin, he glares at me from under his brow. He looks almost dangerous, as if he's about to rush me, rip off my clothes, and fuck me until I beg for mercy. The jokes on him; nothing he'd do would ever force me to beg for mercy.

Nervous anxiety flourishes in the pit of my stomach. "Fun flirting is one thing, but you know we can't take it any further than we already have." I cross my arms over my chest, and he listens intently as I continue. "So, the question remains; what are you doing?"

He stands tall, slips his hands into his pants pockets, and looks at me much the same way. "I want you. I really want you. You're on my mind almost constantly. It doesn't help that I can see you every time I glance away from my desk. I've been burying myself in work, attempting to get you off my mind, but it's futile." His head dips as he scratches the back of it. "Please, Terri, tell me what I can do to make you mine because I'm at a loss."

I look down at the page in my hand to throw off any coworkers who might watch us from below. If it looks like we're discussing anything other than work, rumours will fly.

"Ben, don't. My desire to be with you…" I swallow when the brows above his emerald eyes pinch together. "Well, I might want that, too, but I can't…" I pause and wave my hand in a circle. "This… us… cannot happen."

"Is Sam the reason? Because I wouldn't stop you from being with her."

His expression is serious, but I laugh.

"Of course, you wouldn't! What man in his right mind would stop his woman from having sex with another hot woman? I mean, seriously! You'd want both of us to share your bed. I hate to shatter that fantasy because if you and I were together, I'd want you for myself and wouldn't share you with her. At first, you won't be bothered by her and I spending nights together."

I pace and wave my arms as I talk. "After a while, you'll tolerate it while still holding onto a shred of hope that you might get to play with both of us, but you'll soon realize that'll never happen and your jealousy will take over, and it'll end very badly. We'll fight, the workplace will become a sour place we'll dread coming to, I'll end up quitting, or worse, you'll figure out a way to fire me, and it'll be this whole shit-show. I love my job here!"

He stands beside the desk with his arms crossed over his chest, staring at me with wide eyes and raised brows. I sigh heavily and drop my arms at my sides.

"So, you see it wouldn't work out between us because I won't give up Sam, and I won't share her."

His voice is calm as he speaks much slower than I did. "I wouldn't ask you to share her nor would I stop you from enjoying her company. She has something to offer you that I can't—a female touch. I wouldn't be so selfish as to forbid you from doing what makes you happy, and since she makes you happy…" He sits on the edge of his desk and pinches the bridge of his nose. "I wouldn't be jealous of your love for Sam. I'd be jealous if you were with another man because he has what you can get from me."

If he only knew what I got from JoeSmith, he'd retract that statement. Actually, he'd think I was a warped, mentally disturbed woman and JoeSmith was an abuser who secretly hated women. He'd be dead wrong in his assumptions, but if he doesn't understand the relationship between dom and sub, he'd think the worst.

My tone is low, with hopes to sound more sympathetic. "But I *have* a man in my life. I'm not giving him up, for you or anyone, because he absolutely offers me something you can't." I reach my hand toward him as I step closer. "Now hand me another paper so it looks like we're discussing the case."

I take the random page he hands me and pretend to study it as I shuffle toward the windows before turning my back to my coworkers below, so they can't see my face.

"You couldn't possibly understand the relationship even if I explain it. I need him in my life. He strengthens me." I bite my lips, then drop my eyes back to the page. "I may want you, but I need him."

"Tell me how he strengthens you, and I'll do it," he begs as he rounds the desk with determination in his eyes.

I sigh and walk toward the desk, but still keep my distance. I pretend to shuffle pages and then point to one. He leans in and pretends we're discussing it.

"If it were only that simple," I say, and shake my head. "My relationship with him is… complicated at best, but he's important to me. Please try to understand."

"Terri, I'm trying to, and I hear what you're saying. A little warning; I'm still going to flirt with you. If that's all right." He smiles and fixes his emerald eyes on mine. "I won't pressure you, okay?"

I smile and whisper, "Good. I had hoped you'd still flirt with me."

There's a long silence where we just look at one another. He takes a breath as if he's going to say something but thinks better of it and clears his throat instead.

"I should get back to work," I say as I hand him the pages and he pretends to look at them.

He smiles wide and licks his lips. "You probably should do that now because if you don't, I may just lay you on my desk and have my way with you. But, that's a terrible idea… the papers would get all messed up."

I scrunch one side of my face, cross my arms over my chest, and say, "I'd sweat, they'd stick to my butt, the ink would stain my skin…" I shake my head and sigh, still not smiling. "Oh, the horror!"

He looks very serious as he takes a seat in his chair, but I know he wants to crack a smile. He thinks he's got the best of me. "Definitely not worth it."

As I walk toward the door, I turn and say, "Three seconds in heaven just isn't worth the hour I'll spend scrubbing ink off my ass."

I shrug and pull open the door. He spins his chair, so he isn't facing me.

"You fucking drive me crazy, Terri!" He groans. "Now get out of here before I lose all self-control."

I burst into laughter and descended the staircase. I'm still smiling when I pass Sam's desk. She grabs my arm and tugs me toward her.

"What was all that about?" Her eyes open wide with curiosity.

Loud enough that others will hear, I reply, "He found an inconsistency with the account we're working on." I lean in and whisper. "And we flirted a little."

She stands and follows me to my cubicle. "That man wants you something fierce."

Her eyes skirt up at his office. I follow her gaze and see him at the glass wall, looking at Sam and me, and his brows are pinched together questioningly.

I shrug. "He didn't say so, but I think he wants us both."

"What man wouldn't?" she says as matter-of-fact.

"Exactly." I snicker and pick up my pen so I can tap it on my chin.

"Did he ask if he could?"

Sam's thrilled and her eyes are filled with the promise of her lunchtime fantasy come true. I shake my head.

"No, he didn't, but he knows we're together and said he wouldn't want to break us up."

Simultaneously, the two of us whisper, "He wants us both."

We laugh and the shushes prove we've disturbed our coworkers. Sam returns to her desk and I delve into my files in search of inconsistencies that link to what Ben attempted to show me before the flirting started and we got sidetracked.

Over the next few hours, I find several purchases that don't add up. They ordered some products that never made it into the semi-annual inventory audit report but did in the monthly financial reports, but under different names and expenses.

I take my findings to the copy room and make duplicates. With copies sorted and in the folder, I turn to leave, but Bob's standing in the doorway.

"What can I help you with, Bob?" I ask, trying to keep my annoyance out of my tone.

With his hands in the pockets of his oversized, light-grey dress pants, he bows his head and nervously shuffles his feet.

"I was an asshole at the Christmas party." His eyes tilt up at me, then drop to the floor again. "Please accept my apology. I had way too much to drink, and I ate nothing to absorb it. That doesn't excuse my deplorable behaviour. You're my friend. I mean, you *were* my friend. It'd be a shame if I ruined that."

"You're right, Bob. You were an asshole, but I accept your apology. You should keep in mind that you turn into a total jerk when you drink."

He scratches the back of his head and stands a little taller. "I really am sorry."

I nod and smile, but it fades quickly. "Bob, I want to ask you about something that you said." His eyes meet mine and I walk toward him so I can lower my voice. "You told me that everyone thinks Sam and I are in a sexual relationship. Is that true?"

"Well, um," he pauses and rocks nervously on his heels, "uh, yes. It seems to be the consensus."

"Okay. I just wanted to know. Thanks for your honesty." I pat him on the shoulder as I step around him. "Sorry, Bob, but I must go. I need to talk to Mr. Manning about this account. Are we good?" My hand waves between me and him.

"Yeah, we're good. Again, I'm sorry, Terri." I try to walk away, but he stops me. "Is it true? I mean, I really care about you. If you gave me a shot, I think we could be happy together, unless you, uh…" He stammers. "…um, you *are* with Sam."

He won't let me get away without giving him an answer. He looks like a lost, scared, and curious puppy.

"No, Bob, I don't think we would. You're my work friend and that's as far as I'm willing to take it. I don't want to hurt your feelings, but the whole idea of us? It will not happen. And," I pause to wrinkle my brow, "my sex life is nobody's business in the workplace. I'd never ask you about your personal life, and to be honest, I'm a little offended you'd ask me about mine. Sam's my best friend in the world, and yeah, we're very close, but… Bob, if I were having sex with her, why would I tell you or anyone?"

He frowns, and I cross my arms over my chest, leaving the papers to hang against my side. I crinkle my nose and tilt my head.

"Do you *really* think I'm a lesbian?"

He shrugs and shakes his head as if embarrassed he even insinuated something so farfetched. I exit the room quickly. Hopefully, I changed his thinking or at least have him doubting the rumour. I didn't lie because I'm a terrible liar and he would've seen right through it had I attempted to spew out a full-on denial.

Chapter 32

Blame the Paper Ball

The office comes to life as the final hour ticks. I run up the steps and knock on Ben's door. He calls out, "Come on in."

The door swings closed behind me after I rush in and plop the papers I copied on his desk in front of him.

"I found other issues." My eyes widen when I see disappointment looming on his expression. I add, "Isn't that what I was supposed to be doing?"

"Thought you came back because you changed your mind and want me to lay you out on my desk."

My head tilts and I smile innocently. "Nope. Just paperwork!"

He shakes his head and sighs as he takes the papers I plopped on his desk. He looks them over and I sit in the chair on the other side of his desk. I can smell his cologne hanging in the air. I remember savouring the scent on my skin until I showered at the castle. And I'm reminded of how we made out right over there, in this room and on that sofa. I realize I've been staring at it and quickly turn my attention back to his desk.

"I saw you looking at the sofa. Do you want another go at me?" he inquires, but doesn't lift his eyes from the papers.

I huff. "Yes, but no! After the teasing this afternoon, I don't think I have it in me to stop if we started."

"Good to know." He looks up with a hopeful glint in his eyes. "Everyone will leave eventually, so I'll just keep you here until then."

With my finger pressed to my chin, I scrunch one side of my face and glance up, and then meet his eyes.

"Hmm, great thought, but Sam isn't leaving here without me. We're going for a wax appointment; Brazilian, if you must know."

I rest my hands on the desk across from him as I lean just enough that the front of my shirt hangs, but not enough where he'll have a clear view of my breasts.

"Brazilian, huh?" He shifts in his seat. "Stop it! How do you expect me to concentrate when I'm all worked up?"

"Hey, you started it!" I lift my arms to my sides, palms up. "I'm just keeping the conversation going."

He scans the page aimlessly. His fingertips rub his chin and his eyes skirt up to mine. "Explain what I'm looking at, because I can't concentrate enough to figure it out."

I rise and glide around his desk until I'm standing next to him. His cologne is intoxicating, and my pussy agrees. I lean in until my left breast is inches from his face. Yes, I'm tempting fate. I know it'll tease him and I shouldn't be doing this because I *can't*, but it's so much fun! I feel like I'm in high school and the boy I have a crush on likes me, too.

"Right here, here, here, and here." I point to four spots on two different pages. "Someone's been placing orders that haven't been processed as assets. They line up here, but this over here doesn't. And, there are three employee numbers that don't match people who work here, and companies… I've found six purchasers that don't exist, and I haven't finished looking. It's almost like they're trying to cause confusion in the accounts, hoping they'll get overlooked. But I'm no slouch."

"Now I see it," he says in a different tone, more like Bossman instead of a growly, horny man.

He stands to reach into another stack of papers at the far end of the desk. He flips through a dozen pages and pulls one from the middle of the stack.

"Ah, yes. Right here. You're correct; it's not listed."

He brushes his groin against my ass when he leans around me to take a page from the top of another pile. I don't want him to stop. I imagine he lifts my skirt, yanks down my panties, unzips his fly and fucks me hard for a good, solid minute. I'm sure that's all it would take for both of us to finish. There's been so much sexual tension between us, and we're both wound tightly.

He compares the pages, then pats me on the back. "You've tapped on something here. Now we just need to follow the money trail to see where it leads us, or to whom it leads us. Good job." He turns so his ass leans against his desk and rests his hands gripping the edge on either side. "What kind of bonus would you like?"

I copy his position and offer him a fun challenge. "Why don't you look into my eyes and tell me what you see?"

He gazes at me through slitted eyes, stands, and rests his back against the wall opposite me and then stares seductively into my eyes. He shakes his head and holds his hips.

"Goddamn it, woman! I'm too shy to put that into words." His head tilts and his voice deepens. "I'd have to show you. If you want what I think you want, hike up your skirt and sit on the desk."

He doesn't think I'll do it. Should I be so cruel? I watch his face for a nervous twitch, but there's nothing but confidence.

Ben wants to play? I'll play his teasing game!

I slowly lift my skirt and shift like I'm about to do what he suggested. His face flushes. As if he suddenly remembers where we are, he looks through the glass wall to see if anyone's watching from below and he panics.

"No, don't do it. People can see. That's the only problem with having a glass wall in my office."

Ben takes a deep breath, then walks away from his desk and me. He turns to admire my thighs, which I've left exposed. He's quiet for a moment, probably to run the full scenario through his mind. His fingers comb through his hair and come to rest on his hips.

"Terri, you could get me into a world of trouble. I'm your boss, and you've said you aren't available."

Is he afraid of a lawsuit or fear I'll break his heart?

I should cool it, though; it's not fair to him that I tease but won't satisfy. I suddenly don't feel sexy. I just feel guilty for torturing this poor man. I know submitting to his advances can't happen, so I let the skirt's hem slip down over my knees.

"I should go. People will talk. I'm sure Sam has bitten off all of her fingernails in anticipation. She knows I'm up here and is probably itching to find out if we're behaving ourselves or not." I snicker.

He tilts his head, and with concern on his face, he takes a few steps toward me. "Did you tell her about the sofa situation?"

"Of course. I don't keep secrets from Sam."

He runs his hand through his hair. "Do you think that was a good idea? I mean, what if she goes to Human Resources to file a complaint? She could easily get jealous and seek revenge. You two are in a relationship. What if that goes sour? I could get into a lot of trouble. There could be legal consequences—"

He's panicking, and I need to calm him down.

"You don't know Sam." I gather my original copies and head for the door, leaving the photocopies behind. "I probably shouldn't tell you this, but she wants us to hook up. She would like nothing more than to watch you fuck me until I beg for mercy. So, you have no reason to worry about her going to HR."

He stands with his mouth gaped, trying to think of something witty to say, but he takes too long and I'm halfway down the stairs before he calls my name. I don't turn back, but need to take a breath so I can restrain my excitement. My heart's pounding quicker than usual, and my panties are damp.

I want him! I really, *really* want him.

As I walk past Sam, I answer the question she hasn't yet asked. "I found an inconsistency in that account."

"Sure you did!"

From my desk, I peer up at Ben, who stands at the glass and gazes down at me. I'm curious to know what he's thinking and how many fantasies have run around his thoughts. Because of the pleated dress pants, I can't tell if he's excited by his thoughts. He grins, shakes his head, and walks away.

I'm not sure where he went, but I can't see him in his office. Maybe he's gone to his personal bathroom to release his frustration. The thought has me squeezing my thighs together.

Is he leaning against the back wall with his pants at his ankles and his hand gripped firmly around his solid shaft as he strokes it rapidly? Is his head tipped back with a tight jaw? Will he grab the sink with his free hand to steady himself as a moan escapes his thin lips? When he comes, will his body jerk, followed by a heavy exhale? Will his eyes slowly open and be met with his own flushed reflection draped in a mist of sweat on his face?

A paper ball hits me right in the eye. It hurts instantly. I cup my eye and cry out.

"Oh, dammit! What the f—"

Sam pulls at my hand so she can look. Tears pour from my eye. The light seems to make it sting more, or maybe it's just the air.

"Stop it! Let go of me."

She slaps at my hand. "I'm trying to see if it's cut anywhere. Stop being such a baby! Let me see."

Sam's bossy when she wants to be. I kind of like it when she takes control. Is it weird that I'm aroused even with the looming threat of blindness?

"I can't see anything. Come with me to the lunchroom." Sam pulls me up by my elbow to guide me. "We have to clean off that mess of mascara. Let's get you cleaned up."

"I'll just go to the bathroom."

"No, because the lighting in there is shitty. The lunchroom is much brighter," she insists and redirects me. "I'm so sorry, Terri. I thought you'd see the ball coming at your face and you'd blink like normal people do. It's instinctual, you know. Do you have a blind spot I don't know about?"

She pokes fun at the situation as she sits me on an oak chair she slid from the table closest to the sink. Someone must have recently popped popcorn in the microwave because it smells amazing here. My stomach growls, reminding me I didn't eat much of my lunch.

A small crowd followed us into the light blue room because this is the most exciting thing to happen all week. And who can pull their eyes away from a train wreck? My hand waves dismissively.

"There's nothing to see, people. I'm fine. Everyone, get back to work. Nothing to see here."

I hate when people stare at me, especially when I'm a mess. Unless it's due to a sexual liaison with JoeSmith, of course, but I don't know those voyeurs, so I don't care if I look hideous in front of them. Besides, I think they like it when my mascara runs down my cheeks. People clear a path as Bossman makes his way through the crowd.

"What happened?"

He leans in close to observe as Sam tries to pull open my eyelid despite my protest.

"Nothing, I'm fine," I say, hoping he'll leave, but knowing he won't. Curiosity is strong in humans.

"Dammit, Terri." She yanks my hand away from my face. "I can't help if you don't let me see it!"

"It won't open; it hurts too much when the light hits it!" I yell back. "Just give me a fucking minute, woman!"

Sam backs away and hands me a tissue. I wipe the tears off my cheek only to see the horror of black smeared make-up coating the tissue. I try to open my eyes, but the bright overhead lights have me tearing up.

"Okay, so what happened?" Ben looks at me and says, "Wow! You're a mess."

"Geeze, thanks!" I attempt to roll my eyes, but it has me wincing.

Sam rests her hands on her waist and leans toward him with a silly expression. "She was lost in a daydream about God knows what." She looks at him and squints accusingly. "So, I tossed a paper ball at her and she didn't blink."

Ben teases, "Why the hell would you do that? I thought you were her friend."

"Most people blink when an object is coming directly at them. It's instinct to blink." Sam tries to peer into my eye every time I open it, but it pulls itself closed too quickly. "It's totally my fault, but accidental."

"Do you need to go to a doctor?" he asks.

I smile and shake my head. "No, I'm fine. I just need a few minutes. I'm sure it'll stop watering, and I'll be good to go. Really, I'm okay."

I'm more embarrassed than hurt.

"Okay." Ben waves his arm in the door's direction. "Everyone can go back to work. Terri will be fine. Don't worry."

The people groan and shuffle out of the room like bored zombies.

Sam takes another tissue, wets it under the tap, then wipes away the mascara that's left a trail down my cheek. It blackens the tissue. I'm horrified that the incredibly put-together Ben Manning sees me looking this hideous.

Sam pats Ben's shoulder. "You don't have to stay. I'll take care of her."

Ben puts his hands in his pants pockets. "I have to stay. It's mandatory that she fills out a report. I'm going to stick around and help her do that." He clears his throat. "I can take over. I'll make sure she's tended to."

Sam stands close to him and tilts her head back, so she can look up into his eyes. He squares his shoulders and tilts his face down to look at her. His inexpressive face looks mysterious and therefore more intriguing than when he's flirting.

With a sultry voice, she teases, "I always make sure Terri's *very* well-tended."

Ben doesn't look away. A muscle in his jaw tenses. He clears his throat and grins but says nothing.

Sam turns but holds his gaze until her flirtatious eyes drop to scan his body. She smirks and turns her attention to me and wipes away more of the smeared mascara with a damp tissue and looks up at the ceiling and sighs. She holds my lid open and looks at my eyeball. Both of them stare at my eye and I can't help but erupt into laughter and pull my face away from her hands.

Sam giggles. "What's so funny?"

I struggle to control myself. "You two were just staring at my eyeball." I laugh again. "It just struck me as funny. You two looked hilarious."

Sam walks to the sink and washes her hands. "I think you'll be fine. I didn't see any cuts." She dries her hands and puts her hand on Ben's chest. "She's your patient now, *doctor*. I think she might need some *tending to*."

Sam winks at me before she leaves the room. Ben wears a sexy smirk. He crosses his arms over his chest and turns to ensure the door closed after Sam left.

"Doctor and patient… That would be an interesting role playing fantasy. Wouldn't it?"

I point at my face and frown. "It might excite me if I didn't look so horrible."

He looks serious. "You realize that if we were to play doctor, your make-up would most likely smear. You could start with immaculate make-up, but if I play my role well, you'll look used up when all is said and done."

"But it's my eye that's injured, not the area you'd be tending to. You aren't a very good doctor if you can't distinguish between those two very different parts of the human body." I try to hold back a smile, unsuccessfully.

"But, darling, everything's connected, and I wouldn't be a very good doctor if I didn't do a thorough examination." He stands tall and rubs his chin in frustration. "Dammit, woman! You're extraordinary."

He rests his hands atop his head and looks at the door. He turns back and groans. I dab my tearing eye and snicker.

"Fuck!" He looks me up and down before seriousness takes over him. "If you're all right, I'll head up to my office. You can meet me there when you're ready and we'll fill out a report."

"That's unnecessary. I'm fine, really."

I can't be alone with him in case I can't keep my hands to myself. What if he can't control himself? I'm too weak-willed around him to trust I'll say no.

"The paper ball barely tapped my eyeball. It's good, see? I can see just fine." I blink a lot when I roll my eyes left to right and up and down. "It's good. I'm not filling out a report."

"What if an infection flourishes suddenly and you lose your eye? You'll regret having not filled out a report."

"Seriously?" I shake my head and stand. "I'll be okay. I'm going to go to the bathroom to take the make-up off my other eye so I don't look so ridiculous."

Ben smiles and says, "You can do that upstairs in my private bathroom while I do the paperwork. It'll save time."

He takes my elbow and leads me to the door. I suppose there's no point in protesting because it won't change his mind and I'll come off looking like an unruly child.

Chapter 33

Who Are You?

With his hand on my lower back, he guides me up the stairs to his office. I don't need the help, but I like the heat from his hand.

He digs through the filing cabinet and pulls out a form, brings it to his desk, and takes a pen from the top left drawer. He points to his bathroom before he surveys the form.

I don't bother shutting the door since I'm only going to wash my face. Besides, if I do, I won't hear him ask me questions.

He startles me when he leans around me, opens a drawer under the sink and smiles as he hands me a washcloth.

I wet the soft grey cloth, add a little soap from the pearl and gold dispenser, and then carefully remove the mascara from my unaffected eye. I bend over and splash water to remove the soap when his warm hand rests on my lower back and something brushes along my butt.

I shut off the tap, and a matching grey towel is placed into my hand. When I open my eyes above the towel and look into the mirror, he's beside me and his eyes scream with desire.

Oh, *fuck!*

My pussy clenches as I spin and press my lips to his. With wild enthusiasm, we tongue-fuck one another's mouths. He gives up on the buttons on my blouse and unfastens my skirt and it falls to circle my tan-coloured two-inch heels.

My lacy white panties slide over my hips, and they fall to my ankles. I step out of the left leg hole but they snag on the other shoe, so I leave them to dangle. I reach for his belt, but can't get it to unlatch.

He lifts me by my ass and sets me on the edge of the sink. Without a struggle, he undoes the belt, button, and zipper, and then reaches for something in a drawer as his hot palm slides up my thigh.

Our mouths mash together, but our heavy breathing lessens our kissing skills.

I want him. He wants me. Neither of us is thinking logically, and I couldn't care less about what's-his-name, the guy who refuses to show me his face.

Ben grabs my ass, and I wrap my legs around his waist. He reaches between us and aims his stiff cock. He breaks our kiss and stares into my eyes as he slides into me unhurriedly. It's torturously slow, but watching his lips part and his eyelids sag just before he holds a blink to savour the sensations my pussy brings to him makes the delay worthwhile.

Holy shit! Bossman's cock is buried inside me!

I've dreamed of this for so long and it's happening. He's actually fucking me, and his cock is even thicker than I imagined.

His emerald eyes demand my attention from beneath hooded lids.

When he pushes completely inside me, my head falls back and my eyes squeeze shut. He pulls back and shoves back in. A moan erupts from deep within my soul. His palm covers my mouth, and he shushes me before placing it back on my ass.

He pounds into me so hard my ass lifts off the edge of the sink. I brace my foot against the wall behind him and feel my panties dangle from my ankle.

This is so dangerous! If we get caught—

Anyone could walk in at any moment and find us fucking like wild animals. The thought excites me more. My back arches and he yanks up my blouse, grabs my bra cup, and jerks until my breasts drop free. He sucks one nipple, then the other while he continues fucking me.

I sit up and grab the sleeves of his rolled-up dress shirt that covers his strong biceps. Our faces are nearly touching when an orgasm rushes through me. I clench my teeth and squeeze my eyes shut in a painful display as I battle to swallow my passionate screams.

Holding back my screams is something I've perfected in the playrooms, but here, with Ben, is a completely different ballgame. There's so much more at stake than a simple spanking if I were to cry out.

He lifts me, sets me on my feet, and turns me to face the sink. I put my hands on the mirror. My head still spins when he fills me and my hips slam against the sink. I like this position. The mirror allows me to watch him from a distance while he fucks me.

A light coat of sweat layers across his skin. He stares at me with fiercely passionate eyes that burn into my soul, and he doesn't look away.

He fucks me hard. Is he ever going to cum? Not that I want him to stop, but I've held back the screams from three orgasms. I can't do it again. Even if I were with JoeSmith, there comes a time when I lose control.

People are downstairs, and I can't remember if he shut the office door or not, but the bathroom door is wide open. It's a good thing this room is at the back of his office, where nobody can see us if they look up from the cubicles.

"You have to cum or we'll get caught." I huff and puff, barely able to form words.

He reaches under my shoulder and pulls me back against his shirt-covered chest. His hand spreads wide on my belly and he holds my shoulder with the other.

With my back arched like this, it feels like he's sunk deeper into me and his steely hard cock is teasing my core. This is so much better than I'd dreamed it'd be. I want him inside me forever.

He watches me in the mirror as he slams into me a few final times. His face reddens, forehead creases, and his jaw tightens, but he never looks away. His hips jerk against me, then hold unflinchingly still, and his breath stops. Distant eyes and a mumbled moan finalizes his pleasure.

Ben holds my back against his chest and continues to watch me as our breaths slowly ease. I smile, but his brows furrow. Is he disappointed?

"What's the matter?" I ask, afraid he'll say this didn't live up to his fantasy.

He shakes his head. "Nothing's wrong, but nothing's right either." He takes in a deep breath and eases it out slowly. "You gave in. I didn't think you would. You were so adamant that you belonged to someone else. So, why?"

My boss has completely ruined the moment.

I pull away from him and pull my panties and skirt back on, fix my bra, and exit the bathroom. I pull the door three quarters closed behind me without saying a word.

"Terri!" he calls out to me, but I don't answer.

What the fuck is his problem? He wants me, he doesn't want me. He fucks me, then looks at me as if disgusted with me. Who the hell is he to judge me? I told him about my relationships and he still fucked me. So what's the problem?

With the paper in hand, I round his desk in search of the pen he tossed to the floor just before he ravished me, but I don't see it. I want to fill out the accident form and get the hell out of here before he's finished in the bathroom.

How could I have given in so easily?

I'm upset, but not at him, at myself. How could I do that to JoeSmith, especially after I tried so hard to convince him I wanted to further our relationship? If I tell him, he'll punish me, but only if he can forgive me long enough to want to touch me again.

I feel so dirty, and yet, I'm happy the sexual tension between us is satiated. Wow, can that man fuck!

I can see myself having a relationship with Ben. Maybe somewhere down the line; marriage, kids, and growing old together. He's the kind of guy I could proudly introduce to my family. They'd be delighted that I landed such a well established, handsome man. My sister would turn inside out with jealousy. That alone would be a keepsake moment.

But what about JoeSmith? I can't have a life with him, not really. I'm fooling myself if I think I can. He's all about his lifestyle; at least, I think he is. I really don't know him, but I'd give anything to change that.

Could we have a life together? How would we hide our dungeon desires from my family? My sister would die laughing if she ever opened that secret door. My mother would probably scream the same as she did in my most recent nightmare. My stepfather, Robert, would be so disappointed in me.

But I want JoeSmith in my life. I need him. At least, I think I do.

Not finding the pen, I open the top drawer of Ben's desk to get another, but it's not the neatly arranged stack of pens that stops me in my tracks.

Resting amongst the pens is a little black jewelry box. I glance up at the bathroom and see flickers of movement through the gap in the door. I open the box and I'm met with one glittering diamond earring.

It's mine! The one JoeSmith took from my ear.

But… how?

I stare at the white diamond, hoping to find something that differentiates it from mine, but close the box and set it back in the drawer when I can't. I'm sure it's my earring, or one that looks exactly like it. This can't be a coincidence, can it?

My fingers are numb and I can't stop staring at the slit in the bathroom door. Why has he been in there for so long? Come out so I can drill you with questions.

How did he get my earring? It's probably not even mine. It could just be a crazy coincidence. Someone could have lost it and he picked it up to keep it safe until they come to claim it. It's possible.

My mind races in a hundred different directions, and I can't be here anymore.

Without a sound, I leave his office and nearly trip as I run down the stairs. At the bottom, I gather myself before I come into view of my coworkers, who sit in their cubicles with blank faces.

The last thing I want is to appear as though the boss just fucked me. At least with no make-up on, I don't have to worry about it being smeared. If I look flushed, they'll just think it's because of the paper ball to the eye.

I close my eyes and take a deep breath in through my nose and out of my mouth. I need to appear calm and sane before entering the room. Can I hide the fact that I'm about to lose my mind?

Sam doesn't see me pass her on the way to my desk because she's looking for something in her cabinet. I turn off my computer, close up the folders, stuff them in my drawer, and fling my purse strap over my shoulder. I calmly walk on numb feet to her desk.

Concern overrules her face when I say, "I have to go. I'll call you later."

Sam grabs my arm, but I gently pull it free.

"You're leaving? Are you going to see a doctor, because I'll come with you?"

She attempts to stand, but I rest my hand on her shoulder. She looks up at me and understands that I want her to stay seated and not make a scene.

I smile to calm her nerves. "I'm going home." I nod more than I want to. "I'll call you later, so we can go to the salon together. We can talk then, okay?"

She looks confused when I walk away and leave her with no other explanation for why I'm going home. I can't tell her about any of it right now. Nothing makes sense, and I should figure it out before explaining it to someone else.

What's real, and what's not?

I've been with JoeSmith for over a year and fantasized about him being my boss, but never did I think it could be true.

Is he though?

—To be continued in My JoeSmith: Exposed, Book 2—

Did you enjoy this book?
Please leave a review on your favourite book purchasing site to help readers discover this book, and earn Pebbles free promotional opportunities.
Thank you so much ♥

About Pebbles Lacasse

Pebbles is a contemporary romance and erotica author. She leans toward writing bad boys desiring women who didn't know they have a kinky side. However, she's also known for her women with a dominant nature, and a secret yearning to be loved. Her books and short stories often take her readers into the BDSM lifestyle while revolving around real-life issues, and there's always a happy ending. The captivating stories of romance, love, and tender moments keep her readers coming back for more.

As someone living with Porphyria, Pebbles stays indoors to avoid UV light which gives her plenty of time to write. That's not to say she doesn't love "glamping," fishing, kayaking, and swimming, she just has to do it with protective clothing. If there's something she wants to do, she'll find a way to make it happen.

Pebbles is very family oriented. She and her husband raised their children in southern Ontario where she was born and remains to this day. A 150 lbs Mastiff takes up a lot of room in their home and in their hearts. His best friends are the two rescue cats that think they own the house. The chickens couldn't care less about him until he chases them when they come too close to his outdoor toys.

If you enjoyed MY JOESMITH: ANONYMITY, BOOK ONE,
you may also enjoy:

Full Novels

My JoeSmith: Anonymity, Book One (Coming Soon)
My JoeSmith: Anonymity, Book Two (Releasing Soon)
My JoeSmith: Nurture, Book Three (Releasing Soon)
My JoeSmith: Unity, Book Four (Releasing Soon)
Coaching Rayna, Book One
Coaching Rayna: Bound Hearts, Book Two
Goldilocks & The Three Bear Brothers, Book One
Goldilocks & The Three Bear Brothers: Trifecta, Book Two
Goldilocks & The Three Bear Brothers: Overture, Book Three
Goldilocks & The Three Bear Brothers, Book Four (Coming Soon)
My Wife and Master Jake
Broken Charm

Short Stories

Little Miss Muffet
Hello Officer
Mistress Rabbit
A Run with Charley
Carter's Mistress
Still Waters Burn Deep
Dominatrix for Hire (e-book free with newsletter sign-up)
Dominatrix for Hire (paperback)

Anthologies

Quarantined: A Boxed Set of Pandemic Proportions – Still Waters Burn Deep

To read teasers and see book cover photoshoot photos by Pebbles,
visit www.PebblesLacasse.com

You can connect with Pebbles at the links below

Facebook
https://www.facebook.com/PebblesLacasseEroticRomanceWriter/

Facebook Group
www.facebook.com/groups/pebbleslacasseandfriendsgroup/

Newsletter sign-up
https://bit.ly/pebbleskinkynews

Website
https://www.pebbleslacasse.com

Instagram
https://www.instagram.com/pebbleslacasse/

Twitter
https://twitter.com/pebbleslacasse

Goodreads
http://bit.ly/Goodreads_2y5xJji

Bookbub
https://www.bookbub.com/profile/pebbles-lacasse

Amazon
https://smarturl.it/AmazonPebblesLacasse

Mewe
https://www.mewe.com/i/pebbleslacasse

Youtube
https://www.youtube.com/channel/UC3Jb8ofSw0m3TFn4cMWu5dw

Pinterest
https://www.pinterest.ca/pebbleslacasse/pins/

www.ingramcontent.com/pod-product-compliance
Lightning Source LLC
Chambersburg PA
CBHW050924030726
47503CB00007BB/2447

* 9 7 8 1 9 8 9 9 7 9 1 7 4 *